Somewh... believed that Dominic would never betray her.

But improbable wasn't the same as impossible. And she couldn't take the risk.

Dominic Fabrino had somehow managed to slip past the barriers she'd built around her heart. He'd demanded nothing of her, and not once had he tried to invade her space. He'd been kind and funny, thoughtful and generous.

But what if he'd really kissed her, taken her mouth in a deeper, more primal way? How would she have responded? Would she have welcomed it? Or would she have been afraid? She wasn't sure.

But she wanted to find out.

And therein lay the road to ruin. She'd been wrong about a man once. She could be wrong again....

Dear Reader,

Welcome to Silhouette **Special Edition** . . . welcome to romance. Each month Silhouette **Special Edition** publishes six novels with you in mind—stories of love and life, tales that you can identify with—as well as dream about.

And this December brings six wonderful tales of love! Sherryl Woods's warm, tender series, VOWS, concludes with Brandon Halloran's romance— *Cherish*. Brandon finally meets up again with his first love, beautiful Elizabeth Forsythe. Yes, Virginia, as long as there is life and love, dreams *do* come true!

Heralding in the Christmas spirit this month is *It Must Have Been the Mistletoe* by Nikki Benjamin. This winsome, poignant story will bring a tear to your eye and a smile to your lips!

Rounding out this month of holiday cheer are books from other favorite writers: Trisha Alexander, Ruth Wind, Patricia Coughlin and Mona van Wieren.

I hope that you enjoy this book and all the stories to come. Happy holidays from all of us at Silhouette Books!

Sincerely,

Tara Gavin
Senior Editor
Silhouette Books

P.S.—We've got an extra special surprise next month to start off the New Year right. I'll give you a hint—it begins with a wonderful book by Ginna Gray called *Building Dreams!*

NIKKI
BENJAMIN

IT MUST HAVE BEEN THE MISTLETOE

Silhouette®

SPECIAL EDITION®

Published by Silhouette Books New York
America's Publisher of Contemporary Romance

For my godparents, Larry and Shirley Kuda,
Grandma Elizabeth Hinton, and my cousins: Larry,
Jim, Dave, Sharon, Mark, Joan and Michael—with
fond memories of all the holidays we've shared.
and
Special thanks to my "research assistants"—Greg
"Italian Stallion" Loyacano, Anna (Tiffany White)
Eberhardt and my mom, Marcella Wolff.

SILHOUETTE BOOKS
300 East 42nd St., New York, N.Y. 10017

IT MUST HAVE BEEN THE MISTLETOE

Copyright © 1992 by Barbara Vosbein

ISBN: 0-373-09782-4

First Silhouette Books printing December 1992

Printed in the U.S.A.

NIKKI BENJAMIN

was born and raised in the Midwest, but after years in the Houston area, she considers herself a true Texan. Nikki says she's always been an avid reader. (Her earliest literary heroines were Nancy Drew, Trixie Belden and Beany Malone.) Her writing experience was limited, however, until a friend started penning a novel and encouraged Nikki to do the same. One scene led to another, and soon she was hooked.

When not reading or writing, the author enjoys spending time with her husband and son, needlepoint, hiking, biking, horseback riding and sailing.

Chapter One

"I'm telling you, Mooch, he's got the hots for her."

"I don't think so, Eddie. After he split with Diane, he swore he'd never get involved with another workaholic woman. If that doesn't describe Ms. Townsend, I don't know what does. She works more weekends than we do. And she certainly hasn't given him any encouragement. I've never heard her say more than a dozen words to him when she's been here."

"Maybe she's shy."

"Get serious, will ya? She runs one of the biggest advertising agencies in St. Louis. She isn't shy. She's just not interested. And if you ask me, neither is Dominic."

"Well, if you ask *me,* he is. I've seen the way he looks at her. Talk about hungry eyes. The man's got a bad case of the wants. But I don't think he knows what to do about it."

"Aw, come on, Eddie. Where women are concerned Dominic always knows what to do."

"Not always. Not after Diane. Hey, have you seen my wrench?"

"Yeah, here it is. Catch."

"Ouch. Damn it, Mooch, one of these days..."

Dominic Fabrino stood in his office, coffeepot in one hand, empty mug in the other, his head tilted toward the doorway opening into the long, wide row of covered bays that comprised the main work area of Fabrino's Garage. A frown creased his forehead and dragged at the corners of his mouth.

He'd overheard enough of his employees' conversation to know that they'd been talking about him and Martha Townsend. And he wasn't pleased with what they'd had to say. Not when he'd thought he'd been doing such a good job of concealing his growing attraction to her. And especially not when they seemed as aware as he that the feeling wasn't mutual.

Muttering an oath, he glanced out the window, his eyes roving over the line of vehicles parked on the small lot angling off to one side of the garage. As his gaze settled on the old car hooked on to the back of one of the tow trucks, his frown deepened. He'd seen the car the moment he'd turned into the alley, and mentally cursed the detour to the bank that had delayed him by twenty minutes or more. He saw little enough of her as it was. And even though he knew she'd be back at the end of the day, he wished he hadn't missed her earlier.

She'd been bringing her car to Fabrino's off and on for more than a year. Determined to hang on to the old clunker as long as possible, she'd ignored his advice to invest in something more reliable. So far, he'd been able to keep it running for her, but lately, no matter what he did, it seemed to need work more and more often. As a result, he'd not only seen more and more of Marti Townsend's car, he'd seen more and more of Marti. And the more he saw of her, the more she intrigued him, even though, as Mooch had said, she was precisely the type of woman he'd vowed to keep away from.

Well, maybe not *precisely*. In many ways Marti wasn't anything at all like his ex-wife. Diane wouldn't have been caught dead in Marti's old jalopy. Nor would she have chosen to live in an old Italian neighborhood like the Hill.

Yet, in other ways—ways that really mattered to him— Marti was much the same. Over the past year he'd learned enough about her to know that she was just as intent as Diane had been on climbing her company's corporate ladder. And she seemed just as willing to do so to the exclusion of all else. At least, to his knowledge, she hadn't conned some poor sap into believing he was as important to her as her job. At least, not yet. Too bad he couldn't say the same for Diane.

Granted, his priorities had changed after his father's heart attack. But he'd never demanded that Diane's priorities change, as well. And he'd never asked her to give up all that she'd worked so hard to attain. He'd simply let her know that he wanted a slower, gentler kind of life, a home-and-family kind of life, and he wanted it with her. And she'd led him to believe that's what she'd wanted, too. Why, he'd never know, but she had. And he'd been fool enough to trust in her promises of someday soon—until he'd found out about the not-so-simple little surgery she'd arranged without his—

"Hey, boss, good to see you finally made it."

"Damn it, Mooch! How many times have I told you not to sneak up on me?" Dominic demanded as hot coffee sloshed over his fingers.

"I didn't sneak up on you."

"Maybe you were daydreaming again, Dom." Eddie snickered as he sidled through the doorway.

"Daydreaming about how nice it'd be if I could hire a couple of new mechanics," Dominic muttered, slapping the coffeepot onto the burner.

Trying not to smile, he turned to face the two men who'd helped him save Fabrino's Garage after his father's heart attack four years ago. In more ways than he could count, they were irreplaceable, especially now that he'd decided to expand into the South County area with a second repair shop. And no matter what he said to the contrary, they knew the truth.

"What's going on?" He shifted his mug from one hand to the other and rubbed his wet fingers down the side of his faded jeans.

"We're almost done with Ruzika's Caddy. We've got a couple of tune-ups, an AC repair and another brake job. And Sister Mary Clair dropped off the convent station wagon. Said she talked to you about it last night." Mooch's grin slid into overdrive. "I guess you saw Ms. Townsend's car, too."

"Yes, I saw her car." Dominic raised his cup and took a sip of coffee as he sifted through the stack of papers on his desk.

"And I guess you want to take a look at it yourself."

"Yes, I want to take a look at it myself." He swallowed more coffee, shuffled more papers. "What's wrong with it this time?"

"She said she heard a loud banging noise, then it stopped dead in the middle of the street. When I got there with the tow truck, there was oil all over the place. I'd say she threw a rod. If so, it's definitely DOA."

Moving away from his desk, Dominic peered out the window, eyeing the old car once again. Sipping his coffee with studied nonchalance, he considered Mooch's evaluation for several seconds.

"DOA, huh?"

"If she threw a rod, I'd have to agree with Mooch," Eddie conceded. "Might as well save our time and Ms. Townsend's money and haul it to the junkyard."

Dominic stared out the window a moment longer. Then, easing back, he rested a hip against the edge of his desk. "Put it in bay three and I'll take a look at it."

Setting his mug aside, he shrugged out of the worn black leather bomber jacket he'd worn to ward off the early October chill and pushed up the sleeves of his gray sweatshirt. Despite his employees' avid attention, he couldn't help but smile as an idea he'd been entertaining for weeks came together in his head.

If Mooch and Eddie were right about her car, he'd finally have a good excuse to spend a little time with Ms. Martha Townsend. And a little time should be all it took to convince himself that they weren't right for each other.

He'd been thinking about her—dreaming about her soft voice and gentle smile—way too much, considering all that his ex-wife had taught him about professional women intent on climbing corporate ladders. But he knew that until he dealt with his growing attraction to Marti Townsend, he'd never be able to move on. Until he assured himself that although she seemed different she was really just like Diane, he'd never be able to find the kind of woman he needed, a woman who valued home and family as much as she valued her job.

"Hey, boss, why don't you offer to help her find a new car?" Eddie suggested, digging an elbow into Mooch's ribs as they headed toward the doorway.

"Yeah, why don't you?" Mooch urged, elbowing Eddie in return. "Have a little fun. Get to know the lady."

Dominic scowled at the two men as he reached for his mug and lifted it to his lips. They'd worked for him for more than four years, and they'd become experts at reading his mind as well as his moods. More often than not their uncanny ability worked in his favor. But on days like today . . .

"I already know the lady. And I don't think she's into fun," he said, making a final, probably futile, effort to discourage himself as well as his friends. Setting his empty mug on the desk, he crossed his arms over his chest and tipped his head toward the row of cars parked on the lot. "Unless you guys want to work all weekend, I suggest you get out of here and get busy. I told Ruzika he could pick up his Cadillac at ten o'clock. And I promised Sister Mary Clair the station wagon would be ready by noon."

"You know, if the old clunker threw a rod, she's going to have to buy a new car," Eddie continued, as if Dominic hadn't spoken.

"And a new one won't need work like the old one did," Mooch added, rocking back on his heels and waggling his eyebrows.

"So she probably won't be coming around the way she's—"

"Out—both of you! *Now!*"

"Okay, boss."

"Anything you say, boss."

"Well, well, well. . . . Aren't you the sly one, Ms. Townsend?" Heather Barnes arched one slim, dark eyebrow, her hazel eyes full of mischief. Grinning at Marti, she shook her head in mock dismay, rearranging her mass of shiny brown curls for the umpteenth time that day. "I thought you were just a tightwad. But now I know the real reason why you've clung to that decrepit old car with such single-minded determination."

"Tightwad, huh?" As Marti shifted on the car seat and tilted her head to one side, a wisp of honey blond hair slipped from the neat coil at the nape of her neck. A faint smile tugged at the corners of her mouth as she gazed at her secretary over the top of her horn-rimmed glasses.

Not only was Heather a loyal co-worker, she was honest to a fault. Her irreverent attitude was well-known throughout the office, but Marti couldn't have asked for a more competent executive assistant. She'd learned long ago to take Heather's teasing comments, as well as her caustic criticism, in stride.

"My mistake, Marti. I had no idea your auto mechanic was such a hunk. He's plenty of reason to hang on to that old bomb." Heather fluttered her eyelids as she pressed a hand to her chest. "Be still, my beating heart."

"You mean Mr. Fabrino?" Her smile fading, Marti glanced out the side window. Her gaze settled on the tall, dark man in worn jeans and a grubby gray sweatshirt standing just inside the open doorway of the garage office, clipboard in hand. Even though his shaggy brown hair was badly in need of a trim and his long, square jaw was five-o'clock shadowed, she couldn't deny that he was a handsome man. But she'd never thought of him as a hunk. The term was too sexual for her taste or, for that matter, her peace of mind.

"*Mr. Fabrino!* Marti, please! Against all odds, the man has kept your car running at least a year longer than anyone could have imagined possible. Don't tell me you're not on a first-name basis with him. Where interesting, attractive men are concerned, you are truly hopeless. Unless, of course, he's married."

"No, he's not married. He's divorced," Marti admitted.

"Well, then, what's the problem?" Heather paused for a moment, obviously searching for another alternative. "Is it because he's an auto mechanic and you're the general manager of one of the biggest advertising agencies in St. Louis? Don't tell me you're a snob, Ms. Townsend.''

"After all the years we've worked together you should know me better than that." Making no attempt to hide her anger, Marti turned toward the other woman. "The fact that Dominic is an auto mechanic has nothing to do with how I feel about him. He's managed to keep my car running without charging me an arm and a leg, and of course I'm grateful. But he's just a . . . a business associate.''

"Every eligible man you meet is just a business associate," Heather muttered.

Rather than argue, Marti simply stared at her secretary. Experience had taught her that a silent reprimand often proved most effective where the other woman was concerned.

"Sorry, I was out of line," Heather conceded at last. "By now I should know that when it comes to men, you're an equal-opportunity ice maiden." Though her tone was contrite, the scheming sparkle in her hazel eyes looked anything but repentant.

"Contrary to office gossip, I am *not* an ice maiden," Marti retorted, a defensive edge in her voice. She couldn't count the number of times she'd had similar discussions with her secretary, and she was beginning to grow weary of them. "Pulling the St. Louis branch of Carter and Caisson out of the red hasn't left me any time to socialize. And even if I had the time, it would be foolish for me to get involved with anyone here. You know I want Benson's job, and if I get it, I'll have to move to—''

"He looks awfully glad to see you."

Unable to stop herself, Marti glanced out the window again. Although Dominic was still standing in the office doorway, his eyes were on her instead of the clipboard he held. He waved to her, then turned to speak to the college student who helped out around the garage after school.

"He's probably anxious to close up for the evening. And I know you're anxious to get home, too. It's almost six o'clock." Tightening her hold on her briefcase, Marti opened the door and slid out of the car. Bending down, she met her secretary's rueful gaze for a few seconds. "Thanks a lot, Heather. I really appreciate the ride. See you on Monday."

"Marti..." Heather hesitated. Then, as if aware that she'd be pushing her luck if she said anything else, she heaved a sigh of resignation. "Right. I'll see you on Monday."

Smoothing a hand over her hair, Marti stood at the curb and watched as Heather's car disappeared around the corner. She dearly loved the other woman. They'd become close friends during the years they'd worked together, and Marti understood her concern. With a husband and young son, as well as a demanding job, Heather's life was full to overflowing. In comparison, she obviously found Marti's single life-style rather cold and empty. And lately she'd set about trying to change it. But there were times like tonight when Heather went too far.

Hunk...

The heat of a blush warmed Marti's face. She certainly hadn't thought of Dominic Fabrino in *that* way—at least, not until a few minutes ago. But then, it had been years, seven years to be exact, since she'd thought of any man even the least bit sexually—and she wasn't going to start now. Not even with a man she liked as much as Dominic. He might tempt her to trust again, if she gave him half a chance.

"But I can't... I won't...." she murmured with a quick shake of her head.

She would never forget what had happened the last time she'd trusted a man, a man she'd known far longer and far better than she'd known Dominic Fabrino. The hurt and humiliation had been almost unbearable. If it hadn't been for her job, she wasn't sure how she would have survived. Only by throwing herself into her work had she managed to get past Brent Winston's brutal betrayal. Now the welfare of Carter and Caisson was more important to her than anything. It had to be, she reminded herself sternly, if she intended to get Benson's job.

Straightening her shoulders, she adjusted her glasses with one hand as she tightened her grip on her briefcase with the other. Imagining any kind of relationship with Dominic Fabrino, other than the one she had, was an incredible waste of time. In fact, what she'd found herself daring to wish for in the past few weeks was nothing short of impossible. She had neither the time nor the desire to have a man in her life, especially a man like Dominic. And she could only hope she hadn't given him any ideas to the contrary.

Her fingers fluttered to the front of her tailored, taupe silk suit jacket. As she fastened the buttons she drew in a deep breath, trying to recall how she'd behaved the past couple of times they'd met. She'd been polite, yet friendly. But not too friendly, she hoped. And as long as she maintained her distance, continuing to strike the perfect balance shouldn't be hard. Not if she remained cool and calm and collected.

Once again she smoothed a hand over her hair. Then, suddenly aware of how long she'd lingered at the curb, she took another deep breath. Finally, unable to avoid facing him a moment longer, she spun around, took two steps and walked straight into him.

For an instant, her breasts pressed against the solid wall of his chest and her mouth brushed the warm, bare skin at the base of his throat. She caught her breath as her nipples zinged with sensation despite the layers of clothing she wore. Then she inhaled slowly. The faint odor of gasoline, grease and oil mingled with his distinctively musky male scent—an odd combination, though not unpleasant. Her lips parted as she tipped her head back.

She hadn't realized how tall he was, how broad and...and how hard he was. But then, she'd never been so close to him. And he *was* close, much too close. And he had his hands on her shoulders. A shiver raced up her spine as she realized that he was holding— Holding? *Holding* her.

A flash of fear shot through her. She couldn't stop herself from releasing a startled cry, couldn't stop herself from twisting away from him and stepping back as she tried to break free. Only his firm yet gentle grip saved her from stumbling into the gutter.

"Hey, Marti, take it easy. You don't want to fall and break something, do you?" His voice soft and teasing, Dominic held on to her for a moment longer, wanting to banish the fear flaring in her bright blue eyes, wanting to ease the tension that suddenly stiffened her spine. "I didn't mean to startle you, but you were just standing here, looking like a lost soul." And now she looked like a frightened fawn about to flee, he thought as he finally released her.

Her response to his touch hurt and angered him. In a way he wasn't all that surprised by it. He should have realized that she wasn't the type to welcome fast moves of any kind. Nor did she want anyone invading her space without an engraved invitation. Obviously he wasn't on her "A" list. She'd rather fall into the gutter than have his hands on her.

He was wasting his time and he knew it. If he had any brains, he'd find someone else, someone ready, willing and able to be his girl. But how could he, as long as quiet, classy Marti Townsend edged into his thoughts and dreams on a daily basis?

By getting her out of his system once and for all, that's how.

Shoving his fingers through his hair, he ordered himself to stop staring at her mouth and say something, anything, to break the silence stretching between them.

"I'm sorry I scared you, Marti. But you were about to step off the curb, and I didn't want you to hurt yourself." Sliding his hands into the pockets of his jeans, he raised his eyes and met her gaze.

"I'm the one who should apologize." Taking a deep breath, Marti silently cursed herself for acting like an idiot. Then, smiling slightly, she reached out and touched his arm. The fabric of his worn sweatshirt felt soft and cool against her palm. "If I'd been paying attention to what I was doing instead of daydreaming, I'd never have bumped into you in the first place."

She knew that he'd only meant to save her from a bad fall, yet she'd acted as if he'd intended to harm her. Granted, he'd caught her unawares, but that didn't justify such a violent reaction—such a violent resurgence of the fear that was another man's cruel legacy.

"Hey, don't worry about it. As long as you're okay…"

"I'm fine. Really." She gave his arm a quick squeeze as much to reassure herself as him. Then, eyeing the old car parked on the side lot, she eased her hand away. "Is my car ready?"

"Ready for the junkyard." Dominic turned and headed toward his office, the warmth of her tentative touch fading a little with each step he took.

It had cost her to put her hand on him. He was sure of it. Just as he was sure that he hadn't simply startled her, he'd scared the living daylights out of her. And he didn't like it, not one bit. Because he'd never said or done anything to frighten a woman, not even when he'd been mad as hell at

Diane for deceiving him. Yet he knew that Marti was afraid of him. What he didn't know was why. As he strode across the parking lot, he vowed that one way or another he was going to find out.

Switching her briefcase from her right hand to her left, Marti hurried after Dominic, the heels of her plain taupe pumps clicking on the asphalt. "You've been saying that for months," she chided, trying to keep up with his longer, looser strides.

As she did so, her eyes skimmed the broad line of his back and the narrow curve of his waist and hips, then lingered on the well-honed muscles of his buttocks and thighs, shifting and straining against the worn fabric of his jeans. With a small sigh, she thought of the way his arm had flexed and rippled beneath the softness of his sweatshirt. To her chagrin, she found herself agreeing with her secretary. He *was* a hunk.

"Damn it, Marti, stop thinking about it," she muttered, forcing herself to shift her gaze to the brightly lit building up ahead.

"Swearing, Ms. Townsend?" Dominic asked, glancing at her over his shoulder as he walked into his office.

"At myself," Marti admitted, stopping just inside the doorway.

"Well, I have a feeling I'm going to be next, once I give you the bad news." He turned to face her, settling a hip on the edge of his desk, as she rested a shoulder against the wooden doorframe.

The harsh fluorescent light emphasized the faint shadows under her eyes, shadows he hadn't noticed in the early-evening twilight. Her leather briefcase seemed to tug at her arm like a fifty-pound weight. And though a hint of a smile played at the corners of her mouth, he had a feeling her heart wasn't in it. In fact, she looked so small, so fragile and forlorn, that for a moment he wished he had something good to tell her instead.

"How long will it take you to fix it?"

"The engine threw a rod. I can't fix it. You're going to have to buy another car."

With a low groan, Marti tipped her head back and closed her eyes. From the work area off to the right she could hear the sound of voices, while the smell of gasoline and grime drifted around her on the cool autumn breeze. Dominic's mechanics were obviously still hard at work. But it seemed the time had finally come when nothing they could do would get her car running again.

It wasn't as if she hadn't known that the vehicle was on its last leg. Dominic had been urging her to find another car for months. But having to face one smirking car salesman after another while wondering how badly she was being conned wasn't exactly the way she wanted to spend a Saturday. Actually, another Saturday, she amended. She'd done it twice already. And both times she'd returned home not only frustrated beyond belief but sure that she had a gene missing—the gene that allowed one to separate a good deal from a bad one when buying a car.

Of course, a little researching of makes and models might have helped. But she'd never had time. Or rather, she'd never bothered to make time. And now time had run out on her. She was going to have to buy another car, and she was going to have to do it the following day. Driving a rental would only postpone what she'd put off long enough already.

"But I don't want to buy a car," she muttered, not caring that she sounded more like a stubborn child than a sensible adult.

If her despondent look and disgruntled tone were any indication at all, Marti was less than thrilled with the prospect of finding a replacement for her car. Dominic couldn't blame her. Having to buy a car on the spur of the moment would intimidate almost anyone. But she didn't have to do it alone.

He'd dealt with car dealers on behalf of various friends and relatives in the past. There was no reason why he couldn't do the same for her. All it would cost him was a little time, time he'd be spending with her. He'd make sure she got a good car for her money. And, as he'd told himself earlier in the day, it would be a perfect opportunity to get to know her better. After a few hours in her company, he'd probably be more than ready to accept the fact that they simply weren't right for each other, and never would be.

Of course, there was always the slight possibility that his plan might backfire. He might end up liking her more than he did already. Then he'd really be up a crooked creek without a paddle, wouldn't he?

"I know you don't want to buy a car... But maybe I could make it easier for you," he volunteered at last, willing away the little niggle of doubt that burrowed in the back of his mind. If he didn't make a move one way or another, he'd go crazy wondering "what if?"

"You know of a specific car I can buy?" Marti pushed away from the doorframe, her eyes full of hope as she met his gaze.

"Well, no. But I could help you find one tomorrow. We're going to be closed, so I'm free if you are." Sensing her sudden wariness, he flattened his palms against his desktop and leaned back, offering her his most reassuring smile.

"I appreciate your thoughtfulness. Really, I do." She hesitated a moment, no longer meeting his gaze as she plucked at the buttons on her suit jacket. "But I'm sure you have better things to do than traipse around car lots with me. I don't want you wasting your time—"

"I don't think spending the day with you would be a waste of time," Dominic cut in. She was turning him down as politely as she could, and he didn't like it, not one bit. But aside from making sure she understood how he felt, there was nothing he could do about it. "In fact, I thought it might be fun. But if you'd rather go alone, I understand."

As she met his gaze, Marti saw the hurt in Dominic's dark eyes and mentally cursed herself for being so insensitive. He'd only wanted to give her the help she needed, and she'd been determined to put him off. But why? Because it was either that or give in to the urge to close the distance between them, wrap her arms around him and rest her head on his shoulder.

All at once she realized just how lonely she'd been for the past seven years. She knew that she simply couldn't go on the same way much longer. No matter how hard she'd tried to deny it, she had wants and desires, a woman's wants and desires. If she ever hoped to have them fulfilled, she'd have to learn to trust again.

So why not start with Dominic Fabrino? It wasn't as if he were demanding anything of her. Rather, he'd offered the kind of help one friend offers another. And it was the kind of help she not only needed, but wanted.

"Well, if you're not busy..." She'd dallied so long that he'd probably changed his mind.

"Not busy at all," he assured her, a smile twitching at the corners of his mouth. "It'll be a lot of fun. Wait and see."

"If you say so," she agreed rather doubtfully. Maybe going one-on-one with smirking car salesmen was his idea of a good time, but to Marti it would never be anything but a pain. "What about my old car? Can I use it as a trade-in?" She glanced out the door, her gaze settling on the vehicle.

"Not a chance. I'll have one of the guys tow it to the junkyard on Monday." Reaching down behind the desk, he picked up a small cardboard box. "I cleaned out the glove compartment and the trunk and checked under the seats. If anything's missing, we can take another look before you leave."

"The junkyard?" Marti couldn't hide the sadness in her voice as she took the box from Dominic. She'd traveled so many miles in the old car that she'd begun to think of it as a friend. It was also a reminder of a time when she'd felt truly loved. Her grandmother had given it to her for her sixteenth birthday, despite her parents' protests. *A special gift for my special girl.* "I guess that's the best place for it, huh?" She glanced at Dominic, her mouth tilting up in a wry smile.

"Believe me, it is. Everything there?"

"I think so." She balanced the box on one arm and pawed through it quickly. Maps, flashlight, coins, an umbrella, jumper cables, two coffee mugs she hadn't seen in ages and a camera shifted and jiggled under her fingertips. "Yes, that's everything. If I can use your telephone, I'll call a cab, then get out of your way so you can close up."

"Hold on, I promised a couple of fellas I'd have their cars ready by seven." He crossed to the doorway that opened into the main body of the garage. Though most of his attention had been focused on Marti, he realized it had been unusually quiet in the bays for a while now. "You guys about finished?"

"Just about, boss." Mooch, grinning like an idiot, winked broadly and gave Dominic a thumbs-up.

"Yeah, just about finished, Dom," Eddie agreed, doing likewise.

Len, the college student, stood between the two of them smiling sheepishly.

"Great. I'm taking Ms. Townsend home. I'll be back in fifteen, twenty minutes max. If anybody comes in while I'm gone, you handle it, Mooch. And no matter who needs what, we're closed tomorrow."

"Sure thing, boss. Take your time. We've got everything under control."

"*Out* of control is more like it," Dominic muttered as he turned back to Marti. "Ready to go?"

Before she could voice the protest flashing in her bright blue eyes, he lifted the box out of her hands. He shifted it under one arm and brushed past her, digging his keys out of the side pocket of his jeans as he headed toward his car.

Marti gazed at his retreating back for a moment. Then, tightening her grip on her briefcase, she followed him across the lot once again. No doubt about it, she'd been finessed. And she had to admire his skill. He'd ignored her request to use the telephone, feigning interest in his employees' progress. Then he'd taken custody of her possessions with amazing ease. Now he was standing by the open door of his car, waiting for her.

She paused a few feet away from him, her gaze steady. Just because she'd agreed to go with him tomorrow...

"Don't say it," he advised, tossing the box onto the back seat of the car.

"What?"

"That you can call a cab. I know you can. But it would be silly. Your house is just a few blocks away. So get in."

Ignoring the quickening beat of her heart, Marti debated the wisdom of further argument. Then, with a casual shrug, she stepped forward and slid onto the smooth white leather seat of the beautifully restored tropical turquoise 1957 Chevy. She hadn't gotten as far as she had at Carter and Caisson by fighting losing battles. Insisting on calling a cab would be foolish when they'd be spending most of tomorrow together, anyway. In fact, as long as he didn't insist on coming into her house...

"Don't forget to buckle your seat belt."

She did as he asked. Then, as he backed the Chevy out of the parking lot, she renewed her grip on her briefcase, balancing it on her lap with one hand while she clung to the armrest with the other. Staring out the window, she tried to ignore the expanse of white leather seat that stretched between them, separating yet drawing them together in an oddly intimate way.

As they sped down one quiet, residential street, then another, she suddenly realized that Dominic needed no guidance at all to find her house.

"How do you know where I live?" she asked, frowning slightly.

"I know all sorts of things about you, Ms. Townsend."

Though he seemed to be teasing her, a frisson of fear swept up Marti's spine. "What things?" she demanded, her voice soft and full of uncertainty, her eyes wide as she turned to face him.

"The kind of things printed on a driver's license." Dominic met her frightened gaze for an instant, then focused on the street ahead. If it was the last thing he did, he was going to find out what it was about him that seemed to scare her. But for now he wanted only to reassure her. "Remember the first couple of times you paid for repair work with a check? I asked to see your driver's license so I could find you if it turned out you'd written a hot check."

"I'd never do that," Marti retorted, her simple statement full of righteous indignation.

"I know that now. But a year ago I wasn't so sure. You were new in the neighborhood and looks can be deceiving." Stepping on the clutch, he shifted into neutral and guided the car to the curb in front of a small, two-story, red brick house with dark green trim, a shiny black door and a pair of glowing porch lights. "Well, here you—"

"Oh, yes, here we are." Cutting him off, Marti swung open the car door and stepped onto the sidewalk. "Thanks a lot, Dominic." Twilight had faded into a deepening darkness that pressed around her. She had to get into the house. She had to do it *now*. "See you tomorrow," she added quickly, not meeting his gaze as she slammed the car door.

Spinning around, she groped in her jacket pocket for her door key as she hurried up the walkway. Without a backward glance, she ran up the steps, unlocked the door and slipped inside. As the latch clicked shut, she rested her back against the hard, solid wood. Relaxing her fingers, she dropped her briefcase onto the floor and took several quick, deep breaths.

She had been unforgivably rude. She'd acted like a silly goose. She'd—

The doorbell rang once, twice, a third time, the chimes echoing through the dark hallway.

"Marti? It's me, Dominic. Are you all right?"

Switching on the hall light, she eased the door open just a crack. He was standing on the top step, the width of the porch away, his hands shoved in the side pockets of his jeans, the porch light shining in his eyes, the cardboard box on the concrete between them.

"I'm sorry. I...I...thought you were anxious to get back to the garage," she said, opening the door a little wider.

No matter how lonely she was, she shouldn't have agreed to go with him tomorrow. It wasn't going to work. It couldn't. She was just too afraid....

"I am. But you forgot your stuff. And I was wondering if I could pick you up around nine o'clock?"

He held his breath, bracing himself for her refusal. If she'd reconsidered and didn't want anything to do with him after all, fine. He'd live with it. But it wouldn't be easy. Not when he had no idea why she was so damned afraid of him.

Tell him no. Tell him you've changed your mind. Tell him...

"Nine o'clock sounds fine to me," she murmured, her eyes meeting his.

He held her gaze just long enough to assure himself that she'd meant what she'd said. Then, flashing a quick smile, he turned and walked back to his car.

He had absolutely no idea why he felt so good. She was going to be nothing but trouble. Yet he was already looking forward to seeing her again—and not because he had any intention of getting her out of his system. He already had a feeling that was going to be damn near impossible, at least for the time being.

Long after the Chevy's taillights had faded in the distance, Marti stood in the open doorway, staring into the night, wondering at the wisdom of what she'd done. Finally, shivering slightly at the autumn chill wrapping around her ankles and slipping down the collar of her blouse, she retrieved the cardboard box and went inside again. As she continued down the hallway toward the kitchen, she caught a glimpse of herself in the mirror hanging on the wall.

She was smiling...*smiling,* for heaven's sake. If that didn't prove she needed her head examined, nothing did.

Smiling...

Shaking her head, she dropped the box onto the kitchen table and opened the refrigerator door. She eyed the plate of cold chicken, the bowl of salad greens, the pieces of fruit and bottles of mineral water. Frowning, she slammed the door shut and crossed to the telephone.

"Yes, I'd like to order a medium double-cheese-and-pepperoni pizza and a two-liter bottle of soda to be delivered."

That was the problem with throwing caution to the wind, she mused as she slipped out of her jacket and kicked her pumps halfway across the kitchen floor. Once you started, it was sometimes hard to know when to stop.

Chapter Two

By eight-thirty Saturday morning, Marti was ready to start climbing the walls. She'd been up and dressed since before dawn. She'd eaten toast and drunk tea and read the morning newspaper. Then, knowing she'd be gone most of the day, she'd decided to take a look at the McCaffrey account, one of several she had to review for the Monday morning staff meeting.

She'd opened her briefcase, removed the pertinent papers and set them on the kitchen table. But instead of working she'd spent the next hour alternately staring into space and wandering around the house.

No matter how urgently she ordered herself to concentrate on the task at hand, she finally had to admit she simply couldn't do it. At least, not as long as she kept thinking about Dominic and the day ahead. He'd said it would be fun. And against her better judgment she'd begun to believe that it could be, if she gave it half a chance. In fact, it had been so long since she'd done anything with anyone except work that the prospect of actually enjoying herself while she was with him had gradually become more and more inviting.

"Silly goose," she chided herself softly as she tossed her pen aside. Shifting on the hard oak chair, she gathered her papers together and stuffed them back into her briefcase.

She knew better than to make something out of nothing, yet that was exactly what she'd been doing most of the morning. And what had she gained by it? Nothing but a lot of wasted time, she thought as she scooted her chair back and stood.

It wasn't as if Dominic had any interest in her. He'd simply had a certain amount of sympathy for her situation and, nice guy that he was, he'd volunteered to help her out. Once she found a car, she'd probably never see him again, regardless of whether she had a good time or not. And that was just as well. Wasn't it?

No matter how forlorn she'd been feeling lately she had enough sense to know that she was better off alone. Her job demanded more and more of her time and energy. And she certainly couldn't afford to slack off now. Not if she wanted Benson's job as much as she thought she did. Since a final decision had to be made before the end of the year, the next couple of months would be crucial.

As she'd told Heather yesterday, she couldn't afford to get involved with anyone, and now, more than ever, she realized why. In the hour or more that she'd been trying unsuccessfully to work, Dominic had proven what a distraction he could be. *If she let him.* But she wasn't going to do that, was she? She wasn't going to allow herself to be sidetracked by any man. Not when she was within a hairbreadth of the goal she'd chosen to pursue almost seven years ago.

She'd managed to assuage her loneliness on her own for a long time. And there was no reason why she couldn't continue to do so. She'd invested a small fortune in cameras and a darkroom, and over the past few years her photography had become much more than a hobby. She'd actually sold several of her pictures to local newspapers and magazines. In fact, if it hadn't been for her growing success at Carter and Caisson, not to mention the approval of her parents that had accompanied her achievements there, she might have considered making her hobby a career.

Once again Marti turned away from the table and paced slowly from the kitchen to the front hallway to the living room. She couldn't, *wouldn't,* give up all she'd worked for at Carter and Caisson, not for anything or anybody. And that was that.

As she'd done off and on all morning, she paused to frown at her reflection in the wide oval mirror hanging on the wall above the mantel. It had taken longer than usual for her to decide what to wear, and she still wasn't sure if she'd made the right choices. Nor was she sure why it mattered, since she was shopping for a car, not selling an ad campaign. But somehow it did matter—a lot.

Eyeing herself critically in the beveled glass, she had to admit that there was absolutely nothing wrong with her tailored gray wool slacks, cream silk shirt and dusty rose cable-knit cardigan. And she didn't have any problem with her hair, either. She'd twisted it into a neat coil at the nape of her neck as she did each workday, more out of habit than anything else. But suddenly the single strand of pearls and the antique gold-and-pearl button earrings seemed a bit much for a Saturday morning. A simple gold chain and small gold hoop earrings would probably be more appropriate.

Now if only she could decide what to do about her glasses. They made her look so stern, so…serious. That was all right while she was at the office. But she hadn't wanted to appear that way today. At least, that's what she'd thought earlier when she'd chosen to wear her contact lenses.

As she continued to stare at herself in the mirror, however, she wondered if it was wise to let Dominic see her any way other than he had in the past. She was already more casually dressed than she'd ever been when she'd gone to the garage. And although going without her glasses didn't make a lot of difference, any difference at all could give him ideas. As Brent Winston had taught her seven years ago, that could be a very dangerous thing to do.

"So wear them and be done with it," she muttered almost angrily as she turned away from the mirror.

Glancing at her watch, she hurried down the hallway and started up the stairs. She'd left her glasses on the night-stand in her bedroom. And if she wasn't mistaken, the gold chain and earrings were stashed in the little jewelry box atop the chest of drawers. . . . But it was just ten till nine, surely she'd have more than enough time to—

The doorbell rang before she reached the top step. As the chimes echoed around her, she stopped short. Hesitating for a moment, she clung to the wooden banister. Then slowly, reluctantly, she turned and retraced her steps.

It might not be Dominic, but she wasn't willing to bet on it. Although he was early, he *was* doing her a favor, and letting him stand on her front doorstep while she blithely went about her business would be unforgivably rude. Considering the way her hands were shaking, fiddling with her contact lenses, not to mention a couple of jewelry clasps, would probably take her forever.

Unfortunately, once she opened the door, he'd see her as she was, pearls and all. After that it would be foolish to take the time to make the changes she'd had in mind. In fact, it would be downright stupid since she'd have to ask him to wait in the house while she did it. And inviting Dominic, or any man, into her home was simply out of the question.

"Stop worrying about how you look. You're not going on a date. You're buying a car and you need his help," she cautioned herself quietly as she paused to gather up her purse, keys and the small notebook she'd left on the hall table earlier. "Just think of it as business. Stay cool, calm and collected. Nothing will happen, nothing at all...."

Her resolve renewed, Marti straightened her shoulders and lifted her chin. As she'd reminded herself more than once that morning, she had to find a car. And though she knew that she might regret it later, at the moment she was glad that she wasn't going to have to do it alone.

Keeping that thought in mind, she went to the front door and swung it open. Determined not to allow any lingering doubts to hold her back, she strode across the threshold, a crisp good-morning greeting on the tip of her tongue. But then she raised her eyes and saw him standing on the porch steps.

As her breath caught in her throat, she stopped short and simply stared at the man in front of her. He was definitely Dominic Fabrino, but a new Dominic, amazingly different than she'd ever seen before.

Of course, she hadn't thought he'd appear in worn jeans and a raggedy sweatshirt with his hair falling in his face. To be honest, she'd been too busy culling her own wardrobe to wonder what *he'd* wear. Now she realized that if she had, she probably wouldn't have been surprised to see him dressed in navy pleated plants, a navy-and-white pin-striped shirt and a burgundy V-neck sweater, his hair newly trimmed and neatly combed. And she might not have been quite so stunned at how attractive he could be when he so obviously put his mind to it.

"I know I'm early, but they weren't as busy as I thought they'd be at the barber shop," he said by way of explanation, his deep voice cutting through the silence stretching between them. "And since I was halfway here already, it seemed kind of silly to go home only to have to turn around and come back." Rubbing a hand along the back of his neck, he shrugged almost apologetically.

"No problem. I've been ready," Marti responded more ardently than she'd intended, then mentally chastised herself for gushing as well as gaping at the man.

So much for cool, calm and collected, she admonished herself as she clutched her purse and notebook to her chest. Apparently she wasn't as immune to his masculine allure as she ought to be, as she'd *thought* she'd be. And unfortunately there didn't seem to be anything she could do about it except get past it the way she'd gotten past so many other obstacles over the years.

"Well, then, I guess we should go." He tucked his hands in his pockets, shifting from one foot to the other as he held her gaze, his wry smile warming her as well as reassuring her, despite her every intention not to be so easily swayed.

"I guess we should," she murmured rather dreamily, then gave herself another firm mental shake. She wasn't a lovesick schoolgirl. She was a mature, intelligent woman, and it was time she started acting like one. Tilting her chin at a defiant angle, she attempted to regain control of herself and the situation. "I really must find a car today, so the sooner we get started, the better."

"The sooner the better," he agreed, then paused expectantly, a teasing glint in his eyes.

Marti knew that he was waiting for her to say or do something, but for the life of her she couldn't imagine what it was. She'd already assured him she was ready to go, hadn't she? And surely he must realize there was no graceful way she could get off the porch as long as he was standing on the steps before her.

"So are we going or what?" she asked at last, unable to mask her growing irritation any longer.

"We're going. But I think you'd better close your front door first, don't you?"

"Oh...of course...." Heat climbed her neck and spread across her cheeks as she spun around and grabbed the door handle. More than ever, and in more ways than one, she felt like a fool. And that was exactly how she'd been behaving since she'd walked out her front door.

She might be drawn to Dominic Fabrino, but she had no intention of doing anything about it. After all, she'd been drawn to Brent Winston, too. And no matter how much she wanted to believe that they weren't at all alike, she couldn't afford to think that. She couldn't risk that, given half a chance, Dominic would prove to be as strong and kind and gentle as she wanted him to be. She had already suffered enough pain and humiliation to last a lifetime at the hands of an attractive man. And now she had so much more to lose. If Dominic betrayed her trust as Brent had done...

But she wasn't going to trust him, was she? At least, not the same way she'd trusted Brent. She was going to spend a few hours with him, nothing more, nothing less. And then she'd be on her own again, maybe not the way she wanted to be, but the way she had to be to attain the only goal she had left in her life.

Taking a deep, steadying breath, she pulled her key from the front door lock, then dropped it in her purse as she turned to face Dominic once again. "All done," she confirmed, offering him the same bright smile and brisk tone of voice she used with Carter and Caisson's more recalcitrant clients.

As if aware of her sudden change of manner, he stared at her for several seconds, his dark eyes glimmering with amusement. Then, with a careless shrug, he stepped aside so she could precede him down the porch steps. "After you, Ms. Townsend," he murmured, then nodded toward the sleek black Corvette parked at the curb. "Your carriage awaits."

Somehow she managed to walk past him without falling on her face, but it was no easy task. For the second time in less than ten minutes he'd thrown her for a loop, and she didn't appreciate it, not one bit.

She'd just assumed he'd be driving the '57 Chevy. In fact, she'd been counting on it. Granted, the long, narrow bench seat had made her uncomfortable last night, but only because it had seemed to draw them together in the darkness. However, in the broad light of day it would have put some distance between them, distance she knew she needed now more than ever.

Unfortunately there wasn't going to be much between them but a gearshift in that dark, sexy car, she thought as she moved slowly down the sidewalk. But obviously their close proximity within its confines wasn't going to be nearly as disconcerting for him as it was for her. Otherwise he would have chosen another mode of transportation. Yet she didn't really believe that he'd decided to drive the Corvette just so he could cop a feel. If she did, she'd be back in the house by now.

Maybe he simply liked to drive the big, powerful sports car and the weekends were his only chance to do so. Or maybe he'd realized that spending the day with her was going to be more of a chore than he'd anticipated, and he'd found a way to make it more bearable.

"Wonderful, just wonderful," she muttered, aiming the words at herself in anything but a complimentary way. If she didn't stop assigning ulterior motives to his every move, she was going to end up in the nut house. And it would be just what she deserved, she thought as she paused at the curb.

"Yeah, it is, isn't it," Dominic agreed, halting beside her. He knew that she hadn't been referring to the Corvette, but considering the caustic tone of her voice, he decided it might be wiser to act as if she had. "I bought it with the last bonus I got before I left Comptech. Talk about blowing a wad. If I'd known how things were going to change, I probably wouldn't have done it. But at the time I had the money...and a bad case of the wants," he added ruefully as he opened the car door for her.

"You worked for Comptech?" Once again her eyes widened with surprise.

"For about ten years. From the time I got my MBA until my dad had a heart attack. I took a leave of absence to help out at the garage and never went back."

"I...see...." She gazed at him rather doubtfully, as if unsure that she'd heard him right.

Obviously she was aware of Comptech's reputation as a leader in the computer-software industry. The company was also ranked among the top ten in the country when it came to employee benefits. Job applicants literally lined up for miles when they were hiring. And no one, but *no one,* left Comptech on their own, especially when they'd reached the level he had. Yet Dominic had never regretted the decision he'd made. If Marti thought less of him because he'd opted for the family business rather than Comptech's fast track, he wanted to know it now.

"I realized that I liked working with my hands as well as my head, that I liked being my own boss and watching my own business expand. I also realized how much I was missing working sixty or seventy hours a week. I'll probably never be able to pay cash for a new Corvette again, but I make a decent living and so do the guys who work with me. And it's been kind of nice to be able to take a weekend off whenever I want without feeling guilty," he added, a wry smile tugging at the corners of his mouth.

"What did you do at Comptech?" she asked, tilting her head slightly as she eyed him with sudden interest.

"I was vice president of research and development," he replied, encouraged by her apparent lack of objection to the choices he'd made.

"Vice president?" Her soft voice held a note of utter astonishment. "And you don't miss it? You don't miss being an important part of a company like Comptech?"

"I enjoyed working for Comptech, but I don't miss it. I've been too busy. And I'm a part of Fabrino's now. Actually...I guess I *am* Fabrino's." His smile widened with pride and profound conviction. "And I wouldn't trade it for the world."

"I can't imagine leaving Carter and Caisson. My job's been my life for so long now I'm not sure what I'd do without it," Marti admitted, frowning thoughtfully as she met his gaze a moment longer. "But I may find out, if we don't get going." Ducking her head, she slid into the Corvette, then glanced at him expectantly.

"Why do you say that?"

"I have half a dozen accounts to review for the Monday morning staff meeting. I have to make a final decision on a replacement for our assistant art director while she's on maternity leave. And if I don't get started on next year's budget we won't have one. I'd planned to work all weekend, but..."

"You have to find a car first," he finished for her in a brusque tone of voice, his smile fading as he held her gaze.

She stared at him for several seconds. Then, her bright eyes suddenly shadowed with uncertainty, she nodded wordlessly.

"So let's do it." He slammed the door forcefully, wincing as the window glass rattled. Then, turning on his heel, he took a deep breath of the brisk autumn air and tried to will away the frustration welling up inside him as he crossed behind the car.

He had no right to be annoyed with her. Nor did he have any right to take out his irritation on her. He'd known exactly what he was doing when he brought Comptech into their conversation. He'd wanted her to know where he'd been as well as where he planned to go. And without disparaging the decisions he'd made, Marti had done the same. She'd been honest about her feelings for Carter and Caisson and her determination to improve her position there. In her own quiet way she'd let him know what was important to her. And apparently being with him wasn't anywhere near the top of her list.

Considering the kind of experience he'd had with Diane, he shouldn't have been so surprised. But sometime during the previous night, when he'd been unable to do anything but think of her, he'd begun to hope that he'd been wrong about Marti, that given half a chance she'd show some interest in something other than her job.

He'd forgotten that she was a corporate executive. And that all corporate executives had to be somewhat self-absorbed if they wanted to get ahead. He'd certainly been that way once, and so had his ex-wife. No matter how much he wanted Marti to be different from Diane, he simply couldn't wave a magic wand and make her so. The sooner he accepted that fact, the better off he'd be.

Unfortunately he hadn't planned on having to do it quite so early in the day. In fact, he'd made the mistake of starting to believe he might not have to do it at all, a belief that had been enhanced a hundredfold when she'd first stepped onto her front porch.

For the first time in the year he'd known her, she'd actually appeared approachable. Her classy yet casual clothes accentuated her femininity in a way her business suits never had. And without her horn-rimmed glasses she'd seemed softer and sweeter than he'd ever imagined she could be. He'd had the urge to ask her to take down her hair. But then he'd seen the shyness and uncertainty lurking in the depths of her bright blue eyes. Recalling how she'd run from him the night before, he'd hesitated, not wanting to say or do anything that might scare her away.

Talk about perverse, he thought as he paused beside the Corvette and dug his keys out of his pants pocket. She was the kind of woman he'd vowed to avoid, and considering the exchange they'd just had, he should be more determined than ever to stick to that vow. But, as he had the night before, he sensed that she was afraid of him. And once again her fear disconcerted him, and his vow gave way to a flood of ambiguity that he couldn't ignore.

Instinctively he'd known that she hadn't wanted to be alone with him last night. And a few moments ago the harsh tone of his voice had filled her eyes with apprehension. He would have had to have been blind not to have noticed the way she'd jumped when he'd slammed the car door in anger. Yet this same woman—so easily flustered by him—had managed to rise through the ranks of one of the country's most aggressive advertising agencies to become one of their top executives.

He'd dealt with several ad agencies while he'd worked at Comptech, and he knew for a fact that only the strong survived. A truly timid soul wouldn't have made it past the reception desk, much less gotten as far as Marti had. So that had to mean there was something about *him* that had her running for cover. Whatever it was, he wanted to know. Then at least he could put her mind at ease before they went their separate ways.

However, if he hoped to find out why she was afraid of him, he'd have to set aside his own discontent with his thwarted expectations. She was a nice lady; she certainly didn't deserve to be the butt of what was really his anger at himself.

Drawing in another deep, steadying breath, he opened the car door and slid into his seat. Turning to face her, he smiled at her encouragingly. "Would you like to start with any dealer in particular?"

"Um, no, not...really...." She eyed him warily for several seconds. Then, twisting her purse strap around her fingers, she lowered her gaze.

"Have you been to any yet?" he continued in a gentle tone as he shut his door and stuck the key in the ignition. He was acutely aware of just how much his gruff behavior had upset her. And he knew that it was going to be harder than he'd imagined to find a way to reassure her that she had nothing to fear from him.

Glancing at Dominic again, Marti named two car dealers, both of whom were pretty far down on the bottom of his list. From the look on her face he assumed she hadn't been impressed with them, either, so he immediately eliminated them as possibilities.

"How about a specific make or model? Do you want something small, medium or large? And what kind of price range do you have in mind?"

"Well, I had good luck with my old car so I am partial to Fords," she admitted, a hint of a smile playing at the corners of her mouth. "But I guess I ought to get an idea of what's available from some of the other car makers, too. I'm not fond of big cars, and I'm not wild about spending an enormous sum of money. Otherwise, I'm not sure what I want. And I'm not sure where to start, either.''

''Why don't we try some other car makers first, then hit the Ford dealer?'' Making a mental note that her tension had begun to dissipate once they'd begun to talk ''business,'' Dominic started the engine, shifted into gear and pulled away from the curb. Tapping a fingertip against the notebook she'd laid atop her purse, he continued. ''You make a note of the cars you like best and why. Then we'll stop for lunch and you can make a final decision about what's best for you, all right?'' Sensing her sudden hesitation, he offered her another reassuring smile. ''You don't want to rush into anything, do you?''

''No, but...'' She plucked at her purse strap for several seconds, obviously weighing what he'd said.

''But?''

''But...'' She glanced out the window, then back at him. Returning his smile, she shrugged and shook her head. ''You're right. I don't want to rush into anything.'' She paused a moment as she opened her notebook and slid a pen from her purse. ''So where are we going first?''

''Cowser's on Kingshighway.''

''And what should I do when we get there?''

''Why don't you let me do the talking?'' Just to be on the safe side, he made it a question, then flashed a wicked grin in her direction.

''We'll see.'' A smug expression on her face, Marti settled back in her seat and gazed out the window.

''Sounds fair to me,'' Dominic agreed, more than a hint of laughter in his deep voice as he downshifted and turned onto the highway.

Glancing at her watch, Marti realized it was almost one o'clock. No wonder she was so hungry. It had been hours since she'd had breakfast, yet so far Dominic hadn't seemed inclined to stop for lunch. Granted, she hadn't been all that enthusiastic about their sharing a meal when he'd first mentioned it. But after spending several hours with him the thought of grabbing a sandwich together wasn't quite as disconcerting as it had been earlier.

From the moment they'd pulled onto the first car lot, he'd been all business. He'd shown such aplomb in dealing with the salesmen that Marti had been happy to leave all the talking to him. He'd also addressed her questions and concerns with surprising equanimity. After a while she'd realized that working with him on her search for a new car wasn't much different than working with Charles or Rick or Leo on an ad campaign. With that thought in mind, she'd actually begun to relax and have a good time.

Still, if she didn't take another test drive for the rest of her life, it would be too soon. And if she didn't feed her growling stomach within the next few minutes, she could end up embarrassing herself by gnawing on the Corvette's creamy leather upholstery. Gazing longingly at a steak house as they whizzed by, she hoped that the next dealership would be the last on Dominic's longer-than-anticipated list.

"Just one more dealer, then we'll stop for lunch," Dominic assured her as if reading her mind.

"And then?"

"Then you decide what you want and we go back and get a good deal on it." He paused for a moment, glancing at her questioningly as he waited for the light to change. "Are you leaning toward one car or another yet?"

"Not really," she admitted with a rueful shake of her head. "But once I have a chance to go over all my notes, I'm sure it won't be too hard to make a final choice."

"There's no need to rush into anything. We could give it a couple of days, then go out again one evening after work."

"Oh, no, I couldn't..." She turned to look at him, but he was concentrating on the road ahead as he guided the car through the traffic on Lindbergh Boulevard. "I'll definitely decide today."

"As long as you're sure."

"I will be," she vowed with more confidence than she actually felt.

Though she had several good reasons to buy any one of several equally appealing automobiles, none had jumped off the lot and yelled, "Buy me." But after all of Dominic's hard bargaining on her behalf, how could she tell him that was what she'd been waiting for all along? He'd think she was crazy. And no matter what he said, she had no right to take any more of his time than she already had for what would probably end up a futile search.

Whether she wanted to admit it or not, she simply wasn't going to find a car with her name written all over it, a car that would suit her the way Dominic's Corvette suited him, a car that would make her feel good just looking at it much less driving it, a car—

"Oh, my..." As they pulled onto the lot of Abe's A-1 Ford, Marti turned in her seat, her gaze riveted to the bright, cherry red convertible parked just outside the showroom windows.

"What?" Easing to a stop in a parking space off to one side, Dominic turned, too.

"That's it. That's my car." Without hesitation, she opened her door, slid out and started toward her dream machine.

"Marti, wait." Catching up with her in a few quick strides, Dominic grabbed her hand and tugged gently in a vain attempt to slow her headlong rush across the car lot. "Remember what I told you about playing it cool?"

"I remember. But I'm going to buy that car no matter what." Tipping her head back, she eyed him steadily, all but daring him to disagree.

"You are?" From the amazed look on his face as he met her gaze, she could have sprouted wings. Maybe she had.

"I am," she replied, her voice full of conviction as she stopped beside the car and smoothed a hand over the black leather seat on the driver's side.

With the black top down and the sun sparkling off the windshield, the little Mustang all but begged her to come and play. And, more than anything, that was what she wanted to do. As she imagined her hands wrapped around the steering wheel and the wind in her hair, somewhere deep inside her something cold and hard and tight shifted and eased with surprising suddenness.

"I want to drive it. *Now.*"

"Your wish is my command." A salesman sidled up to them and dangled a set of keys in front of her face.

"Thanks, pal. We'll be right back," Dominic advised as he snatched the keys out of the other man's hand.

"Sure thing." Ignoring Dominic, he winked at Marti. "Have fun, sweetheart."

"Oh, I will." She offered him a wide smile, then turned to Dominic and held out her hand. "Keys, please."

"I'll 'keys, please' you," he muttered as he pulled her around to the passenger side and opened the door for her.

"Dominic, I want to drive."

"I know. And so does he." He nodded toward the salesman hovering a few yards away. "And believe me, right now the price is being driven up, not down."

"So?"

"So try to act nonchalant. And hard as it may be, defer to me. Then maybe, just maybe, this won't end up costing you an arm and a leg.'' He held her gaze as he gently squeezed her hand. ''All right?''

Though she wanted to argue, she knew he was right. It was never wise to be too eager. And despite what she'd said a few moments earlier, she had no intention of paying more than what Dominic thought the car was worth.

''All right,'' she agreed. ''But once we're a couple of blocks away from here I get to drive.''

''Yeah, you get to drive...sweetheart.'' Imitating the salesman, Dominic winked broadly and led her into the car with a bow.

''So you've made up your mind.''

''Yes. I'll have the double steak-burger platter with a salad, fries and a cherry cola.'' She tossed her menu aside and sat back in her chair, a smug smile tilting the corners of her mouth.

''About the car, Marti, the *car.*'' Dominic eyed her over the top of his menu with no small amount of exasperation. ''You left your notebook in the Corvette. So you've already decided to buy the Mustang, regardless of how it compares to the other cars we looked at today. Right?''

''Right.'' She nodded her head for added emphasis, then glanced at the waitress who'd stopped to take their order. ''Hi. I'll have the steak-burger platter...''

Dominic added his order to Marti's, then turned his attention back to her. ''I just want you to be sure about it.''

''You said it's a nice car.''

''It's a very nice car.''

''And you said you ought to be able to get the salesman to come down at least a couple of thousand off the sticker price.''

''If you play it cool when we go back to the dealership.''

''Then I'm sure.''

"Good."

As Marti picked up her fork and dug into her salad Dominic opened the little bag of oyster crackers that came with his chili and dumped them into it. Stirring the mess together with his spoon, he smiled inwardly, still amused by the change that had come over her the moment they'd pulled onto the Ford lot.

Until then she'd searched for a new car with a kind of quiet intensity. She had taken notes, asked questions and verbally weighed the pros and cons of various makes and models as earnestly as if her life depended on her decision. Then she'd totally lost it the moment she'd seen the little Mustang convertible, revealing a side of her that Dominic had convinced himself didn't exist. And he was intrigued by her all over again.

He had a feeling that she wasn't quite as staid and serious as she pretended to be. Buried beneath her reserve was an adventurous spirit that occasionally broke its bonds. And he'd been lucky enough to catch a glimpse of it. But why only a glimpse? What had caused her to conceal the best part of her, the part that made her come alive in a way he would have never imagined possible?

Had something happened in her past to make her so cool and distant? Or was there something about him that made her withdraw, that made her afraid? He knew of only one way to find out: start voicing some of the questions he'd been keeping to himself. And he intended to do it—now.

"You mentioned that you grew up in Kansas City. Does your family still live there?" he asked, settling back in his chair as the waitress set their burgers and fries on the table.

"Yes." Without looking at him, she picked up her burger and took a big bite.

Frowning at her obvious ploy, he salted his fries, then liberally doused them with ketchup. "So you have parents, grandparents, brothers, sisters, aunts, uncles?"

"Just parents. My grandparents are dead and I'm an only child of only children."

"Must have been kind of lonely for you."

"It wasn't too bad. My grandmother, my mother's mother, lived with us. We were really close. My old car originally belonged to her. She died a few months after my sixteenth birthday."

"I'm sorry."

"It was a long time ago." She shrugged as she reached for her cherry cola.

"You went to Mizzou, didn't you?" he continued doggedly, referring to the University of Missouri in Columbia by its popular nickname. With each question he asked she seemed to retreat a little more, but he refused to back off. Getting to know her obviously wasn't going to be easy, but he firmly believed it would be worth it.

"Yes."

"And then you went to work for Carter and Caisson?"

"Actually, I worked at a bank in Kansas City for almost a year. But I didn't like it much. I wanted to do something creative."

"So how long have you been with C and C now?"

"About seven years."

Stabbing at his fries with his fork, Dominic hesitated for several seconds as he considered which track to take next. They'd discussed their business backgrounds earlier and, to be honest, he was more interested in her personally than professionally at the moment. But although she didn't seem to be frightened by his inquisitiveness, there was no denying her reluctance to talk about herself. Ah, well, in for a penny, in for a pound, he thought, eyeing her steadily across the table.

"Ever been married?"

"No."

"Ever come close?"

"Not . . . not really." Pushing her empty plate away, she lowered her gaze, but not before Dominic had seen the flicker of fear in her eyes. "Going to work for Carter and Caisson meant a move to St. Louis. I didn't know anyone here, and my new job kept me awfully busy. I didn't have much of a chance to socialize outside of the office. And I don't believe in dating co-workers or clients. So there hasn't really been anyone. . . ." She paused, then glanced at him, obviously ill at ease despite her smile. "Gosh, all I've done is talk about myself. What about you, Dominic? Parents, grandparents, brothers, sisters?"

"My parents and my grandmother, my father's mother, live on the Hill. My sisters, too. They're both married. Rose has three kids, two girls and a boy. And Carmen is expecting her first baby in February," he replied, returning her smile. He knew that she wouldn't talk about herself any more today unless he pushed. But he felt that he'd pushed hard enough, at least for the time being.

"Did you go to Mizzou?"

"For my undergraduate degree. I got my MBA at Northwestern, in Illinois."

"Then you went to work for Comptech until your dad had a heart attack." She folded her napkin into a neat square and set it on the table. "I remember you told me once that you'd been married."

"Yeah, I've been married. I've been divorced for about three years now." He stated the facts simply and easily. The worst of the hurt and anger had dissipated a long time ago.

"How long were you married?"

"Almost eight years. We met at Comptech. We worked in different divisions. Diane's general manager of marketing for the southern United States. She's based in Dallas now."

"Eight years?" She stared at him in surprise, hesitating as if she was unsure about how deeply into his past she wanted to probe. In the end, curiosity got the better of her. "What happened?"

"After I left Comptech and took over my dad's business, I wanted to start a family. She agreed, just like she agreed with my decision to get off the fast track. Then she had her tubes tied without telling me. I found out about it when I opened a piece of her mail by mistake. It was a statement from a gynecologist in Houston. She'd had it done on one of her business trips."

"But...why? Why deceive you?" Marti stared at him, her eyes wide.

"She thought I'd come to my senses eventually and go back to Comptech. In her words, she didn't want to be stuck with a squalling brat as a result of my mid-life crisis." Folding his fingers into a fist, he turned away from her as a wave of anger washed over him.

"Oh, Dominic, I'm sorry. I had no right..."

As Marti's fingertips grazed the back of his hand, he faced her again, forcing himself to smile. Telling her about Diane had been more difficult than he'd expected. But he was glad that he had. He'd learned the hard way that it was far better to lay all your cards on the table at the beginning. And he wanted to believe that for Marti and himself today was definitely a beginning.

"Hey, we've been doing business together for almost a year, haven't we?" With a deft twist of his wrist he caught her hand in his. "Don't you think it's about time we finally got to know each other?"

"Of course," she agreed, her soft voice lacking conviction as she slid her hand free and fumbled for her purse. "Lunch is on me," she continued brightly, glancing back at him.

"I don't think so." He palmed the check before she could, scooted his chair out and stood.

"But you've spent all day helping me find a car. It's the least I can do." Slipping her purse strap over her shoulder, she stood, too. A frown tugged at the corners of her mouth.

"No, the least you can do is invite me to dinner," he suggested, keeping his tone light and teasing. Again he saw the flicker of fear in her eyes, and for just a moment he was tempted to back off. But he didn't. He'd never do anything to hurt her, but unless he spent some time with her how could he make sure that she knew it? "You can cook, can't you?"

"Yes, but—"

"So dinner at your place whenever you want, and we'll call it even. Okay?" Not waiting for a reply, he turned and headed for the cashier.

As she stared at Dominic's retreating back, Marti realized just how completely she'd been finessed. He'd all but invited himself into her home, and she'd allowed him to do it. If she'd had half her wits about her, she'd never have gotten herself into such an awkward position. But she'd let down her guard after he'd told her about his ex-wife. Now she was going to have to find a graceful way to get out of her predicament. Of course she'd repay him . . . somehow. But he wasn't having dinner at her house. At least, not in this lifetime.

Reminding herself that within an hour or two at most she'd have her car and be home again, Marti joined Dominic at the cash register and waited patiently while he paid their bill. As they walked to his Corvette, she thanked him for lunch, then sat quietly while they drove back to the Ford dealership.

"Nervous?" Dominic asked as they walked toward the showroom.

"A little. I've never bought a new car before."

"Just—"

"Be cool and let you do the talking?"

"Yeah." Reaching for the door handle, he grinned at her. "I think I can handle that."

"I think you can, too. Still want to pay cash?"

"Yes."

"Then let's go for it, okay?"

"Okay."

It took less time than Marti had expected for Dominic to make a deal for her. In fact, before she knew it, she was the proud owner of a brand-new, cherry red Mustang convertible. But contrary to her original plan, she wasn't going to be able to drive it home until Tuesday. Not only did her check have to clear the bank, but she had to arrange for an increase in insurance coverage, too. On Tuesday, though, the sporty little car would be all hers. Now if only the mild weather would hold out a few more weeks so she could drive with the top down, she'd be truly happy.

"How does it feel to be a new-car owner?" Dominic asked as he turned down her street.

"Pretty good," she admitted, then frowned. "Why are you driving so slowly all of a sudden?"

"Because I want you to promise me something."

"What?" She eyed him suspiciously. If he thought she was going to cook for him tonight or any night, he had another think coming.

"I want you to promise that you'll let me walk you to your front door."

"That's it?"

"That's it."

"Okay, I promise you can walk me to my front door."

"Thank you, Ms. Townsend. You don't know how much that means to me."

He sounded so sincere that Marti glanced at him suspiciously again. But his teasing wink back told her she must be imagining things.

True to her word, she waited for him to come around and open her car door, then walked with him to her front porch. Pausing at the base of the steps, she turned to face him.

"I really appreciate all you've done, first with my old car and with helping me find a new one. I couldn't have done it on my own."

"Oh, I imagine you could have. But it wouldn't have been as much fun, would it have?" He smiled slowly as he gazed down at her.

"No, it wouldn't have," she admitted, realizing that she meant it. In fact, for just an instant, she wished their day didn't have to end. But it was almost four o'clock, and she had a ton of work to do. "Well, thanks again, Dominic."

"You're welcome, Marti." He hesitated for several seconds. Then ever so gently he smoothed a wisp of her honey blond hair away from her face. "See you."

Without a word, Marti watched him turn and walk away. Her heart pounded in her chest, her hands trembled and she didn't need a mirror to know that her face burned bright red. Even as she let him go she considered calling him back. But in the end she couldn't do it. She stood where she was, alone in the shadowy sunlight, until he'd gone. And then slowly, sadly, she climbed the steps, unlocked the door and once again sought her solitary sanctuary.

Chapter Three

Just after noon on Sunday, Marti finally called it quits. With a sigh of resignation, she tossed her pen onto the table, stood up and crossed the kitchen. Bracing her palms on the tile counter on either side of the sink, she gazed out the window at her neatly landscaped little yard and wondered what she was going to do. In all the years she'd been with Carter and Caisson, she'd never faced a Monday morning staff meeting unprepared. But there was a first time for everything. And at the rate she was going, tomorrow would probably be one.

Though she'd been trying to work for more than three hours, she'd accomplished nothing at all. No matter how hard she stared at the papers she'd spread out in front of her, she couldn't seem to concentrate on anything even vaguely related to Carter and Caisson for more than a minute or two. Then, despite her best efforts, her mind would wander, and before she knew it, once again she'd be thinking about Dominic Fabrino and the time they'd spent together.

"As if dreaming the night away hadn't been enough," she muttered with a rueful shake of her head.

Had anyone ever suggested that she could be so distracted by a man, she'd have thought they were crazy. Now she was starting to wonder if maybe she needed her head examined. Surely she had more worthwhile things to do than daydream about Dominic.

"So why aren't you doing them?" she chided herself softly as she turned away from the window and leaned against the counter. Crossing her arms over her chest, she tipped her head back and stared at the ceiling for several seconds, as if searching for the answer to her question. But she was only fooling herself. Though she might not like to admit it, she knew only too well why she couldn't work.

It had been quite a while since she'd had as much fun as she'd had with Dominic, and unfortunately the novelty of it had yet to wear off. Suddenly she had some good memories to supplant the bad, and foolish though she knew it was, she didn't want to let them go—not when she knew those few good memories would be all she'd have.

Looking back, she couldn't believe how fearful and uncertain she'd been about him. He'd behaved like a perfect gentleman the entire time they'd been together. And he'd treated her like a friend and associate in much the same way that the men she worked with did. At least, he had—until he'd walked her to her front door....

Turning to gaze out the window again, Marti thought of the moment when he'd touched her hair, and wondered if she'd only imagined it. He'd done it so quickly, so simply, that it might not have happened at all. And he'd made no other move in that direction. He'd merely said that he'd see her. Then he'd gone on his way without a backward glance.

But they weren't going to see each other again and she knew it. Her new car wouldn't require the services of a master mechanic, so she had no reason to return to Fabrino's. And Dominic had more than done his *duty* where she was concerned. While he'd been kind enough to help her find a car, she knew that she couldn't expect his benevolence to extend any further, especially now that he'd gotten to know her.

After the conversations they'd had yesterday, surely he'd realized as well as she that they simply weren't right for each other. She'd meant what she'd said when she'd told him that her job was her life. And he'd left no doubt in her mind that a wife and family were of primary importance to him. Obviously their wants and needs were poles apart. *Obviously.*

For just a moment Marti remembered a time when she'd wanted, *needed,* a husband and family—a time before Brent Winston.

But she'd put all that behind her, hadn't she? She'd pulled herself out of the abyss of pain and humiliation that had been a brutal man's cruel legacy. And in so doing she'd chosen to pursue one set of hopes and dreams rather than another. After what Brent had done to her, she'd known that she could never be any man's wife. But one day she could rise to the top of Carter and Caisson.

And now certainly wasn't the time to be having second thoughts. Not when she was so close to her ultimate goal. Now was the time to reinforce her normally steadfast determination to be a success. And to accept, once and for all, that despite her growing attraction to him the few hours she'd spent with Dominic would be all she'd have.

Unless she invited him to dinner....

But she wasn't going to do that, was she? While the thought of having him in her house wasn't nearly as frightening as it had been a couple of days ago, she wasn't foolish enough to tempt fate one way or another. Nor was she going to start something she couldn't finish. And although Dominic had suggested a dinner invitation as an appropriate way to repay him, she wasn't about to give him the idea that she was interested in him more personally.

As she'd decided sometime around midnight last night, she'd show her appreciation in a more detached manner, just as she did with Carter and Caisson's clients. She could send him a gift certificate for dinner for two at Tony's or Giovanni's or that posh little restaurant in the Ritz Carlton Hotel.

But what if he felt obligated to invite her to join him? That would defeat the purpose. Then again, what if he didn't? Standing in her kitchen, staring out the window, Marti realized that she didn't really relish the thought of Dominic Fabrino dining out with another woman.

Better to have something sent from one of the little specialty shops in Clayton or Kirkwood, she thought, turning her back on the bright, sunny day. Perhaps a case of wine or a selection of gourmet coffees. Or chocolates or fruit and nuts or a honey-baked ham.

"While you're at it, Marti, why not have Dierberg's deliver groceries to his door once a month for a year?" she muttered sarcastically, moving away from the kitchen counter. "That would certainly pay your debt, wouldn't it?"

Not that Dominic had made her feel as if she owed him anything. Except a home-cooked meal....

The urge to scream almost overwhelmed her as she paused by the table and stared at the various files spread out atop it. She was back to square one. Again. For all her mental gyrations she'd done nothing but increase her level of frustration. And she was no more able to settle down to work than she had been fifteen minutes ago.

Glancing over her shoulder, she gazed out the window for several seconds. Beyond the glass the sun shone brilliantly in the clear blue sky. When she'd gone out earlier to pick up her paper, the air had been cool and crisp and . . . inviting. But she'd been too determined to work and had not accepted what had been inevitable all along.

Before she could even think of changing her mind, she crossed the kitchen, walked down the hallway and ran up the stairs. In her bedroom she grabbed her camera, a sweater, her keys and some cash, then headed for the front door. Tower Grove Park would be full of people on a beautiful day like today. And she could walk there in thirty minutes or less.

Surely some fresh air and exercise would clear her head. Then maybe, just maybe, she'd be able to get something done when she returned. And if she didn't? Well, there was always tomorrow. She'd been the one who'd originally chosen Monday morning for staff meetings. So if she wanted to change them to Tuesday mornings, she had every right to. And she probably would, she thought, smiling as she paused on her front porch to draw in a deep breath of the autumn air. Then, lifting her face to the sun, she started down the sidewalk.

She wanted to photograph the old music stand and the romantic ruins surrounded by fall colors. And if she was lucky, she'd come upon some children playing in the piles of leaves near the dovecote picnic pavilion. She could just imagine them running and jumping, then laughing out loud as the leaves scattered around them. Her smile widening, she quickened her pace. She'd get some wonderful pictures today, just wonderful. . . .

Just after seven o'clock on Sunday evening Dominic finally headed for home. He'd been at his parents' house since early afternoon. He'd stopped by to tell his father the good news about closing the deal on the property that would be Fabrino's South County sometime after the first of the year. He'd ended up staying to watch a football game with the old man, even though he wasn't all that interested in the sport anymore. Then, when he'd realized that his mother was making lasagna, he'd invited himself to dinner, stretching out his visit well beyond what he'd originally intended. In fact, if it hadn't been for the senior citizens' social at St. Ambrose that they'd planned to attend, he'd probably still be sitting in his parents' living room.

He'd been too restless to work on the bills and book-keeping the way he'd planned, but he hadn't really been in the mood to socialize with anyone outside his family. And since he'd spent the night before playing poker with his sisters and their husbands—and losing every hand—he hadn't wanted to impose on them again. Especially not when they'd already given him a hard time about "the blonde" his brother-in-law Tony had seen him with on Saturday afternoon.

Talk about getting the third degree, he thought as he climbed into his car and started the engine. It had taken every ounce of skill he possessed to avoid answering his older sisters' probing questions. But then he'd had lots of practice over the years. And this time he'd obviously been more than moderately successful at deflecting their interest since there was no sign that word had gotten back to his mother.

Had Carmen or Rose said anything to their mother, she would have been all over him about it. But neither his mother nor his father had mentioned Marti, so he assumed his sisters had wisely chosen not to get their hopes up. Which was just as well, because where Marti was concerned there was definitely no hope. At least not the wife-and-kids kind of hope his mother was increasingly eager to entertain.

"So if there's no hope, why are you driving by her house again?" he chided himself as he turned onto her street. Talk about a waste of time. Especially considering he'd done so twice already since he'd left her standing on her front doorstep, and had gained nothing by it either time. Not even peace of mind.

At midnight last night her place had been so dark and still that he'd spent hours wondering if she was all right. And when he'd cruised by that afternoon the house had appeared equally abandoned, thus increasing his concern.

Certainly she'd been on her own for a long time. And over the years she would have had to have learned to take care of herself. Yet he hadn't liked the idea of her being all alone in that closed and quiet house without any means of transportation. Not that he'd had any guarantee that she was alone or, for that matter, without a way to get around—which was probably the real reason why he'd been so antsy all day, he thought, slowing the Corvette to a crawl.

To his relief he saw that there were lights on in her front windows, both upstairs and down. And there weren't any cars parked on the street nearby. More than likely she was not only home alone but perfectly all right. But maybe he ought to stop and say hello just to be sure.

Then again, maybe not, he decided, pressing down on the accelerator and pulling away from the curb. Some sixth sense warned him that ringing her doorbell at seven-thirty on a Sunday night wouldn't be wise, that it would scare the living daylights out of her. And that was the last thing he wanted to do. He'd actually made some progress with Ms. Martha Townsend the previous day, and that progress meant more to him than he liked to admit.

Although she hadn't lowered her guard completely, after a while she'd shown some signs of enjoying his company. She'd laughed and talked with less reserve than she ever had before. And when he'd given in to the urge that had been riding him all day, when he'd finally touched her golden hair, she hadn't flinched away from him as he'd feared she would. She'd gazed at him with wide, wondering eyes. And when he'd turned to go he'd been almost certain that her wonder had suddenly been tinged with regret.

Yet she hadn't made any move to stop him. She'd let him go without a word.

"And if you had any sense at all, you'd stay gone," he admonished himself as he turned the corner and headed for home. "Because you want a lot more than a *relationship*. And she obviously wants a lot less."

It was good advice and he knew it. But he also knew that he wasn't going to take it, at least not yet. One day with Marti hadn't been nearly enough to quell his growing interest in her. In fact, he had to admit that the time they'd spent together had left him more intrigued than ever. And he realized that getting her out of his system was going to take a lot longer than he'd originally anticipated.

"Yeah, sure, like getting her out of your system is what you really have in mind," he growled as he pulled into the garage behind the little two-bedroom bungalow he'd bought after the condo in Clayton had been sold.

In fact, what he'd *really* had in mind, at least most of last night, was pulling the pins from her hair and holding her in his arms and kissing her soft mouth until the last of her resistance was gone. And if he didn't get his mind on something else soon, he'd be up all night again.

He'd already wasted one good night's sleep wanting what he'd probably never have. He wasn't about to waste another. Unless he could find a legitimate way to see her again, any thoughts at all in her direction would be fruitless. And thoughts of holding, kissing and touching would be downright frustrating.

So he couldn't show up unexpectedly on her front doorstep, especially at night. But he could call her on the telephone. And, knowing that she was without a car, he could offer to give her a ride to work in the morning. Considering how efficient she seemed to be, she'd probably already made arrangements. But what could it hurt to call and ask? At the very worst, he'd at least get to talk to her, if only for a few minutes.

Still, he didn't head straight for the telephone after hanging up his jacket in the hall closet. Instead he took his time, storing the pan of leftover lasagna in the refrigerator. Then he took a brownie from the bag his mother had sent home with him and wandered into the living room.

Savoring the dark, rich chocolate, he considered the possible consequences if he chose to pursue Ms. Marti Townsend. He knew he'd be setting himself up for more hurt. But he was also honest enough to admit that he wouldn't be the only one at risk.

Marti was a nice woman with specific goals and aspirations for the future, goals and aspirations that simply weren't compatible with his own. Throwing roadblocks of any kind in her way would be unfair, especially if he did so only to assuage his masculine pride. He'd be meddling with her emotional well-being, and that was something he didn't want to do to anyone. Not after all he'd gone through with Diane.

He'd learned the hard way that wanting someone to change wasn't enough to make it happen. If a person didn't choose to change, they wouldn't, no matter what you said or did. Diane hadn't chosen to change. Yet he'd allowed himself to believe that she would, even though, looking back, he'd had no reason to.

They'd been so much alike when they'd first met at Comptech. They'd both wanted a "better life" than their blue-collar upbringings, and they'd both been willing to work for it to the exclusion of all else. But then his father had had a heart attack, and Dominic had known that without his help the older man would lose his business. So he'd taken a leave of absence and gone back to Fabrino's.

Within weeks he'd begun to realize that his life as a corporate executive hadn't necessarily been "better," just different. He'd realized that home and family meant more to him than he'd ever admitted. And he'd realized that money and power weren't true measures of a man's success. What he *hadn't* realized, but should have, was that for Diane they were, and they always would be.

Growing up on a small farm in central Missouri as the eldest of eight children, she'd done without much more than he had. She'd done her fair share of hard, physical labor. Plus she'd been given much of the responsibility for raising her younger brothers and sisters. Yet she'd found time for her schoolwork, won a college scholarship and eventually began to live the kind of life she'd dreamed of for so long. And she'd had no intention of giving up even a small part of it to have his child—or any child—ever.

He might have been able to deal with it if she'd been honest with him. Instead she'd led him on, allowing him to believe that she shared his dreams, when all the time she'd been deceiving him while waiting for him to come to his senses. And that's exactly what he'd finally done, the night he opened a piece of her mail by mistake and saw the statement for a tubal ligation from a doctor in Houston.

Yeah, he'd come to his senses, all right. And in the three years since then, he'd refused to get involved with anyone who even vaguely resembled his ex-wife in thought, word or deed. But then Marti Townsend had wandered into Fabrino's Garage, and it had been downhill ever since. And the slide would continue until he got her out of his system once and for all, something he couldn't do as long as he kept avoiding her.

He eyed the telephone on the table next to his chair, searching unsuccessfully for a way to justify what he knew he was about to do. He was going to call her. And he was going to offer her a ride to work. Period. If she accepted, fine. If not, that was fine, too. He'd find another way to see her. Just one more time. Just to be sure he'd made the right decision. For her good, as well as his own.

When the telephone rang at eight-thirty Marti was tempted not to answer it. She hadn't talked to her parents in almost a month and was afraid it would be them. She was in no mood to answer their probing questions about her life in general and her job in particular. They'd only find fault with something she'd done or planned to do and end up ruining what remained of her weekend.

But guilt got the better of her after the third ring. If she had to talk to her domineering mother and her pompous father, she might as well get it over with tonight. In fact, it might actually be easier while she was still basking in the mellow glow that had followed her home from the park and into her darkroom, where she'd spent the past couple of hours printing pictures. Then, of course, it might not be her parents calling after all. It might be someone from work with a problem that needed her immediate attention.

She lifted the receiver on the fourth ring, took a deep breath and said hello.

"Hey, Marti. It's me...Dominic. Just thought I'd call and see how you're doing."

She hesitated for several seconds, surprised by the deep voice coming from the other end of the telephone line. Dominic Fabrino was the last person she'd expected to call. Yet she was more pleased than she wanted to be that he had.

"I'm, um, just fine. How about you?" she asked as she twisted the telephone cord around her fingers.

"I'm fine, too." He paused, as if unsure what he wanted to say next, then finally continued. "Have you been doing all right without a car? Do you need anything from the store or ... anything?"

"No, not really." She hesitated again, searching desperately for something more to say. For someone who prided herself on being good with words, she was having an awfully hard time coming up with anything intelligent.

She could ask how he'd spent the day, but it wasn't really any of her business. And she didn't think he'd be interested in her walk to the park or her picture taking. She imagined he'd only called to dispense with any lingering sense of obligation he might feel toward her. Making it easy for him was the least she could do.

"I've got more than enough stuff on hand to tide me over until my car is ready. But I really appreciate your concern. Thanks so much for call—"

"How about work tomorrow? Have you made arrangements to get to the office in the morning?" he asked, cutting her off in mid-farewell.

"Gosh, I ... I hadn't really thought about it," she said. It was a white lie, and she was glad that they weren't standing face-to-face. The hot flush heating her cheeks would have given her away in an instant.

But she didn't want to tell him that she'd planned to take the bus. She wanted to see if he'd offer an alternative, one she had every intention of accepting, despite all the warnings she'd given herself earlier in the day.

"I wouldn't mind taking you downtown."

"I appreciate the offer, but I don't want you to go out of your way. I can always take the bus," she admitted, her conscience prodding her in a way she couldn't ignore.

"I don't think that would be a good idea. At least, not tomorrow. There's a cold front coming in tonight, and the weather's supposed to be wet and nasty in the morning. And you've got a two, maybe three-block walk to the nearest stop, don't you?"

"Almost four..." She hesitated one last time, then continued. "And I hate walking in cold, wet, nasty weather. So if you're sure you don't mind, I'll be more than happy to take you up on your offer."

She could have called a cab, but she wasn't about to say so. She'd been honest enough to give him an out, and he'd chosen not to take it. Now it was time to be honest with herself and acknowledge the fact that she wanted to see him again.

"If I minded, I wouldn't have asked." He stated the simple fact in a reassuring tone of voice. "What time do you usually leave the house?"

"About seven. But if that's not convenient—"

"Seven, it is. See you then."

"Yes, of course. See you then," she agreed, just moments before he hung up.

Smiling, she cradled the receiver, then set about unwinding the cord from around her fingers. That done, she stood by the kitchen counter for several minutes more. Finally, giving herself a firm mental shake, she returned to the table, determined to get something done in the hours ahead. This time Marti faced the facts head-on: she wasn't going to be getting any sleep—again.

Despite the cold, damp wind whipping through the trees, scattering leaves in all directions, Marti was standing on her front porch waiting for him when he pulled to the curb at seven o'clock sharp Monday morning. Muttering a curse, Dominic jumped out of the Chevy and sprinted to the sidewalk. He hadn't expected her to wait for him out in the cold, but in a way it made sense. He was beginning to realize that it was just like Marti to feel she ought to.

In fact, he'd been waiting for her to call and cancel the ride to work since just after six. He was glad that she hadn't, much too glad for his own good. Especially since the woman hurrying toward him bore only a faint resemblance to the woman he'd been with on Saturday.

His soft, sweet Marti had changed, literally overnight, into Ms. Martha Townsend, Carter and Caisson Advertising Incorporated's cool and distant general manager. Once again she'd scraped her hair back and pinned it up. And once again she wore her horn-rimmed glasses. He'd lay odds that underneath her tailored, black cashmere coat was another of her boring little business suits, probably dark gray to match her low-heeled pumps, along with the requisite silk shirt.

As he swung the passenger door open for her, he eyed the briefcase she clutched in one leather-gloved hand and barely quelled the urge to curse out loud. He'd seen her similarly dressed often enough in the past. But after Saturday...

Hell, what had he expected? She *was* Carter and Caisson's general manager, and it was her responsibility to look the part. Whether he liked it or not, there was nothing he could do about it, nothing he *would* do about it. Because she wasn't *his,* and as he'd told himself last night, she never would be.

"You didn't have to wait outside, Marti. I would have come to the door," he growled, stepping aside as she moved past him.

"I thought you might be in a hurry. Anyway, I'd only just come out when you pulled up to the curb." She slid into the car, then jumped when he slammed the door shut.

Maybe he wasn't a morning person, she thought, watching him cross in front of the Chevy. But, no, he'd been in a good mood when he'd come to the house on Saturday. Hadn't he? And taking her to work *had* been his idea. He'd also readily agreed to be there at seven, so it wasn't as if she'd rousted him out of bed before he was ready. All she'd done was walk out her front door a minute or two before he'd arrived. So why was he being so surly?

As he climbed into the car the scent of his spicy aftershave whispered around her on the gust of cold air he brought in with him. Settling her briefcase more securely in her lap, Marti glanced at him out of the corner of her eye. He was dressed in faded jeans, an old sweatshirt and a shabby, brown leather bomber jacket—his usual work wear.

To her surprise Marti realized that she actually liked him better in his simple work clothes than the more fashionable attire he'd worn on Saturday. For some reason she also felt more comfortable with him this way. She couldn't deny that he'd looked good in slacks and a sweater, but the jeans, sweatshirt and leather jacket enhanced his rugged masculinity in a way that made her feel more feminine than she'd ever felt before. And it was an extremely pleasant feeling.

However, he had an odd look on his face—half angry, half exasperated—that she found somewhat disconcerting. And she wasn't sure what to do about it. She didn't like to think that she'd done something to upset him, even unknowingly. Not when he was doing her a favor. Again.

But what could she say? What *should* she say?

At this point she didn't think it mattered, as long as she said something to break the silence stretching between them. Just to be on the safe side, though, she'd be as gracious as possible. If graciousness worked with her more cantankerous clients, surely it would work with Dominic Fabrino. And if it didn't? Well, then, she'd think of something else. She had no intention of spending the rest of the day blaming herself for leaving him moody and ill-tempered.

"You were right about the weather. It's as bad as you said it would be." Shifting on the wide seat, she turned to face him as he started the engine and pulled away from the curb. "I'm really glad you called and offered me a ride to work," she added with a smile.

Steering the Chevy down the street, he stared out the windshield, not saying anything for several seconds. Marti was beginning to wonder if he'd heard her when he finally met her gaze.

"I'm glad I did, too," he said, returning her smile, his voice reassuringly warm. "I'd have felt pretty bad if I'd found out later that you'd walked four blocks to the bus stop in this mess." He paused for a moment, shifting his attention to the street ahead, then continued more casually. "So did you get any work done yesterday?"

"Actually, I played hooky. I walked to Tower Grove Park around noon and spent the rest of the afternoon taking pictures," she replied, barely restraining a sigh of relief at his sudden change of mood. He'd obviously set aside whatever had been bothering him. Or else she'd imagined it. "What about you? Did you do anything special?"

"I went to see my folks. Watched a football game with my dad. Then I let my mother talk me into staying for dinner. I'm a sucker for a home-cooked meal, ya know."

He glanced at her and grinned in a way that made her heart flutter. As a flash of heat flew up her cheeks, she ducked her head. Avoiding his gaze, she tightened her grip on her briefcase and willed the moment to pass. She was not going to invite him to dinner. She *wasn't*. No matter how guilty and ungrateful she felt. There were other, less personal ways to show her appreciation. Before the day was over she'd ask Heather to help her choose the one that best suited the situation.

"Sounds like you had a nice day, then," she murmured noncommittally as she risked a quick glance in his direction. He seemed to be concentrating intently on his driving. Rain was pounding on the windshield.

"Sounds like I wasn't the only one. You enjoy taking pictures, huh?"

"It gives me a chance to be creative, something I've missed since moving to the business side of advertising. But I seem to have less and less time for it lately. What about you? Do you have any hobbies?"

"You're riding in it," he said as he turned onto Market Street and headed in the general direction of her building.

"The Chevy's your hobby?"

"When I bought it over two years ago it was a beat-up old rust bucket. Now it's almost completely restored to mint condition. Guess I'll have to start looking around for another old classic that needs some TLC after the first of the year. Although I won't have nearly as much free time on my hands once the new garage is open."

"New garage?" Marti gazed at him thoughtfully as he halted the car in front of the tall, gray stone building that housed the St. Louis offices of Carter and Caisson. "Are you moving to another location or expanding?"

"Expanding. Grubman finally accepted my offer for his place on South Lindbergh. The buildings need some renovation and at least half the machinery has to be replaced. But Fabrino's Number Two should be ready for business sometime in January."

Hearing the pride in Dominic's voice and seeing it in his dark eyes as he turned to face her, Marti couldn't help but smile. "And here I thought you'd had it with working sixty hours a week," she teased softly.

"Business has been pretty good lately, but I'm not planning on being *that* busy."

"Oh, I don't know. You might be surprised. I've recommended you to dozens of people over the past year. And I'm sure I'm not your only satisfied customer."

"Well, thanks. I really appreciate the free advertising. At least, I will until I have to start working every Saturday again."

"I guess that would be a fate worse than death, huh?" she asked wryly.

"Not necessarily. But there *are* lots of other ways I'd rather spend my weekends," he replied, the corners of his mouth hitching into a wicked grin.

"Oh, really? Such as?"

"Such as how I spent the past weekend."

His grin faded as he held her gaze, and Marti realized that he wasn't just talking about the time he'd spent with his parents. He was including the hours they'd been together. And he wanted her to know it.

"Well, gosh, I guess I'd better get going," she murmured, shifting on the seat. "I think Officer Friendly down the block has been eyeing us for the past few minutes, and now he's heading this way. I don't want you to get a ticket or anything."

"That's Joey Donatello. We went to high school together. He's not coming over here to give me a ticket. He's coming over here to drool on my Chevy."

"In any case, it's getting late and I really should..." As she groped for the door handle, he rested a hand on her shoulder, gently turning her to face him again.

"Marti, it's pouring out there. Stay put while I come around with an umbrella, okay?"

Not waiting for her to reply, he pulled an enormous black umbrella out from under the front seat and opened his car door. Ten seconds later she was tucked under his arm, walking beside him as fast as she could toward the double bank of glass doors, the cold wind whipping around her ankles.

He didn't let go of her until they were standing in the lobby. And as he did, Marti realized that she didn't want to move away. She wanted to savor the warmth of his closeness for as long as she could.

"So what time do you want me to pick you up this evening?" he asked, his voice husky as he smoothed a few wild wisps of hair away from her face.

She blinked twice as she gazed up at him, the intimacy of his touch cutting into her soul. Then she quickly shook her head as his words finally sank into her befuddled brain. "You don't have to..."

She saw the warning in his dark eyes and her words trailed away. He wasn't going to take no for an answer. And to be honest, "no" wasn't the answer she really wanted to give.

"Six o'clock would be fine."

"Six, it is." He smiled, apparently pleased with her answer, then continued. "Just so you won't have to worry about it, why don't you plan on riding to work with me tomorrow morning, too? Then I can take you over to the car dealer tomorrow night."

"All right."

"And, Marti, do me a favor, will you?"

"What's that?"

"Stay in the lobby until I get here tonight. I don't want you to end up with pneumonia. Okay?"

"Okay."

He nodded his head once as if to seal their pact. Then he swung around and strode through the doors, disappearing into the growing crowd of office workers who had begun to arrive.

"Well, well, well . . . Ms. Townsend. And wasn't that *Mr. Fabrino?*"

"Heather!"

"Good morning to you, too, boss."

Spinning around on her heel, Marti marched toward the bank of elevators at the opposite end of the long, narrow lobby, her face burning what could only be a bright red. "What are you doing here so early?"

"I thought I was going to be typing next year's budget so it would be ready to hand out at the staff meeting. But something tells me I could have slept an extra thirty minutes."

"Oh, Heather, I'm sorry." Marti turned to her assistant as they waited for an elevator. "I completely forgot."

"Why am I not surprised?" Heather waggled her eyebrows as she grinned at Marti. "Is he as good as he looks?"

Although Marti didn't think it was possible, her face seemed to grow even hotter as she turned away from the other woman's avid gaze. "Honestly, Heather. I wouldn't know."

"Oh, please, I saw the way you were looking at each other."

"It's not what you think."

"Then what is it? Tell me, tell me. *Tell me,*" Heather demanded in a strident whisper as they squeezed onto an elevator.

"Upstairs, all right?"

"All right," she murmured, drawing out the words with childish glee.

Talk about luck, Marti thought, shifting her briefcase from one hand to another as the lighted numbers all too

quickly marked off the floors. But then if anyone from the
office had to witness her little scene with Dominic, she supposed she'd just as soon it be Heather. At least she was loyal
and understanding. And she kept her mouth closed when it
really counted. She did, however, have a bad habit of
jumping to conclusions, and once she got something into her
head, it was almost impossible to get it out. But Marti had
set her straight in the past, and there was no reason why she
couldn't do it again.

"Okay, Marti, we've been up here alone for all of twenty
seconds. What gives with you and the hunk?" Heather
wheedled, following Marti down the hallway and into her
office, switching on lights along the way.

"My car finally gave out, so I had to shop for a new one
on Saturday. Dominic offered to go with me and I accepted. He also offered me a ride to work. And again I accepted. End of story." With studied nonchalance Marti
dropped her briefcase onto her desk, then shrugged out of
her coat and hung it up in the corner.

"Oh, no, you're not getting off that easy. I saw you together, remember?" Not bothering to remove her coat,
Heather slouched into one of the chairs facing Marti's desk.

"How could I forget?" Marti muttered as she sat in her
desk chair and opened her briefcase. "But you didn't see
what you thought you did. Believe me, you didn't." She
sifted through the papers she'd pored over the night before,
then glanced at her secretary. "Are you going to make coffee or should I?"

"I'll make it."

"Today?" Marti prodded when Heather made no move
to leave.

"Very funny." She eyed Marti a moment longer, then
stood and huffed out of the office.

Though Marti wanted to believe the confrontation was over, she knew better. She stared out the window and tried to brace herself for round two. Sure enough, within ten minutes Heather had returned with a mug of hot coffee in each hand. She plunked Marti's down in the middle of her desk.

"It was nice of him to help you find a car, wasn't it?" she prompted, taking her seat again.

"Very nice."

"And I imagine you'd like to do something nice for him in return, wouldn't you?"

Momentarily lulled by the other woman's change in tactic, Marti agreed. "I thought maybe I'd send him a case of wine. Or maybe a selection of gourmet coffees from that little shop in Clayton. What do you think?"

"I think you ought to invite him to dinner. You could make your beef Stroganoff. And the chocolate cake with pecans and cinnamon and double-fudge frosting. You know what they say about the way to a man's heart...."

Marti groaned out loud as she covered her face with her hands. If she didn't know better, she'd think the two of them had gotten together and plotted against her. "I am not, repeat *not,* inviting Dominic Fabrino to dinner."

"Why not?"

"Because I don't want to."

"But he must have spent most of Saturday helping you find a new car. And he brought you to work this morning. A case of wine or a selection of gourmet coffees seems like rather shabby thanks for that kind of time and trouble. If you ask me—"

"Well, I'm not," Marti cut in as firmly as she could, determined to end their conversation before it went any further. "Now if you don't mind, I'd like to get some work done before the phones start ringing."

"What about tonight?"

Marti gazed at Heather warily. "What *about* tonight? Is there something special on the calendar?"

"Oh, no. I was just wondering if you needed a ride home. I'll be happy to take you."

"Um, no, I don't."

"How about tomorrow?"

"My car will be ready tomorrow," she hedged.

"Hey, great. What did you get?" Heather asked, finally standing and heading for the door.

"A red Mustang convertible."

"Not really?"

"Really," Marti admitted with a grin.

As she paused by the door, Heather grinned, too. "Sure you're feeling all right, Marti?"

"Just fine, Heather, just fine."

"Oh, I almost forgot. What about the budget? If you want me to have it ready for the staff meeting, I'd better get started on it right away."

"Actually, it's . . . not ready. And I thought maybe we'd have the staff meeting tomorrow. Let everyone know as soon as they're here, all right?"

"All right. But first I'd better find the thermometer. I have a feeling you're coming down with something. Something serious!" Whirling around, she slipped through the door, Marti's gold pen sailing after her.

Chapter Four

"Well, Ms. Townsend, I want you to know that it's been a real pleasure doing business with you. I hope you enjoy your new car."

From several feet away Dominic watched as the salesman handed Marti the keys to the Mustang, then swung open the door for her and all but bowed her into the driver's seat.

"I'm sure I will." Apparently oblivious to the fact that the man was undressing her with his eyes, she smiled up at him as he draped himself over the door in a way that made Dominic see red.

His hands stuffed in his jacket pockets, he sauntered over to join them. As he paused beside the car, he just managed to stifle the urge to grab the guy by the scruff of his neck and shake him. He couldn't blame the guy for making a pass at her. Even in her corporate gear, Marti was irresistible. But that didn't mean he had to stand by idly and allow such flirtation to continue.

"If you have any questions or any problems at all, call me. You've got my card, haven't—?"

"Yeah, we've got your card," Dominic growled, his dark tone full of one-man-to-another warning as he rested his hip against the side of the car.

Losing some of his cockiness, the salesman straightened up and stepped back immediately, more than willing to allow Dominic to stake his claim.

"Well, then, I guess that's everything," he said, not quite meeting Dominic's steady stare. "Thanks again, Ms. Townsend. Mr. Fabrino..." Not waiting for a reply, he turned quickly and walked back to the showroom, leaving them alone on the brightly lit lot.

"You were kind of curt with him, weren't you?" Marti asked, glancing at him rather quizzically. "He was only being nice."

"He was getting ready to slobber all over the upholstery. I didn't think you'd appreciate the mess."

"Well, in that case, thanks... I think." A hint of a smile flitted across her face as she held his gaze.

"You're welcome." He hesitated for a moment, wanting to return her smile, but oddly unable to do so.

Despite her severe hairstyle and horn-rimmed glasses, she looked so pretty sitting in the little car. And suddenly, inexplicably, he wanted to capture the moment, to bury it deep in his soul. Because he knew that their time together was almost at an end. And though by all accounts he should be ready by now to be done with her, the thought of never seeing her again was too much to bear.

But he'd run out of excuses to continue his pursuit. While she'd accepted his help on Saturday as well as the taxi service he'd provided the past couple of days, she'd done so with a certain amount of trepidation. And she hadn't given him any encouragement at all. She'd voiced her appreciation for all that he'd done without ever seeming to care that it was *he* who had done it. So now he'd see her home one last time, and that would be that. Dominic Fabrino had better things to do than beat his head against a brick wall, no matter how desirable that brick wall might happen to be.

"Ready to go?" he asked, his voice a shade or two gruffer than it had been earlier as he finally broke the silence surrounding them.

"Oh, yes." Obviously unaware of his change of mood, she smiled as she turned away from him and smoothed her hands over the steering wheel in childish anticipation.

"Do you have to make any stops or are you heading straight home?"

"Straight home."

"Good. I'll be right behind you."

"Oh, but..." She faced him, her smile fading, prepared to protest once again. But something of his determination to see her safely home must have shown in his eyes, because she stopped short of actually saying anything aloud. Instead she merely shrugged as she slid the key in the ignition and started the engine. "Fine. See you there."

"Yeah, see you there," he echoed. Then he quietly closed her car door, turned and walked away.

Not quite thirty minutes later Dominic followed her into her driveway. As she pulled into the garage, he climbed out of his car, then stood beside it, waiting for her to join him. Though his mood was no less grim than it had been when they'd left the dealership, he couldn't deny the glimmer of hope in his heart that she'd say something, *anything,* to let him know that he meant more to her than the means to an end. But as the garage door closed and she moved toward him, he knew he was hoping in vain.

"I can't tell you how much I appreciate all you've done for me the past few days," she said, her smile cool and distant as she offered him her hand across the narrow distance between them. "Thanks, Dominic. Thanks so much."

"You're more than welcome," he replied in an equally detached manner. He took her hand in his for just a moment, then released her. "Goodbye, Marti."

She stared at him for several seconds, a puzzled, expectant look in her eyes, but he said nothing more. Nor did he make any move to escort her the few remaining feet to her front door. He refused to get that close to going inside with her, only to be left out in the cold yet again. He'd rather wait by the car.

"Goodbye," she murmured softly, taking one step back, then another. Finally she turned away from him, crossed to the front porch and climbed the steps. Without a backward glance, she unlocked the door, opened it and walked into the house.

As her front door closed and lights came on in the windows, Dominic slowly turned away. Whatever he'd had with Marti Townsend, it had been fun. But it was over now. Whether he liked it or not, it was over. Unless she called him. Then maybe he'd consider seeing her again. Maybe...

"Don't kid yourself, Fabrino. If she calls, you'll come running, and you know it," he muttered derisively as he slid into the Chevy and started the engine.

He glanced at the house one last time and wondered what she would do if he rang the doorbell. Finally, convincing himself that he'd really rather not know, he backed out of her driveway and headed for home.

As the sound of Dominic's car faded in the distance, Marti dropped her briefcase onto the floor, leaned against the door and closed her eyes. She should have said something, *done* something. Something besides turning and walking away with no more than a murmur of thanks.

But as they'd stood together in her driveway, the darkness closing in around them, fear had caught her in its trembling grip yet again. And despite the trust that had begun to grow inside her, she hadn't been able to cross the line she'd drawn seven years ago. She hadn't been able to invite him into her house, to offer him a drink as any normal woman would have.

"But you're not *normal,* are you? Not anymore. Not since Brent Winston shoved you against a wall and ripped off your clothes, and...and hurt you," she muttered, pushing away from the door as anger welled up inside her. Anger at Brent for what he'd done, and anger at herself for what she'd allowed herself to become—a lonely, fearful woman.

Somewhere deep in her heart she believed that Dominic would never betray her as Brent had. But in her head she knew that improbable wasn't the same as impossible. And she couldn't take the risk of following her heart rather than her head. She'd never be able to cope with the emotional anguish of another brutal violation. And if she couldn't cope, she'd lose everything she'd worked so hard to attain.

Yet the only alternative was to go on in the same frightened, forlorn way she'd been living for so long. And suddenly, inexplicably, she wasn't sure she could do it. Not if it meant never seeing Dominic Fabrino again.

In the time they'd spent together over the past few days he'd somehow managed to slip past the barriers she'd built around her heart just by being...himself. He'd demanded nothing of her, nothing at all. And not once had he tried to invade her space beyond the bounds of simple friendship. He'd been kind and funny, as well as thoughtful and generous. And when he'd been insistent it had only been on her behalf, to help her, not to hurt her.

He'd teased her about his love of home cooking, but he hadn't forced the issue in an embarrassing way. And neither last night—when he'd brought her home from work— nor tonight—when he'd followed her from the car dealer's—had he made a false move. He could have insisted that she invite him into her home, especially tonight. But he hadn't. Nor had he even laid a hand on her.

Yet all she'd offered him in return for so much consideration was a cool, rather curt dismissal.

She'd seen the hurt in his eyes when she'd wished him good-night. Obviously he'd expected more from her than that. And he'd had every right to, after all he'd done. But he hadn't pressured her in any way. He'd let her go with no more than a final word of farewell. And she'd gone, despite the decisiveness in his deep, soft voice that had assured her he'd meant what he'd said when he'd said goodbye.

She had been so sure that she'd be glad to see the last of him, she thought as she moved down the hallway and started up the stairs. But then the moment finally had come to say goodbye, and she'd been far from glad. And by then it had been too late to call him back.

But she could call him now, couldn't she? She could call him and tell him . . . what?

She flicked the light switch as she walked into her bedroom, then crossed to the dresser. Pausing in front of the mirror that hung above it, she studied her reflection for several seconds, as if searching for answers to her questions. Finally, more annoyed with herself than ever, she turned away and went to sit on the edge of her bed.

There wasn't much she could say to him to compensate for her earlier rudeness, and she knew it. Words were cheap, and "sorry" alone simply wouldn't do. Not when she owed him so much more than an apology.

Of course, she couldn't discount the possibility that Dominic Fabrino no longer wanted anything at all from her, including what would only prove to be a poor excuse. In fact, if she called him tonight he might very well hang up on her. Considering her behavior out in the driveway, she knew she couldn't blame him. He *had* said goodbye. And he'd said it without a moment's hesitation and in a tone of voice that hadn't encouraged any argument. Not that she'd wanted to argue with him then. But now . . .

No, not now. Better to wait until tomorrow to talk to him, she cautioned herself as she slipped out of her shoes and unbuttoned her suit jacket. By then his recollection of her icy withdrawal would have faded, and surely he'd be more willing to hear what she had to say. Whatever it happened to be. She'd have to give it some more thought.

He'd probably get the case of wine she'd sent him first thing in the morning. Then he'd realize that she wasn't as unappreciative as she seemed. Heather had balked at the idea, saying it was a rather cold way of showing her thanks, and Marti had had second thoughts about the decision all day. But now she knew she'd made a wise move.

Come to think of it, knowing what a gentleman he was, she could almost count on him calling her, if only to let her know that he'd received her gift. And when he did, she'd casually suggest . . . something. Maybe dinner at Tony's or Giovanni's, her treat, or . . . well, *something*.

Her decision made, she shrugged out of her jacket, then lay back on the bed and stared at the ceiling. She hadn't seen the last of Dominic Fabrino after all, she assured herself. And she wouldn't, at least not until she'd repaid his thoughtfulness in a warm and gracious way. And the sooner the better.

She would set something up for Saturday night, she decided as she closed her eyes. When he called. Tomorrow . . .

"Oh, and here's a message for you from *Mr. Fabrino,* too," Heather said, tossing another slip of paper atop the others littering Marti's desk.

At the sound of Dominic's name Marti set aside her pen, raised her head and stared at her secretary. "When did he call?"

"Just before I went to lunch. Since it wasn't urgent I stuck it in with all the—"

"Why didn't you put him through?" she demanded, frowning as she sat back in her chair. "I was in my office then. And I don't recall asking you to hold my calls."

"He didn't want me to disturb you. Said he knew how busy you were. And he just wanted you to know that he got the wine."

"That's all he said? That he got the wine?"

"That's all he said."

"You should have put him through," Marti snapped, making no effort at all to hide her displeasure as she stood and crossed to the window.

"If you'd told me you wanted to talk to him, I would have," Heather shot back, valiantly holding her ground.

Staring at the street several stories below, Marti drew in a deep breath and slowly counted to ten. Heather was right. She always let her know when she wanted to talk to someone personally. Otherwise her secretary was authorized to use her own judgment concerning incoming calls.

But she hadn't wanted to say anything about Dominic. She hadn't wanted to stir up Heather's insatiable curiosity any more than she'd done already. And she'd just assumed that when Dominic called he'd ask for her. She hadn't expected him to leave a message.

Of course he would expect her to be busy. But then why call her at the office rather than at home? Maybe he'd just wanted to let her know as soon as possible that he'd gotten her gift. Maybe he'd call again tonight to talk to her personally. And maybe the moon was made of green cheese.

In any case, she owed Heather an apology. Turning away from the window, she returned to her desk.

"I'm sorry, Heather. I had no right to be angry with you. You were only doing your job." Smiling hesitantly, she eyed her secretary for several seconds before she continued. "Apology accepted?"

"Apology accepted." Heather smiled, too, then waved a hand at the slips of paper on the desk. "Who first?"

"See if you can get Neal Dobbs for me." Marti sat in her chair and began to sort through the other items awaiting her attention. "If not, try Jason Smallwood. He should be in the office by now."

"What about Mr. Fabrino?"

"What about him?" Marti asked, glancing at her secretary for just a second.

"Are you going to call him?"

"No."

"I think you should."

"Well, I don't."

"What if he calls you again?"

"Then I'll talk to him. All right?"

"All right. I guess...." Heather replied airily, then whirled around and walked out of the office without another word.

Actually, she *could* call him, Marti thought as she sat back in her chair again. Just to let him know she'd gotten his message. But what if he was busy? Then she'd have to leave a message. And that would be silly.

Better to wait and see if he called her tonight. If he did, she could easily take it from there. And if he didn't? Well, then maybe she'd call him. Maybe...

As the buzzer on her intercom went off, she sat forward and reached for her phone. Lifting the receiver, she gave herself a firm mental shake. She had work to do, a lot of work, and too little of it had gotten done over the past few days. If she didn't get her mind back on business and keep it there, she was going to be in trouble, big trouble.

"Yes, Heather?"

"Neal 'Slick As a Banana Peel' Dobbs on line one, Ms. Townsend."

"Heather, please, he's one of our best clients."

"I know. Ain't it a shame?"

"Yeah, it is," Marti agreed with uncommon irreverence. Then, making a conscious effort to wipe the smile off her face, she punched in line one. "Neal, sorry I missed you earlier. What can I do for you?"

He didn't call on Wednesday night. Nor did he call on Thursday. Finally, sometime around eight o'clock Thursday night, Marti realized that if she wanted to see Dominic again, she'd have to take the initiative. And though she'd tried to deny it for two days now, she knew that she wanted to see him again. She wanted it more than anything.

Odd how quickly she'd begun to miss him, she thought as she prowled around the house, hands stuffed in the pockets of her old blue wool robe. But then she'd enjoyed being with him more than she'd wanted to admit, even at seven in the morning. She'd enjoyed talking with him and laughing with him as they'd shared bits and pieces of their days. And she didn't like to think that they'd never do it again.

Pausing by the kitchen counter, she eyed the phone for several long moments. Almost a week earlier she'd talked herself into trusting him enough to spend a day with him. And he'd done nothing to betray her.

Now she knew that she had to trust him enough to spend an evening with him alone in her home. Because if she couldn't do that, she'd be better off forgetting him, forgetting his wide smile, his kind eyes, the gentle touch of his hand on her hair.

Actually, that's what she ought to do, anyway. She didn't have time to torment herself with more wishful thinking. But she couldn't forget, she *wouldn't* forget, until there'd been some kind of closure between them. And there couldn't be any closure until she'd repaid him for all he'd done.

Her mind made up at last, she lifted the receiver and dialed his number as quickly as she could, then sent up a silent prayer that he'd answer. She absolutely, positively couldn't go another round alone with herself or she'd end up in a mental—

He answered on the third ring, his voice as dark and rich as she remembered. He greeted her warmly. Well, not *her* exactly, since he didn't yet know who was calling.

Stop wandering, Marti, and speak to the man.

"Hello, Dominic. It's me ... Marti."

"Hey, Marti, how are you doing?"

"Um, fine. How about you?" He didn't exactly sound thrilled to hear from her, but at least he hadn't hung up on her.

"I'm fine, too. How's the new car running?"

"Great, just great." She shifted from one slippered foot to the other, then began to wind the phone cord around her fingers. As if cutting off the blood supply to one of her extremities might actually help her think of something scintillating to say. "I thought I'd miss my old car, but I don't." *I miss you.*

"Well, good."

"Mmm, yes," she murmured, then caught herself counting her heartbeats in the sudden silence stretching between them. "Um, actually, I was calling to see if you're busy Saturday night...."

She paused, hoping he would respond, but he said nothing. Obviously he wasn't going to make it easy for her, but then he had no reason to. Not after the way she'd treated him.

"Because if you're not, I thought you might like to come to my house for dinner," she continued at last, the words tumbling out of her mouth one after another.

Again he said nothing for several seconds. Then, finally, he replied. "I'd like that a lot, Marti," he said, his voice several degrees warmer than it had been at first.

"You...you would?" she stuttered, surprised by his sudden acceptance of her rather poorly offered invitation.

"Sure. Unless you're planning to serve something totally gross like brains à la mode," he teased in a way that made her smile.

"Actually, I was thinking more along the lines of beef Stroganoff."

"Ah, one of my favorites. Goes so well with red wine. And I just happen to have an entire case of a truly fine cabernet sauvignon. Shall I bring a bottle with me?"

"Oh, by all means."

"So, Saturday night. What time?"

"Seven?"

"Seven, it is. See you then."

As she said goodbye and hung up the phone, Marti wasn't sure if she wanted to laugh or cry or dig a hole and hide. Inviting Dominic to dinner had been easier than she'd imagined, but she wasn't going to fool herself. Talking to him on the telephone and entertaining him in the privacy of her home weren't the same thing at all.

While she knew him better than she'd known any man over the past seven years, trusting her judgment, not to mention trusting *him*, was going to be tough. Yet she liked what she knew of Dominic Fabrino, and she wanted to know more. And there was only one way she could do that. She had to put the past behind her. And she had to believe in him. Or at least, she had to be willing to try.

And she was, Marti realized, smiling softly as she curled up on the couch in the living room. Then, with a sigh of resignation, she reached for the papers she'd left on the coffee table. Neal Dobbs would be expecting an outline for his company's new ad campaign when they met in the morning. And unless she put Dominic Fabrino out of her mind and got to work, he wasn't going to get it.

At five minutes till seven on Saturday night Dominic pulled up to the curb in front of Marti's house. He shut off the lights and the engine, but made no move to leave the car. Instead he sat back and studied the brightly lit house, asking himself yet again what the hell was he doing there—besides wasting his time?

He wanted to believe she'd invited him to dinner simply because she'd wished to see him again. But he was wise enough to know better. She'd made it clear that she was too busy to see a man socially. Hadn't she? So her invitation couldn't be anything more than a last bit of business between them, or perhaps just another way of expressing her gratitude. To Dominic Fabrino for services rendered: a case of expensive red wine, a plate of beef Stroganoff and one last thank-you-very-much.

He should have settled for the case of wine and let her off the hook like any real gentleman would have. He could have told her he'd already made plans for Saturday night. He'd certainly been tempted to do just that. Unfortunately the temptation had lasted less than five seconds, or about as long as it took for him to remind himself that it wouldn't behoove him to cut off his nose to spite his face.

When it came right down to it, he was here because he'd missed her, because he'd wanted to see her again. And if she hadn't called him, he probably would have called her. *Probably?* Hell, he'd started to dial her number at least half a dozen times before eight o'clock Thursday night. Had she waited another ten or fifteen minutes, he'd have been the one doing the asking, and he knew it. He'd made reservations at Tony's, hadn't he? And he hadn't planned to go there alone. Or with anyone else.

In any case, he was here now. And regardless of why she'd invited him to dinner, he was going to make the most of it. He didn't want tonight to be the last time they spent together. And in the hours ahead he intended to do whatever he could to persuade Marti that she didn't, either.

He'd tried to stay away from her, for her good as well as his own, but after less than forty-eight hours he'd been dialing her number. If he intended to get her out of his system, as he knew he should, obviously it was time to try another tack. And there was always a possibility that familiarity *would* breed contempt. Of course, there was also a possibility that given a pair of paper wings he could fly.

Shaking his head at his foolishness, he reached for the bottle of wine and bouquet of flowers he'd brought her. Then he climbed out of his car, took a deep breath and started up the walkway to her front porch. High above him the moon shone brightly in the night sky amid a scattering of sparkling stars. All around him the crisp autumn air smelled faintly of wood smoke and cedar spice.

As he stepped into the warm, welcoming glow of the porch light, his heart beat a little faster. Soon, very soon, he would see her. And before the evening ended, if she wanted what he wanted, he would hold her, touch her, taste her . . .

Going very still, he stared at her front door. *Where* had he gotten that idea? And more importantly, why? She certainly hadn't led him to believe she wanted anything from him at all, much less the kind of intense, physical encounter he'd just been imagining. In fact, she'd more than kept her distance whenever they'd been together. And he had no reason to think tonight would be any different.

"So behave yourself, or you'll frighten the living daylights out of her," he ordered as he rang the doorbell, then stepped back so she could see him through the peephole.

A few seconds later the door swung open and Marti stood before him. Gazing upon her, he drew in another deep breath, then barely resisted the urge to let it out in a long, low whistle of masculine approval.

As she had on Saturday, she'd left off her glasses. Her hair was coiled at the nape of her neck loosely enough for a few wisps to softly feather her forehead and the sides of her face. Her simple, long-sleeved, black wool dress clung to her curves, enhancing her feminine appeal in an unexpected way, while her sheer black stockings, slim black heels and single strand of pearls emphasized the elegance of her fragile beauty.

"Dominic, it's so good to see you again. Come in," she invited, smiling shyly as she stepped back, allowing him to enter.

"I'm not too early, am I?" As he moved through the doorway into the long, narrow hall, he offered up a silent prayer of thanks that he'd chosen to wear a coat and tie instead of jeans and a sweater. Obviously he hadn't been the only one who'd wanted tonight to be special.

"Not at all." She shut the door, then turned to face him. Her eyes met his, and she hesitated, her smile slipping slightly, as if she was momentarily at a loss. Finally, shifting her gaze, she continued. "I see you remembered the wine."

"Oh, yeah. And these are for you." He handed her the bouquet of pink roses and white carnations nestled in green tissue, but held on to the wine.

"You shouldn't have, but I'm glad you did." Bending her head over the flowers for a moment, she breathed in their fresh fragrance and her smile reappeared. "I'd better put them in water." Again she hesitated. Then, as she moved past him toward what he assumed was the kitchen, she continued. "Would you . . . would you like a drink?"

Aware of her skittishness, Dominic waited until she was several steps ahead of him before he followed her down the hallway. "I'll have whatever you are, if you're having one."

"Actually, I'm having a beer," she admitted, sounding rather sheepish as she turned through a doorway off to the left. "But you're more than welcome to have something else. I've got Scotch and bourbon and vodka and gin and all sorts of mixers."

"A beer sounds good to me." Eager to catch a glimpse of at least the first floor of the house before he joined her, Dominic slowed his pace a bit.

To his right, an archway opened into a reasonably sized, comfortably furnished living room. A traditional sofa and two wing chairs upholstered in sturdy fabrics in muted shades of burgundy and hunter green, a couple of cherry-wood end tables and a coffee table had been arranged around a fireplace. An antique armoire, one of its doors cocked open to reveal a small stereo that was playing mellow jazz, took up most of one wall. And a chrome-and-glass étagère filled with framed photographs angled out from a far corner.

To the left an identical archway opened into the dining room. The oval table had been set with lace and linen, china, crystal and silverware. A basket of rose and cream silk flowers and a cluster of crystal candlesticks fitted with tall tapers served as a centerpiece. The room also held an antique buffet and matching china cabinet. Several watercolors of various sizes hung on the walls.

If he'd been hoping not to like what he saw, Dominic would have been disappointed. There was nothing fake or frilly, nothing wildly extravagant or frightfully pretentious anywhere he looked. The warmth, the elegance and simplicity of Marti's style was evident all around him, and he found that reassuring. Her home reflected the kind of woman she was—the kind of woman he had believed her to be.

Lured by the lingering scent of her perfume as well as the rich aroma of simmering beef Stroganoff, Dominic moved past the hall table, barely glancing at the array of photographs atop it. Maybe he'd have time to study them more closely later in the evening. But right now he knew that if he loitered any longer, Marti might begin to think he was up to something. And the last thing he wanted to do was worry her.

He crossed the brightly lit kitchen and, keeping a little distance between them, joined her at the counter as she tucked the last of the flowers into an art-glass vase.

"Are you sure about the beer?"

"I'm sure." As she moved to the refrigerator and got a can for him, he reached for the corkscrew she'd set out and went to work on the wine bottle.

"Dinner's almost ready. I just put the rolls in the oven. And it shouldn't take long for me to toss the salad." She poured his beer into an old-fashioned frosted mug and set it in front of him. Then she moved to the refrigerator again to retrieve a crystal bowl of salad greens mixed with various chopped fresh vegetables.

"Don't rush on my account." He set the open wine bottle aside and reached for his beer.

"I'm not." She returned to the opposite end of the counter and put the bowl down without glancing at him.

"Anything I can do to help?" Savoring a mouthful of icy brew, he eyed Marti as she poured herb vinegar, olive oil and assorted seasonings into a bottle and shook it, her hands trembling slightly.

"Not really."

Dominic took another swallow of his beer, and another. Then, carrying his mug in one hand, he wandered over to the table, pulled out a chair and sat down. Almost immediately Marti seemed to relax, her movements slowing appreciably as she dumped the dressing over the salad and began to toss it.

Dominic sighed inwardly and shook his head. So much for holding, touching and tasting anytime tonight, he thought dispiritedly, swirling the last of his beer around the bottom of his mug.

Although they'd spent several hours together over a period of several days, and although she'd invited him into her home, he obviously still made her uneasy. But why? He hadn't made any fast moves. He hadn't made any moves at all. And he wouldn't, couldn't, as long as she seemed so skittish. He'd give her as much time and space as she needed. But once she was sure that she had nothing to fear from him ...

For just a moment he closed his eyes and imagined her writhing, hot and naked, in his arms. Then, barely suppressing a groan of frustration, he drained the dregs of his beer.

"Would you like another?" Marti asked, glancing at him over her shoulder as she crossed to the oven to check on the rolls.

"No, thanks." He set his mug on the table and sat back in his chair, willing himself to think about something, *anything,* other than what he had been thinking about. It wasn't easy. Not with her bent over the oven in such an alluring way. "I really like your house," he offered at last. "At least, what I've seen of it. How many bedrooms do you have?"

Even if he hadn't known as soon as the words were out of his mouth that he'd said the wrong thing, Marti's reaction would have clued him in immediately. As the oven door slipped out of her hand and slammed shut, she straightened quickly and glanced at him again, a flicker of fear in her bright blue eyes.

"Three originally, all upstairs," she replied. Returning to the counter, she picked up the bowl of salad, then headed toward the doorway that opened into the dining room. "But I had the wall between the smallest bedroom and the hall bathroom knocked out so I could use it as a darkroom."

"Sounds like you're pretty serious about your photography."

"As serious as I can be with the amount of spare time I have to devote to it." Back in the kitchen again, she grabbed a pair of pot holders and removed a couple of covered dishes and the pan of rolls from the oven. "And since this is our busiest time of year..." She shrugged as she began transferring the steaming rolls into a cloth-lined wicker basket.

"Bad week?" Without waiting to be asked, Dominic joined Marti at the counter. Using her pot holders, he carried the casserole dishes into the dining room, then returned for the wine.

"I've had worse. Of course, I've also had better," she admitted, setting the rolls on the table. As he poured the wine, she lit the candles, then dimmed the chandelier. "How about you? Have you been busy, too?"

"More than I thought I'd be. You wouldn't believe the paperwork I've had to do just to apply for the loan to buy the new property." Relieved that he'd finally hit upon a reasonably safe topic of conversation, he seated Marti, then moved to his place at the table. More than anything he wanted to put her at ease, and if it meant talking business for a while, then that's what they'd do.

And that's what they did, trading impersonal, albeit amusing anecdotes as they ate. By the time he'd finished his second helping of salad and beef Stroganoff over buttered noodles, Dominic knew quite a bit about the highs and lows of running an advertising agency. And he'd told Marti a lot more about Fabrino's and his growing plans for expansion than she'd probably bargained for.

But she'd honestly seemed to be enjoying herself during dinner. And, as he helped her clear the last of the dishes from the dining-room table, he realized that she was much more relaxed than she had been more than an hour earlier.

At first he'd thought that maybe the alcohol had loosened her up. But she hadn't finished either her beer or her wine, so he knew that wasn't the case. And he was glad. He wanted her to be at ease with him but not because she was too loaded to know better. He wanted her to be just as aware of what was happening between them as he planned to be.

"We can have coffee and dessert in the living room if you'd like," she suggested, plugging in the coffeemaker. "You do like chocolate cake, don't you?" She smiled as she glanced at him over her shoulder.

"Do bears live in the woods?"

"Good." Turning away again, she began to arrange cups and saucers on a wicker tray. "Why don't you light a fire in the fireplace, then? The logs and kindling are stacked and ready to go, the flue is open and the matches are on the mantel. I'll be in to join you as soon as the coffee's ready.''

"Yes, ma'am. Anything else, ma'am?" he teased as he crossed to the doorway.

"Oh, yes. I almost forgot. Would you like a glass of brandy, too?"

"No, thanks." He felt as if he'd been given a special gift— coffee and dessert in front of a fire with the woman he…with a woman he liked a lot. And if he wanted to make the most of it, he'd have to keep his wits about him.

On his way to the living room, he stopped at the hall table and, as he'd promised himself earlier, took a few seconds to study the arrangement of photographs atop it. Three were studio portraits and appeared to be fairly recent. There was one each of a fiftyish man and woman, and one of them together. From the look of them, Dominic decided they were probably Marti's parents. The fourth was an old, rather amateurish black-and-white photo of an elderly woman, probably Marti's grandmother, the one who'd given her the car, he thought as he crossed to the fireplace.

Thanks to the little gas jet, he had the fire going in a matter of minutes. He replaced the fan-shaped screen, then wandered over to the étagère to look at the photographs set out in small groupings on the glass shelves. There were several of a young couple with a little boy, playing in a park, celebrating a birthday, splashing in a mud puddle, each one radiating the joy the three of them shared just being together. Dominic wondered who they were, and how they'd come to be a part of her life. Obviously she cared for them quite a bit. And for that he envied them greatly.

Disconcerted by the sudden rush of almost unreasonable jealousy he'd felt for the three strangers, he turned his attention to the other photographs Marti had chosen to display. As he studied first one, then another and another, he frowned thoughtfully.

All of them were of children, but each one was different, distinct. And each one, in its own special way, was extraordinarily beautiful. In one a boy with a devilish grin hung out of a tree. In another a girl in a hot pink parka swirled and twirled in a patch of new-fallen snow. A boy in a bright red jersey leapt into the air, sending a soccer ball spinning away. And a small girl arced into the summer sky on a wooden-seated swing.

The last of the photographs had been set apart on the top shelf, angled on either side of a small stack of books on art and antiques. One was of a woman sitting on a park bench gazing down at the sleeping baby cradled in her arms. The other was a silhouette of a tall man holding the hand of a toddler as they ambled down a city sidewalk.

He'd had no idea how gifted she was with a camera, no idea at all. When she'd told him that she'd gone to the park to take pictures, he'd assumed it had been the fall colors or an unusual architectural landmark she'd wanted to capture on film. Now he knew that what she'd sought was something more elusive. Was it something she wanted, but thought she couldn't, or wouldn't, have?

He reached out and lightly traced a finger over the glass covering the photograph of the man holding the little boy's hand, and a feeling of warmth washed over him. Then, hearing the faint, rhythmic click of Marti's heels against the tile floor in the kitchen, he drew his hand back and turned away. He didn't want her to know how deeply he'd been touched by what he'd seen in her photographs. Instinct warned that it was too soon to reveal the hope he felt in his heart. Hope for her, for him, for them.

He paused in front of the only painting in the room, an oil of an old woman and a young girl who vaguely resembled Marti. Although the medium was different, the style was similar to that of the watercolor landscapes he'd seen in the dining room.

"That's one of my mother's early works," Marti said as she crossed from the doorway to the coffee table and set down the tray she'd been carrying.

"It's very nice. You and your grandmother?"

"Yes. I was about three. Gran had just come to live with us. And my mother had just decided to get serious about her artwork."

"She did the watercolors in the dining room, too, didn't she?"

"Years ago. But they weren't up to her usual standard. She was going to toss them out until I talked her into letting me have them." She sat on one side of the sofa and poured coffee into their cups.

"Do you paint, too?"

"I used to try, but I wasn't very good. I still sketch occasionally, although it's usually something work related. But at least my mother can't say the time she spent trying to mold me into her image has gone completely to waste."

Moving past her, Dominic returned to the étagère and picked up a photograph of the young couple. "If you took these, then you should be glad you weren't molded into anybody's image but your own. They're very, very good, Marti."

"Thank you." A hint of pink tinged her cheeks. She avoided his gaze as she set first his cup and saucer, then a dessert plate with a huge slab of chocolate cake, on the coffee table.

"People you know?"

"Only the couple. Heather's my assistant, and that's her husband and son. The others are just . . . strangers." She hesitated a moment, head down, then raised her eyes. "Ready for dessert?" she asked brightly.

He put the picture back in its place, then crossed the living room to join her by the coffee table. He considered sitting in one of the wing chairs, but only for an instant. Offering what he hoped was a reassuring smile, he sat down at the opposite end of the sofa and picked up his plate. He also considered letting her get away with changing the subject, but nixed that idea, as well.

"You like kids, huh?" he asked, digging unabashedly into his cake.

"I...guess so. Except for the time I've spent with Heather's son, I haven't really been around them that much. But I do enjoy taking pictures of them."

"Why?"

"Why?" she echoed his question, eyeing him uncertainly. "I'm not sure." She shrugged, setting aside her half-eaten cake and reaching for her cup. Then she glanced at him quickly, a startled expression on her face. "I'm not a weirdo or anything."

"I didn't think you were," Dominic assured her softly, aware that he'd upset her. Suddenly he wished he *had* changed the subject. But there was so much he wanted to know about her, so much he needed to know, and getting her to talk about anything personal was almost impossible.

She put her cup down, her coffee untouched, then sat back and folded her hands in her lap. When she finally met his gaze she smiled ruefully, as if ashamed that she'd jumped to the wrong conclusion about his curiosity. "Actually, they're really fun to photograph. Especially when they don't know you're doing it. They're so honest about everything. And they're so bright and funny, so full of hopes and dreams, so full of...life...." She shook her head wryly as her words trailed off. "Don't get me started. I'll bore you to death," she warned, reaching for her cup again.

"Not a chance." Dominic returned his empty plate to the table, then swallowed the last of his coffee. "In fact, you've got me ready to give it a try. Unfortunately I don't know one end of a camera from another. But maybe you could give me a few pointers. Then we could try our luck with my nieces and nephew."

"It's not really that difficult, especially if you have an automatic thirty-five-millimeter camera. You just aim and shoot." As if surprised at her own enthusiasm, her smile faded, and she glanced at her watch. "You shouldn't have any problems." She looked at him somewhat awkwardly, then glanced again at her watch. "Would you like more coffee?"

Dominic sighed inwardly. She was still just being polite, polite and distant and diverting, and he hated it. Of course, he probably had only himself to blame. He *had* mentioned the possibility of seeing her again.

But why should that put her off? She'd been the one to offer tonight's invitation. And she'd been the one to make the evening more than it had to be. She'd been the one to make it a special china-and-crystal occasion. He wasn't egotistical. Yet he couldn't understand why she'd bother if he meant nothing to her. Especially since she'd already repaid him for his "services" with a case of fine wine.

"What I'd like, Marti, much more than coffee, is to see you again," he said at last, turning to face her.

"Oh, Dominic, I'm not sure—"

"I'm not talking about anything serious," he hedged. "Just dinner at a nice restaurant or an afternoon in the park, popcorn and a movie, or a little jazz at one of those clubs on the riverfront." He waved a hand at the stereo that had been playing just that all evening. "I know you're busy.

I am, too. But you know what they say about all work and no play, don't you?"

"I know," she admitted. But as she met his gaze, her eyes were full of doubt. "But I—"

"Don't say anything one way or another now. Just think about it, okay? And we'll talk again in a few days." He stood quickly and started toward the doorway leading into the hall. "Guess I'd better get going. It's late." He didn't have to look at his watch to know that it wasn't. But he was afraid that if he stayed any longer she'd come up with a reason not to see him again, one he might find hard to refute.

To his relief, she trailed after him without a word. But when he reached the front door he realized that she'd hesitated halfway down the hallway. He could have opened the door and let himself out, but he didn't. He stood aside and waited for her to close the distance between them. After several seconds, she finally did so, pausing a foot or two away from him.

"You don't have to rush off," she murmured at last, her hand on the doorknob as she looked up at him.

He'd expected to see uncertainty in her wide eyes. What he saw was something else altogether, something so much like longing that it made his heart ache. But underlying it there was also a hint of fear. "Yeah, I think I do." He paused, wanting to touch her. Instead he tucked his hands in his pockets, then continued. "Tell me something, will you?"

"What?"

"Are you afraid of me?"

"No, of course not," she replied, no longer meeting his gaze as her words tumbled out too fast.

"Good, because I'm not a *weirdo* or anything," he said half-teasingly, using her own words to reassure her. "And I swear I'll never hurt you, Marti. Never."

Slowly she raised her head, her eyes searching his. Then finally she smiled. "I didn't think you would."

He felt as if he'd been given a very special gift, and for one long moment he didn't know what to say. In the end he settled for what was easiest, as well as most appropriate.

"Thanks for dinner."

"You're welcome."

"Well, good night."

"Good night."

He knew he should just go, but he didn't. Instead, ever so slowly, he bent his head and brushed a feather-light kiss over her slightly parted lips. Then, not trusting himself to speak or to stay, he slipped out the door and hurried down the walkway, the sound of Marti's soft sigh echoing deep in his soul.

Chapter Five

She didn't sleep at all that night. She tossed and turned, muttered and grumbled and punched her pillow more times than she could count. Once again, thoughts of Dominic and the hours they'd just spent together whirled around and around in her head, the possibilities tempting, the improbabilities taunting in a most upsetting manner.

Her carefully orchestrated evening had been going so well. Dominic had been a perfect gentleman and her initial uncertainty had faded. For a while she'd actually enjoyed herself much more than she'd expected. But then he'd mentioned her photographs, and suddenly things had gotten out of hand.

Since his questions had been anything but subtle, she'd known very well what he was getting at. He'd thought that she was using pictures to take the place of something she wanted but had chosen not to have. And his implication had disturbed her. Because she wasn't doing that at all.

She wasn't.

She'd wanted children once, a whole houseful of children, she reminded herself as she threw back her blankets and slipped out of bed. But then she'd wanted to be married, too. The one had always gone with the other. Then she'd decided that marriage would be out of the question...after Brent.

Of course, she knew that there were ways to conceive a child without having sex. She'd read about artificial insemination and embryo transplants, but after the kind of childhood she'd had, she'd never felt especially well equipped to handle single parenthood.

Having padded down the stairs, Marti paused by the hall table. She picked up the photograph of her grandmother and tipped it toward the dim glow of the night-light she'd left burning. Though she could barely make out the details, she gazed at it for several seconds. Then, returning it to the table, she wandered into the living room.

During the years that Gram had lived with them, Marti knew she'd done her best to fill the empty places left by her mother, the artist, and her father, the physician. Still, her nurturing couldn't quite substitute for that of two loving parents.

But her parents had been too busy pursuing their personal goals to give her the kind of care she'd needed, the kind of concern she'd craved. They'd been cold and distant and rather rigid about her upbringing. And although Gram had tried to smooth away some of the rough edges, Marti had always secretly feared that one day she'd turn out just like her parents.

Walking through the shadowy darkness, she moved toward the étagère, oddly drawn to her photographs. She couldn't see them through the darkness, and yet, she could. The pictures flashed across her mind. A boy leapt into the sky, a girl swirled in the snow. A father held his toddler's hand. A mother cradled her sleeping babe.…

She'd realized long ago that she knew too little about warm and loving relationships to have a child on her own. And now, with the kind of job she had, not to mention the kind of job she planned to have, a child was definitely out of the question. She'd made her choices, and she'd had no regrets. None…until Dominic Fabrino came along, and suddenly she'd begun to wonder.

Turning away from the étagère, she crossed the living room and headed for the stairs, hands clenched at her sides. She'd meant tonight to be an ending, but he'd obviously had other ideas. And she hadn't tried very hard to dissuade him, had she? He'd started talking about seeing her again, and she'd done nothing to discourage him. She should have told him about her pending promotion, her upcoming move to Chicago. She should have, she *would* have…

But he'd been so sweet, so sincere, that she hadn't wanted to put him off. She hadn't wanted to be callous or unnecessarily cruel.

Oh, please, Marti, let's face facts—you didn't want to let him go knowing you'd never see him again.

She sat on the edge of her bed and stared out the window, one hand pressed against her lips. A sliver of moonlight shivered through the bare branches of the old elm nearest the house, piercing the darkness as the memory of his kiss pierced her heart.

He'd bent his head and taken her mouth so slowly, so gently, that she might have imagined it. And she hadn't been afraid. To her surprise she'd been left wanting more, so much more than she'd ever wanted before. And hours later, to her chagrin, she was still beguiled by the belief that she could have it.

As she slid under the blankets and settled back against her pillows, she wondered if she would have felt as warm and safe and secure as she'd thought she would have if he'd put his arms around her. And if he'd really kissed her? If he'd taken her mouth in a deeper, more primal way, how would she have responded? Would she have welcomed the unexpected intimacy? Or would she have been afraid? She wasn't sure, not sure at all. But she knew that she wanted to find out.

And therein lay the road to ruin. She'd been wrong about a man once. She could be wrong again.

Or she could be right....

He'd been so patient and understanding. And he'd seemed to care for her enough to go carefully, to be the kind of gentle lover she'd only begun to realize she wanted, needed, to make her whole again. She'd been alone, and lonely, for so long that she should have learned by now to accept it as her way of life. But she hadn't. And now she had a feeling she never could.

Still, the alternative involved no small amount of risk, albeit a different kind of risk than she'd first feared. Already she was drawn to him in an unsettling way. Already she'd begun to hope, to dream. What would she do if she fell in love with him? How would she leave him when the time came?

Because eventually she knew she'd have to leave. She'd have to go to Chicago to take Benson's job, to move another step forward on her road to success.

Sometime around dawn, too exhausted to argue with herself any longer, Marti finally dozed off. But although she'd slept soundly for several hours, when she awoke she was anything but refreshed. And she had no more idea of what to do about Dominic Fabrino than she'd had twelve hours earlier.

Of course, she probably wouldn't have to do anything about him today, she thought, pulling on an old pair of jeans and an oversize sweater. He'd said they'd talk in a few days. But just in case he changed his mind, she'd turn off the telephone and let the answering machine take her calls. That way she could get some work done without being distracted. Why, if she put her mind to it, next year's budget could be ready to submit to Chicago before the end of the week.

She tried to work. Really, she did. And although she seemed to spend more time checking her answering machine for messages than checking the columns of figures on the papers covering her kitchen table, she got quite a bit done. But she didn't enjoy doing it. Not in the same way she had in the past, when she hadn't had other options that seemed so enticing. Suddenly work was...work. Something she had to do as opposed to something she wanted to do. And what she wanted to do was simply out of the question. Because it was *his* turn to call her.

But he didn't. Not on Sunday or Monday or Tuesday. That was how Marti came to realize that in some cases a few days could actually be equated with eternity. Yet pride, coupled with a lingering hint of self-doubt, prevented her from doing the dialing herself. Perhaps he'd had second thoughts. And perhaps it was just as well.

By Wednesday night she'd given up hope of hearing from him again. In fact, she'd even begun to work on the part about not caring. And then, just after eight, the phone rang. She moved off the sofa so fast she fell over the coffee table. Rubbing her shin, cursing under her breath and limping as fast as she could, she managed to answer before the fourth ring.

"Hey, Marti, this is Dominic. Did I catch you at a bad time?"

"Oh . . . no . . ." she assured him, trying to get her breathing under control as she fished around in the freezer for some ice. "I was getting caught up on my reading." Actually she'd been watching sitcoms while listlessly thumbing through back issues of several trade publications.

"Anything interesting?"

"Not really."

"I had a nice time Saturday night."

"Me, too." She wrapped several ice cubes in a towel, then pressed it against the bump on her leg as she tried to think of something else to say. Her eyes strayed to the vase on the kitchen table. "The flowers you brought are still lovely. I've really enjoyed them."

"I'm glad." He hesitated, as if bracing himself for something more than the small talk they'd been exchanging. "Have you thought about what I said Saturday night?"

"About going out?" she hedged, wanting to give herself a little more time even though she'd already made up her mind.

"Yeah."

"I'd . . . I'd like to."

He didn't say anything for several seconds, and Marti began to wonder if she'd given the wrong answer. Maybe he'd only called because he'd said he would. Maybe he'd only called to say goodbye.

"Are you busy Saturday night? I know it's Halloween, and I understand if you've already made plans. Lots of parties and stuff going on. But if not . . ."

"No, I don't have any plans for Saturday night." Heather *was* having a costume party, and Marti *had* been invited. But she'd already tendered her regrets because she hadn't wanted to go alone.

"Then what do you say we go trick-or-treating?"

"You're not serious, are you?" He sounded as though he was teasing. Still, she wondered what he had in mind.

"Well, yes, I am. You see, my sister and brother-in-law are going to a party, so I promised to take my nieces and nephew around the neighborhood. And I thought maybe you'd like to come with us. We're having burgers and fries first, and we'll be kid-sitting afterward, but Rose promised she and Drew wouldn't be out too late. So?"

"Do I have to wear a costume?"

"Just come as yourself. Unless you have one of those little French maid outfits—short black skirt, fishnet stockings, three-inch—"

"I'll come as myself," she assured him with a laugh.

"So it's a date?"

"It's a date."

"Great," he replied, making no attempt to mask his pleasure. "The kids want to hit the streets by six-thirty. And, of course, we'll need time to eat first. How about if I pick you up around five?"

"I'll be ready."

"Oh, and Marti?"

"Yes?"

"Bring your camera, okay?"

"Okay."

"I hope you like belly bombers."

"What?" Marti tucked her purse and camera on the floor by her feet. Then, sure that she'd heard him wrong, she sat back in the passenger seat of Dominic's Corvette and eyed him curiously as he pulled away from the curb in front of her house.

It was just after five on Saturday night, Halloween night. And, much to her surprise, she was looking forward to the evening ahead with more anticipation than anxiety. Meeting Dominic's sister and her family should have made her nervous, and it did, but only a little. She couldn't imagine anyone related to him being anything but nice. And when she thought about it, she liked the idea of getting to know them.

"Belly bombers. You know, those miniature hamburgers. Don't tell me you've never had one?"

"I've never heard them called that," she admitted. "And, no, I've never had *one*." She loved the little hamburgers, but she normally had a minimum of three or four, especially if she was hungry.

"Ah, you're addicted, too, huh?" he teased, pulling into line for the drive-through window.

"I wouldn't say addicted." Addicted was once a day. She'd gotten herself down to once a week.

"How many do you want?"

She shrugged noncommittally. "How many do you usually have?"

"Right. A dozen ought to do it for us, plus a dozen for Rose and Drew and a dozen for the kids makes three dozen. Fries?"

"I might eat a few."

"And four large fries," he added, turning to the window to place their order.

It was all Marti could do to keep from snitching a burger from the bags of fragrant food warming her lap on the short drive to his sister's house. She hadn't eaten much earlier in the day, and thanks to the combination of good food and good company, suddenly she was starving.

"Get ready for total chaos," Dominic warned as he pulled into the driveway of a neat, two-story brick house just a few blocks away from Marti's.

"That bad, huh?"

"You tell me." He took two of the bags from her so she could pick up her purse and camera. Then, grinning wickedly, he helped her out of the car.

She'd thought he was kidding...until they walked through the front door and she was swept into a vortex of light, sound and bright colors. Suddenly she knew how Alice had felt tumbling down the rabbit hole.

His sister's house was a whole other world inhabited by three medium-to-small strangers, all laughing and shouting at once as they gave new meaning to perpetual motion. Toys and clothes and an odd mix of sporting goods littered the living room floor and furniture. A tiny red dachshund with long, silky hair and a whirlwind tail scampered around, alternately barking and growling at anything and everything.

Her first instinct was to turn and run, and it must have shown on her face.

"You okay?" Dominic asked, slipping an arm around her shoulders and gently drawing her close.

"Um, yes, I think so." She accepted his embrace gratefully as she eyed the teeming horde heading their way.

"I swear they won't bite, not even Butch."

"Butch?" She gazed up at him uncertainly.

"The dog."

"Oh." She stared at the little red dog now lying on its back, tongue lolling, at her feet. *"Butch?"*

"Hey, Mom, Uncle Dominic's here. And he brought his girlfriend with him," the eldest of the three, a girl of about twelve, wearing white makeup and an old prom dress, yelled up the stairs, then stepped over a soccer ball and headed their way. "Mom didn't tell us you had a girlfriend, Uncle Dominic."

"Ah, big deal, Angela. What counts are the bombers. Can we eat right away? I'm starving. And Mom said I couldn't squirt any ketchup on myself until after dinner." A boy of about ten with a rubber ax sticking out of the top of his head grabbed Marti's bag of burgers and disappeared through a doorway off to the right.

"Listen, all of you settle down a minute and let me introduce you to my friend. All right?" Dominic demanded, raising his voice several decibels in an attempt to be heard. When they quieted, he continued. "Marti, this is Angela." Grinning, he gave the older girl an obvious once-over. "Going as Frank's bride again this year, Angie? Nice, real nice." Pausing a moment, he gestured toward the empty doorway. "The guy who just snitched your bag of burgers is Andy. And this little squirt is Amy." He scooped up a girl of about six, dressed in pink tights and a tutu, and held her in his arms. "Hi, cutie. Whatcha know good?"

"I know you're good, Uncle Dominic." She gave him a hug, then smiled shyly at Marti. "I'm a ballerina."

"And a very pretty one," Marti said with a shy smile of her own.

"Yeah, but I need a hairdo." The little girl patted her long, dark hair with one hand. "Like yours," she added.

"Well, maybe Ms. Townsend can help you with that after we eat," Dominic suggested.

"Miz, huh?" Angela drawled, her grin a lot like her uncle's. "So when are you two getting married?"

"Oh, Uncle Dominic, are you getting married? Can I be the flower girl? Oh, please, can I, can I?" Amy pleaded.

Utterly stupefied, Marti stared at the two girls as a blush spread across her cheeks. What she wouldn't do for a rabbit hole now, or any hole, as long as she could fall into it. *Married.* She glanced at Dominic out of the corner of her eye and caught him looking at her, a bemused expression on his face. However, it vanished completely as he turned back to his nieces.

"Angela, I think your mother's looking for you. And you, too," he added, nodding at Amy, who was still gazing up at him hopefully.

"Oh, no, she's not," Angela replied rather huffily. "She's the one who told us to scope out the *situation.*"

"Angie, honey, why don't you take Amy into the kitchen and give her something to eat." A woman wearing a red yarn wig hurried down the stairs.

"But, Mom—"

"*Now,* Angela." The woman paused beside Marti as the girls turned and headed for the doorway. When they were gone, she faced Marti and offered a welcoming smile. "I may look like Raggedy Ann, but I'm really Rose Gardner. And this is my husband, Drew." She gestured toward the grown-up Raggedy Andy who had followed her downstairs, then continued. "It's so nice to finally meet you, Marti, although I apologize for the current state of affairs around here." She waved a hand at the living room.

"It's nice to meet you, too," Marti replied, her earlier discomfort at the mention of marriage quickly dissipating as Dominic hugged his sister and shook hands with his brother-in-law.

They exchanged a few words, catching up on what had happened in their lives since the last time they'd talked. Then Rose took one of the bags Dominic had been holding and, apologizing once again, went back upstairs with Drew to finish dressing.

"Guess we'd better eat, too, before our food gets cold," Dominic suggested. Casually slipping his arm around Marti's shoulders, he guided her toward the kitchen.

He was really proud of her. Not everyone would have held up so well under a Gardner Gang onslaught, complete with a mention of marriage in the first five minutes. But she'd been a real trooper. Once she got used to the noise level and the incessant activity, she'd be fine, just fine.

It was clear to Dominic, whether she wanted to admit it to him or not, she liked children. Her photographs had assured him of that. And although they had a penchant for smart mouths and a "your business is my business" mindset, his nieces and nephew were nice kids. Before the evening was over, he had a feeling she'd end up enjoying herself enormously. In fact, he'd been counting on just that when he'd invited her.

She'd told him that her job was her life. But after last Saturday night he'd begun to wonder if that was the way she really wanted it. Perhaps all she needed were some alternatives. And what could it hurt to find out?

The kitchen wasn't quite as bad as he'd expected it to be. Either Andy and the girls had managed to keep most of the food in their mouths, or poor Butch, sitting beside Amy's chair and smacking his chops, was going to end up with a major bellyache.

"Why don't you put your purse and camera on top of the refrigerator?" he suggested as he moved ahead of her toward the table. "They should be safe up there. Right, guys?"

"Don't look at me, man. I'm out of here." Ketchup bottle in one hand, Andy slid out of his chair.

"Hey, clean up your mess," Angela commanded as she stuffed a handful of cardboard cartons into the trash can under the sink.

"Make me."

"Andrew, put down the ketchup bottle and clean up your mess. Then the two of you can leave us to eat in peace," Dominic said as he set the remaining paper bag on the table and began to clear a space for them.

"Yeah, eat in peace," Amy piped up. "Then my hairdo. Right, Miss Marti?"

"Right, Amy," Marti agreed without hesitation.

Glancing over his shoulder, Dominic saw that she was still standing by the refrigerator. But she wasn't paying any attention to him. She was watching Andy elbow Angela out of his way. And she was smiling. "Grab a couple of sodas and come eat before everything's cold," he suggested, setting out paper plates and napkins.

"Don't forget, we're leaving at six-thirty *sharp*," Angela advised as she flounced toward the doorway.

"And we're going up and down *every* street for miles and miles," Andy added, snitching the ketchup bottle and making a run for it.

Once again Dominic glanced at Marti. And once again she wasn't paying any attention to him. Somehow she'd slipped her camera from its case without anyone noticing. As he looked on she calmly shot a picture of an unknowing Amy feeding Butch a wiggly french fry.

Smiling to himself, he quickly turned away and began pulling burgers and fries from the bag. She was going to be fine, all right—more than fine.

"Hey, why do you have eight burgers and I only have four?" Marti demanded when she finally joined him at the table a few seconds later.

"Well, what would you consider an equal division?"

"Six and six. That equals twelve," Amy answered precociously.

"It certainly does." Marti winked at the little girl as she grabbed two of Dominic's burgers and set them next to her plate. Then she smiled at Dominic. "You can have all the fries."

"Gee, thanks."

They ate in companionable silence for several minutes, relishing the oniony flavor of the little burgers while they were still warm and juicy.

"So we're going up and down every street for miles and miles," Marti said at last. "I'm glad I wore my walking shoes." She wiped her mouth on a napkin, took a sip of her cola and reached for her fourth burger.

"Don't worry. They usually last about an hour or an hour and a half max. By then their bags are so full of junk they can hardly carry them. And I won't let them eat any of it until we have it X-rayed at the hospital. So they should be ready to call it quits by seven-thirty or eight. With luck we should be back here by nine, and all of them should be in bed by ten at the latest."

"Uh-uh, Uncle Dominic. Mommy told us we could stay up real late if we wanted to, and I want to. Do you like to play Candyland, Marti? Uncle Dominic does."

Uncle Dominic groaned out load. "No, no, *please*. Not Candyland. Anything but Candyland."

"Oh, silly." Amy laughed.

"That bad, huh?" Marti asked, laughing, too, as she met his gaze.

"Once again, I'll let you see for yourself."

"I seem to remember you saying the exact same thing right before we walked into bedlam."

"Yeah, and you handled it real well, didn't you?" he replied, unable to hide his growing admiration for her.

"Piece of cake," she murmured, blushing a bit as she stood and began to gather up their empty plates.

Dominic stood, too, and gently touched her arm, drawing her attention back to him. "Having fun?" he asked softly, solemnly.

"Oh, yes," she breathed, gazing up at him, her eyes sparkling.

"Hey, no mushy stuff, Uncle Dominic," Amy interrupted. "It's time for my hairdo, isn't it, Marti?" Impatiently she hopped from one foot to the other, dancing around them.

"It certainly is," Marti agreed, shaking her head rather ruefully as she handed him the plates and turned to face his niece. "Have you got a brush and hairpins?"

"Right here." Amy scampered over to the counter to retrieve them.

"Okay, come and sit in my lap and tell me how you want it."

"Just like yours. All neat and pretty."

"All neat and pretty, it is," Marti agreed, smoothing the brush ever so gently through the little girl's long dark hair.

Dominic stood watching them for several seconds. Then, setting the plates on the counter, he moved across the kitchen to where he'd left his jacket. As quietly as he could, he pulled the little automatic thirty-five-millimeter camera he'd bought just yesterday out of his jacket pocket and began to take a few pictures of his own.

At six-thirty sharp they said goodbye to Rose and Drew, who wouldn't be leaving until seven. Then, in the company of Frankenstein's bride, a gruesome, bloody monster and a neat and pretty ballerina, Dominic and Marti walked up one street and down another for almost two hours, laughing and talking, and after the first block, holding hands.

Since Dominic had lived in the neighborhood most of his life and knew many of the people there, he felt the children were reasonably safe. But he only allowed them to stop at houses where the porch lights were on. And he not only insisted on having their candy X-rayed at a nearby hospital that offered the special service, he also enlisted Marti's help in scrupulously checking for any suspicious-looking items when they returned to his sister's house.

"Actually, he's looking for peanut-butter cups so he can snitch them," Angela said, inching her pile of goodies a little farther away from her uncle.

"Yeah, he *loves* them," Amy added.

"Am not," Dominic defended himself, about to take a bite of chocolate and peanut butter.

"Are, too. And you're not getting any more of mine." Using both arms, Andy scooped his loot off the kitchen table and back into his bag.

"Mine, either." Angela's candy disappeared off the table, too. "Come on, Andy, let's go watch one of the monster movies Mom rented for us. You, too, Amy." She turned to Dominic and continued with all the authority of a first-born. "She said we could watch it on the television in her bedroom so you could be *alone.*"

"But I don't like monster movies," Amy said, her voice low and a little trembly.

"Then why don't you stay down here and play Candyland with me and Uncle Dominic," Marti suggested as she helped her scoop the last of her candy back into her bag.

"But then you won't get to be alone."

"That's okay, squirt," Dominic assured her. "We can be alone another time, can't we, Marti?" Though he wanted to look at her, to gauge the sincerity of her response, he concentrated on unwrapping the last of the candies he'd swiped during inspection.

If he had anything to say about it, they'd have lots of time alone together. But he still wasn't sure if she felt the same way. If she did, he'd hear it in her voice. If not, he didn't want to see rejection in her eyes.

"I hope so," she said at last, her voice soft.

"I hope so, too." He reached out and squeezed her hand gently for just an instant, then let her go as Amy plunked down the game box onto the table between them.

"Youngest goes first," the little girl declared.

"And second and third and fourth," Dominic added, shuffling the cards.

"Oh, Uncle Dominic, you're being silly again."

"Hey, I'm just a silly kind of guy." He glanced at Marti and winked. And much to his surprise, she winked back.

They played three rounds of the game before Amy began to droop. Finally, about halfway through round four she laid her head on the table, closed her eyes and fell sound asleep. Sharing a smile with Marti, Dominic stood and walked around the table, then carefully scooped the little girl into his arms.

"Want to help me get her settled?" he whispered as he headed out of the kitchen.

"Sure."

Marti trailed after him through the dark, silent living room and up the dimly lit stairs, pausing when he did in the doorway of his sister's bedroom. Angela and Andy were stretched out on the bed with Butch between them, wide eyes fixed on the flickering TV screen.

"How's the movie?" Dominic asked softly.

"Totally scary," Angela replied in an equally hushed tone of voice. "Will you watch it with us in the living room now that Amy's asleep?"

"Yeah, sure." As he sighed, Marti tried, unsuccessfully, to hide her smile. "It's not funny," he muttered, glancing at her as they continued down the hallway. "They're determined not to leave us alone for five minutes."

"From what I could see the movie did look kind of scary for them to be watching it alone," Marti said as she moved ahead of him into Amy's room. Guided by the warm glow of a night-light, she crossed to the little girl's canopy bed and turned back the comforter.

"Too scary? For those two? How can you say that after seeing the way they were dressed tonight? Now *that* was too scary."

"Well, now that you mention it..." Laughing softly, Marti stood back while Dominic settled Amy, tutu, tights and all, in the bed. Then she stepped forward to draw the comforter up around the sleeping child's shoulders. "She really is a little sweetie, isn't she?"

"She can be a handful if she doesn't get her way. But most of the time she's a good kid. Angela and Andy are good, too."

"How could they be anything else? They have two parents who obviously love them, they have each other and they have you. And others, too. Your grandmother, your parents, your sister and her husband..." she murmured wistfully.

As she straightened and stepped back, she realized she envied them on all counts. She'd missed so much when she was growing up. And now she was growing older and missing even more. But she'd made her choices. And she had a good life. She did.

"A big family can have its advantages, especially if everyone gets along as well as we do," he admitted as they turned to go. "Sometimes, when we're all together, talking and laughing, we can be kind of intimidating. But once you get used to us, we're not so bad. And we're definitely not a closed community. There's always room for one more. And considering how good you are at playing Candyland..."

"My entree, huh?" Despite her wry tone of voice she was touched by the reassuring warmth of his words. Glancing up at him as they walked down the hall, she smiled gratefully, glad to have been a part of his family if only for one night.

"Hey, you won two out of three games, didn't you?" he asked, wrapping an arm around her shoulders and giving her a quick hug, then releasing her as they came to the stairs.

"Mmm, I did, didn't I?" she agreed, slightly flustered by the sudden, close contact with him. Hanging on to the rail, she followed him down the steps, her face flushed, her heart beating fast. It had been a long time since anyone had hugged her, so long that she'd forgotten how wonderful it could be.

In the living room Angela, Andy and Butch were already sprawled on the floor in front of the television, and all three of them, dog included, seemed to be once again engrossed in their totally scary movie.

"At least they left us the sofa," Dominic muttered, taking Marti's hand and pulling her down beside him. "Come on, sit close so the monster won't get you."

Marti did as he suggested, and almost immediately Dominic put his arm around her, drawing her closer still. Then he reached up and switched off the lamp on the end table, and they were plunged into semidarkness. For just an instant she hesitated, then she relaxed against him, her head on his shoulder, her legs tucked up under her.

"I think a monster has her already, don't you, Andy?" Angela asked her brother, not quite under her breath.

"Not funny, Angie, not funny at all," Dominic growled.

"Then why is Marti laughing?"

"Angie, shut up, will ya? I'm trying to watch the movie." Andy poked his sister with his elbow, and of course she poked him back.

"You're not supposed to say—"

"All right, you two, *quiet.*"

Mindful that their uncle had obviously had enough, Angela and Andy hissed a few final words at each other, then settled down to watch the movie. Marti willed herself to do likewise, but she was too aware of Dominic to concentrate on anything else.

As she leaned against him, his body heat warming her, she could hear the slow, steady beat of his heart, she could smell the spicy tang of his after-shave, she could feel the gentle brush of his lips against her hair as he stroked her arm. Her eyes riveted to the ghostly image shimmering and swirling on the small screen, she rubbed her cheek against the soft fabric of his plaid flannel shirt, then rested her hand on his denim-clad thigh.

He drew in a deep breath, then went very still, and Marti sensed that he was waiting, waiting... And suddenly she knew that if she turned her head, if she tipped her face up, if she raised her eyes and met his gaze, he would kiss her. But not as he had the other night. Here, now, he would really kiss her. All she had to do was turn her head... tip her face up... raise her eyes—

"Hi, everybody, we're home."

At the sound of his sister's voice Dominic switched on the lamp, and Marti sighed with profound regret. If only she hadn't hesitated, if only she'd had the courage to go after what she'd wanted. If only... But she hadn't, and now it was too late. Easing away from Dominic, she swung her legs to the floor and sat up straight.

"How were they?" Rose asked, shrugging out of her coat and pulling off her yarn wig at the same time.

"We were perfect little angels, weren't we, Uncle Dominic?" Sitting Indian-style, Angela offered her mother a suitably beatific smile.

"Well, perfect little angels, why don't you wing it up to bed? It's almost midnight," Drew said as he joined them in the living room.

"Oh, right, *now* they have to go to bed," Dominic muttered, eyeing Marti with such exaggerated woe that she had to smile. Then, as the kids trudged up the stairs, grumbling at each other every step of the way, he turned his attention to his sister. "So how was the party?"

"More fun than I expected. Everybody dressed up and some of the costumes were really original," Rose said. Flopping onto a chair, she kicked off her shoes and wiggled her toes.

"Yeah, you should have seen Denise Miles. She came as a belly dancer. Talk about hot." Drew waved one hand as if it were on fire.

"Oh, that wasn't original. That was...that was..." At a loss for words, Rose shook her head as she traded smiles with Marti. "How about something to drink? I can make coffee."

"No, thanks." Dominic stood and stretched, then grabbed Marti's hand and pulled her to her feet. "It's getting late, and I've got to work tomorrow," he added as he headed for the kitchen to get Marti's purse and camera as well as their coats.

"Me, too," Marti admitted, barely stifling a yawn.

"Well, thanks again, Dominic." Rose hugged her younger brother, then turned to Marti and hugged her, too. "And thanks to you, too, Marti. I hope they weren't too bad."

"They weren't bad at all," Marti replied, surprised and unaccountably pleased by Rose's show of affection.

"Did you hear that? She doesn't think they're bad," Drew teased as he joined his wife at the front door. "Please, Ms. Townsend, come back anytime. And don't feel you have to bring Dominic with you."

"Hey, I like you, too, Drew," Dominic said, grinning at his brother-in-law as he took Marti's hand and guided her toward his car. "Good night, everybody."

·   "They're so nice." Marti sighed as she settled into the front seat of the Corvette. "Thanks for inviting me."

"Had fun, huh?" Dominic started the engine, backed out of the driveway and headed toward her house, which was only a few blocks away.

"Oh, yes, a lot of fun."

"I kind of thought you would."

"Oh, really? Why?"

"I'm not sure. I just did."

They drove the rest of the way in silence, but Marti didn't mind a bit. It seemed so right to be with Dominic, riding down one dark street after another in the quiet car, so right that she wished they could ride on forever. But sooner than she'd anticipated, he pulled up in front of her house. And suddenly, unexpectedly, a tiny prickle of fear crept up her spine.

While she'd left lights on inside, she'd decided to leave her porch lights off so as not to disappoint any would-be trick or treaters. As a result, her front porch was shrouded in darkness. And in a moment or two, she'd be walking into that darkness with Dominic.

With *Dominic*—kind and understanding, warm and gentle Dominic. She had nothing to fear from him and she knew it. Why, only a short while ago she'd wanted to kiss him, really kiss him. And darkness or no darkness, she realized that she still did.

"Something wrong, Marti?" He stood by the open car door, waiting for her to get out.

"No, nothing at all."

Almost tentatively he slipped his arm around her as they walked up the sidewalk. Without hesitation she moved closer to him, grateful for the warmth he provided against the cold night air.

"So, you have to work tomorrow," she said, picking up on what he'd told his sister earlier.

"One of my best customers couldn't get his car started this afternoon, and he needs it for an out-of-town business trip first thing Monday morning. I told him I'd do whatever I could to get it running for him." Pausing as they reached the porch, he took her key and unlocked her door but didn't turn on the light. "Sounds like you'll be busy, too." He pressed her key into her hand, then took a step back.

"One of *my* best customers wants his entire ad campaign revamped before the first of the year and, honestly, I haven't a clue where to begin."

"Maybe all you need to do is sleep on it."

"Maybe." She tipped her face up, meeting his gaze, allowing the single, wistful word to hang between them. The last thing on her mind was Neal Dobbs's ad campaign.

"Well, then, I'd better let you go before it gets any later. Good night, Marti."

As he had the week before, he slowly bent his head and gently brushed his lips over hers. Then he took another step back, and another.

"Dominic, wait." Unwilling to let him go without a real kiss, Marti moved toward him. Resting one hand on his chest, she tipped her head back and pressed her lips against his.

In an instant he drew her into his arms and opened his mouth over hers. Instinctively she parted her lips for his gently probing tongue, sighing with pleasure at her first taste of him, then reveling in the smooth, sensual glide of his tongue against hers as she returned his caress. Moaning softly, she pressed against him, wanting more, wanting . . .

Slowly Dominic raised his head. Smiling down at her, he smoothed a wisp of hair away from her face with a trembling hand.

''What's wrong?'' she whispered, afraid that he'd ended their kiss because, with her lack of experience, she'd done something wrong.

''Not a thing. In fact, I'd say everything was right.''

''Then why did you stop?''

''Because . . .''

''Because why?'' she prodded.

''Just plain old because.'' He hugged her close for one long moment, then set her away from him. ''I have to go, Marti. While I still can.''

She stared at him as she weighed his words, and suddenly she understood what he was saying. He wanted more than deep kisses and gentle caresses. If she didn't let him go, he'd assume that she did, too. And with that assumption he'd feel free to take what he wanted.

Shivering slightly, she moved away from him, fumbling for the door handle as she did so. ''Yes, you'd better . . . better go,'' she agreed, her voice barely above a whisper. ''Thanks again for—for tonight. Good—goodbye.''

''Good night, Marti.'' Shoving his hands in his jacket pockets, he turned and walked down the steps.

For just an instant she longed to call him back. Then common sense came to the fore, and she quickly slipped inside her house and closed the door.

She should have known better than to tempt him. He'd been a perfect gentleman, but still she'd been playing with fire. And she couldn't afford to be burned. She simply couldn't afford it at all.

But kissing him, really kissing him, had been better than she'd ever imagined. And already she wanted to do it again, and again. If she hadn't let him go . . .

''If you hadn't let him go, he wouldn't have stopped with a few kisses,'' she warned herself as she dropped her purse and camera onto the hall table and slipped out of her jacket.

"And then what would you have done?" As she turned toward the stairs, Marti realized she wasn't sure.

And that frightened her more than anything, considering her certainty that she had so much to lose.

Chapter Six

Late the next morning, after coffee and sweet rolls from the bakery up the street and a thorough perusal of the Sunday paper, Marti settled down at the kitchen table, spread out the necessary information in front of her and, through sheer determination, kept her mind on the Dobbs account rather than Dominic. By mid-afternoon, much to her surprise, she actually had several ideas down on paper.

Granted, her concepts were far from brilliant, but Neal Dobbs was relatively easy to please. While she might not have given it her best shot, as long as she had something to show him when they met the following day, he'd be happy. And at the moment that was all that mattered to her. In fact, at the rate she was going, if she didn't move on to something else soon, she never would. It was already after two o'clock, and she'd barely made a dent in the other, equally important work she had to do before tomorrow.

Sighing, she eyed her open briefcase without enthusiasm. Then, shifting her gaze to the blue sky and bright sun framed by the kitchen window, she recalled how delightfully warm the air had been when she'd walked to the bakery earlier. With winter just around the corner, there wouldn't be many more days like today, when she could go for a drive with the top down, then stop to have a picnic in the park.

She had to eat sometime, she reasoned, moving away from the window to pull a loaf of bread from the bread box. Having worked most of the morning and into the afternoon, she really did need a break. In fact, a couple of hours out in the fresh air and sunshine might help to clear the cobwebs. Why, she might actually feel like working again if she got away for a while.

Humming softly to herself, she set ham, cheese, mustard and mayo and four slices of bread on the counter. She paused for a moment, then added four more slices. Dominic had planned to work today, too, hadn't he? And if he was still at the garage, he'd probably be ready to take a break, too. She could call Fabrino's and find out. Better yet, she could simply arrive with her picnic basket packed. If he was there, and he wanted to join her, fine. If not, she'd understand. Really, she would. And she'd go on her own as she'd always done.

But after last night going alone didn't hold the same appeal that it had in the past. In fact, her idea of having a picnic in the park probably had a lot more to do with Dominic than she liked to admit. Going alone would be all right, but going with him would be something else altogether. Going with him would be fun. They could laugh and talk, just as they'd done every other time they'd been together.

And maybe, just maybe, he'd kiss her again....

"And then what?" she demanded in a low voice, suddenly angry at herself, as well as confused by the trail her thoughts were taking.

He'd made it plain that he wasn't going to settle for kisses, at least not for long. But kisses were all she had to give. She might want more, need more, but in her heart of hearts she knew she wasn't ready for that kind of relationship. And to allow Dominic to think otherwise, to lead him on, to tempt him or tease him in any way, would be wrong.

Frowning, she crossed to the pantry and pulled out a wicker basket for the sandwiches, chips and cookies, and a small cooler for the soft drinks. As she had off and on for the past three weeks, she wondered if it might not be best to end whatever they had between them before it went any further. Surely there'd be less hurt all around if they ended it now rather than a few weeks or months from now.

But how could she, when just the thought of him banished the aching, empty loneliness that had haunted her for so long? How could she, when he made her feel whole again, when he warmed her with his laughter and touched her with his kindness? She couldn't. She simply couldn't.

But she could be mindful of the fine line that separated a friend from a lover. And she could be very, very careful not to cross it in the future. A week ago he'd made it clear that he didn't expect anything serious to come of their seeing each other. So if she, in turn, let him know that she only wanted to be friends, surely he wouldn't object.

He obviously knew as well as she did that they just weren't meant to have any kind of permanent relationship together. He wanted a wife and a mother for his children, while she wanted her hard-earned vice presidency at the Chicago headquarters of Carter and Caisson. And she doubted that a few kisses had altered his ultimate goal any more than they'd altered hers.

But if a few kisses hadn't caused either of them any problems, surely a little picnic in the park wouldn't hurt any. She packed the basket and cooler quickly, before she could talk herself out of it.

Upstairs she tied her hair back at the nape of her neck. Pinning it up as she usually did would be a waste of time since she planned to drive with the top down. Then she pulled an emerald green sweater over the plaid shirt and faded jeans she already wore and shoved her bare feet into an old pair of loafers.

Outside, the weather was as luscious as she'd expected. Settling back in the driver's seat of her little red Mustang, she tipped her face up to the sun, relishing its warmth as the cool wind whispered around her, teasing at her hair. With luck, Dominic would be at Fabrino's. They'd go for a drive, have their picnic in the park, then they'd each go their separate ways. And she'd have one more precious memory to hold in her heart for all the ever-afters when they would forever be apart.

Holding her breath, she turned the corner and headed toward the garage. Halfway down the block she saw Dominic's Chevy parked on the lot and sighed with relief. Now if only he wasn't too busy to take some time away, she'd be truly happy.

As she slowed the Mustang to turn into Fabrino's she saw a car on the rack in one of the bays, but otherwise the garage seemed to be deserted. She doubted that he'd gone off somewhere while the place was open. Yet for just an instant she was tempted to let well enough alone, to simply drive on. But then he walked out of his office, wiping his hands on an old rag, saw her and smiled. And Marti smiled, too, as she eased to a stop beside the Chevy.

"Ready for a break?" she called as she switched off the ignition and opened the car door.

"How'd you know?" Dominic paused several yards away and tried, unsuccessfully, to will away the wild rush of pleasure welling up inside him at her unexpected arrival. It meant nothing at all that she'd taken time off to stop by the garage, and he knew it. More than likely she was just bored and restless, as bored and restless as he'd been all day, and the lovely weather had lured her out.

But she hadn't gone off alone. She'd come looking for him. And Dominic wanted to know why. Was there more to their relationship than he'd allowed himself to believe? Did she care for him as much as he cared for her? And, equally important, did she want him in the same way he wanted her? Even after the way she'd kissed him last night, he hadn't thought so because she'd let him go. But now, as she smiled and waved and started toward him, he wasn't quite so sure.

"Just lucky, I guess." She paused, her smile widening for a moment as if she'd thought of something funny. "Actually, I was climbing the walls and decided to get out for a while," she continued with a casual shrug. "I thought I'd go for a ride, then have a picnic lunch in the park. And I thought if you weren't too busy, you might like to join me. It's nothing fancy, and I wasn't planning on being gone for more than a couple of hours."

"Sounds good to me. Can you give me a few minutes to get cleaned up?"

"Sure."

As he turned and headed back to the office with Marti trailing along behind him, Dominic finally realized that she hadn't simply stopped to see him for a minute or two. She'd come to invite him to spend what was left of the afternoon with her. And considering her casual clothes and hairstyle, he had a feeling she'd probably done so on the spur of the moment. But that made her overture even more endearing. She'd thought of him when she'd least expected to, and despite her hesitation in the past, she'd dared to do something about it.

While Marti waited in his office, he went back to the washroom and scrubbed down as best he could. His grubby jeans and boots would have to do. At least he kept a clean shirt and pullover sweater hanging in the supply closet for emergencies. He changed in no time. A few moments more and the garage was closed and locked, and he and Marti were on their way to her car.

"Want me to drive?" he asked with a teasing grin.

"Sure." She tossed him her keys.

"Really?" He almost missed catching them, so surprised was he at her answer.

"Hey, I get to drive it every day. And, anyway, if you drive it I figure you'll be able to tell if it's running the way it should." It was her turn to grin as she slipped into the passenger seat.

"Ulterior motives, huh? And here I thought you just wanted to be with me." He sighed dejectedly and eyed her solemnly for several seconds from the driver's seat. Then, inserting the key in the ignition and starting the engine, he grinned again. "Ah, well, I guess I'll live. As long as I get to drive."

"Why am I not surprised?" Marti muttered wryly as he pulled out of the lot.

"Has it been giving you any trouble at all?" Dominic asked, heading for the highway. He could put the Mustang through its paces much better on the open road. And he could also take Marti by the new place and let her have a look at it. It wasn't quite ready for business, but it was shaping up nicely.

"Not a bit. But I'd still feel better if you checked it out for me." She tipped her head against the headrest, turned and smiled at him as the wind tugged at loose strands of her sun-gilded hair.

For a heartbeat or two, as he met her gaze, the world narrowed to the small space between them, to the warmth in her eyes and the sweetness in her smile. Then, realizing where he was and what he was supposed to be doing, he shifted his attention to the road ahead. If he wrecked her car, she'd never forgive him, much less let him drive again.

The Mustang ran as well as he'd expected, and within fifteen minutes he was pulling onto the lot of the soon-to-be, new Fabrino's.

"Is this your new place?" Marti asked, hopping out of the car as soon as he stopped and walking toward the three large buildings that made up the complex. "It's much bigger than the one in the city, isn't it?"

"About one and a half times bigger. That's one of the reasons I bought it. There's nowhere to expand in the city. And with people hanging on to their cars longer and having to keep up with maintenance, we've started to have more work than we can handle there. I have lots of customers who live out in the suburbs, too. Having another garage here will make it a lot more convenient for them." He knew he was rattling on, but he was proud of how far he'd brought the business in the past four years. And he had a feeling that, unlike Diane, Marti would understand just how much it meant to him.

"How far along are the renovations?" She peered through a window at what would be the office, then moved down to another window that opened into one of several work areas.

"Barring any major problems, we should be ready to open just after the first of the year."

As she turned to face him, she frowned thoughtfully. "Are you going to do some advertising before your grand opening?"

"I'm going to advertise the new location, but I hadn't really thought about doing it in advance. And I hadn't thought about having a grand opening, either."

"Oh, I think advance ads in local newspapers and magazines, as well as a few spots on the local cable TV channels coupled with grand-opening specials, would really help bring in the business from day one." She led the way back to her car, her excitement and enthusiasm more than obvious. "You know, it wouldn't take me long to work up some ideas for you," she continued, glancing at him over her shoulder. "In fact, I think it would be kind of fun."

"I appreciate the offer. But Carter and Caisson is a big agency with fees to match." He shrugged ruefully as he held the car door open for her. "I'm afraid you're way out of my league, Marti."

"If I worked on it personally, I could do most of it in my spare time. Then I wouldn't have to bill you for as many hours as I would if I gave it to one of my staff. Kind of like you did for me with my old car." Turning sideways, she grinned at him impishly as he slid back into the driver's seat and started the engine. "Keeping that old car running would have cost me a fortune anywhere but Fabrino's, and you know it as well as I do."

He did, but he was still hesitant about accepting her offer. For one thing, he knew that she had quite a bit to do already. In fact, he had no doubt that she worked at least sixty hours a week as it was. And for another, he could think of a lot better ways for her to spend what little spare time she had than on more of the same, even if it would be for him. He'd much rather have her spend a few hours with him than working for him any day.

"Again, I appreciate the offer. But, Marti, from what you've said, it doesn't sound like you have any spare time."

"I've been busy lately, but not so much so that I couldn't fit Fabrino's into my schedule. I wouldn't have offered otherwise. Really, Dominic, I wouldn't," she added, so earnestly that he almost acquiesced.

"Let me think about it, okay?" he asked at last. Allowing Marti to work for him would be one way to maintain their growing relationship. But if it cut into the time they could spend together, it would end up being less of a help and more of a hindrance. There were enough obstacles in their way already.

"But—"

"I'll think about it," he repeated firmly, cutting off whatever objections she'd been prepared to raise. "Now why don't we find a place to have our picnic? Got any ideas?"

When Marti didn't answer immediately, Dominic braced himself for an argument. He knew she hadn't gotten as far as she had in the advertising business by being overly amenable. If she was determined enough, he figured she could debate her side with the best of them. However, in the end, she didn't push it.

"Since we're heading back to the city, how about Tower Grove Park? It's fairly close to the house and, along with Shaw's Garden, it's one of my favorite places."

"Mine, too," he admitted, barely concealing his sigh of relief.

They found a parking place without a problem and quickly unloaded the car, then followed a walkway past several clusters of tables, most of which were already occupied. By mutual agreement they continued on a little farther to a more secluded spot under a huge old tree, and there, on the crisp bed of leaves beneath it, they spread out the old quilt Marti had brought along.

Both of them were hungrier than they'd imagined, so they didn't say much as they ate, concentrating instead on the simple fare that Marti had prepared. But by the time she opened the little bag of anise wafers and almond macaroons she'd bought at the bakery that morning, they were sated enough to settle back against the broad tree trunk and savor their surroundings along with their dessert.

"Want to take a walk?" Dominic asked as he dug another anise wafer out of the bag. He was addicted to the crisp, golden cookies. But his mother only made them around the holidays and, given his penchant for sweets, he'd learned to stay away from the bakery except on special occasions.

"Mmm, I don't know. It's kind of nice just sitting here, isn't it?" Her hand brushed against his as she reached for the last macaroon.

"Yeah, it is." More than happy to remain where he was, he stretched his legs out in front of him. Then, shifting slightly, he casually put an arm around Marti's shoulders and drew her close. When she relaxed against him willingly, without hesitation, he couldn't help but smile, sure that he'd been right about the signals she'd been sending. "You were a big hit last night."

"Really?" She tilted her head back, her eyes bright with unspoken pleasure as she met his gaze.

"My sister called this morning to warn me that I'd better bring you back again soon or the kids would never forgive me. Especially Amy. She insisted that Rose fix her hair just like you did last night."

"All neat and pretty...." Marti murmured. Then, as if realizing her hair was anything but neat and pretty at the moment, she straightened a bit and tried, unsuccessfully, to smooth some of the windblown wisps back into place.

"Here, let me," Dominic offered. Not giving her a chance to protest, he tugged on the narrow green ribbon until it came loose, then ran his fingers through the silken length of her hair, fanning it out over her shoulders.

"Oh, Dominic, you shouldn't have…" She grabbed at the ribbon, but before she could get her hands on it, he stuffed it in a pocket of his jeans.

"Why not?"

"Because…" Blushing, she turned her face away and shrugged with seeming uncertainty. "I never wear my hair loose."

"Well, you should." He traced the line of her jaw with his fingertips, then gently tilted her head up. "You look so soft and pretty." Bending his head, he kissed her slowly, lingeringly. And as he stroked her lips with the tip of his tongue, she sighed and leaned against him, opening her mouth to him.

He tasted of almond and coconut and a hint of licorice, and suddenly Marti couldn't get enough of him. Whimpering softly, she leaned against him, flattening her palms against his sweater-clad chest, sliding her tongue against his, delighting in the hot, wet thrust and parry with every fiber of her being.

When he raised his head and eased away from her, she wanted to object. But instead, common sense finally coming to the fore, she laid her head on his shoulder and quietly closed her eyes. She should have opted for a walk, a long, brisk walk around the park, she thought, rubbing her face against the nubby texture of his sweater. That's what friends would have done. But his kisses warmed away the chill of her loneliness, and in his arms she felt so safe, so incredibly secure.

Opening her eyes, she saw the sun dip behind the trees, sending shadows scuffling all around them. The afternoon was almost over and their interlude must end. But not yet, she prayed as he gently caressed her hair and murmured her name. Not just yet....

Mentally tossing aside the last of her self-imposed strictures, she curled closer to him, then lifted her head and pressed her lips against the bare skin at the base of his throat. He growled softly, his hold on her tightening. An instant later, he shifted her onto his lap. He held her gaze for several seconds, as if assuring himself of something. Then he dipped his head and claimed her mouth again, more fiercely, more possessively than ever as he smoothed his palm down the front of her sweater to cover her breast.

Even through several layers of fabric Marti felt the heat of his touch, a heat that coursed through her and pooled deep in her belly. Moaning softly, she arched into him, wrapping her arms around his neck, not sure what she wanted, only... only wanting, as he slid his hand away and gently ended their kiss.

"I think we'd better go," he muttered, his voice rough as he threaded his fingers through her hair. "It's getting late, and parks after dark aren't as safe as they used to be." Tipping her face back, he dropped a quick kiss on her lips, then eased her off his lap. "Why don't you grab the basket and cooler while I get the quilt?"

Without a word, she did as he suggested, then stood off to one side as he shook out the quilt and doubled it twice. Most of the people she'd seen earlier had already gone, and the few remaining stragglers all seemed to be on their way out, as well. She'd never been in the park so near dark and had no idea how deserted it could become.

"All of a sudden everybody's gone," she said, shivering slightly at the hint of chill in the night breeze. "I didn't realize..."

"I would have been hurt if you had," Dominic teased. Grinning suggestively, he put an arm around her and hugged her close as they started toward her car.

Glancing at him, she smiled uncertainly. Once again, despite her better judgment, she'd behaved in an obviously wanton way. She could only imagine what Dominic must think of her, not to mention what he must expect. And she didn't like to think what he might say or do when he realized that his prospects actually weren't all that good.

Mentally cursing her earlier lack of prudence, she deemed it time to put some distance between them, literally as well as figuratively. Slipping away from him, she moved ahead to set the basket and cooler on the back seat. "I think we ought to put the top up. It's starting to get cold, isn't it?" she asked brightly. "And I suppose it would be easier if I drove. That way you can just hop out at the garage."

He eyed her quizzically in the deepening dusk as he set the quilt on the back seat, too. "Something wrong, Marti?"

"No, of course not. I'm just ready to go home and get back to work. And I bet you've got a lot to do at the garage, too."

"Actually, I was just about finished when you showed up." He dug her keys out of his pocket and tossed them to her, then opened the car door for her.

"Oh, well, then I guess you're anxious to get home." She slid into the driver's seat, careful not to brush up against him, then slipped the key into the ignition and hit the switch that raised the top.

"Not half as anxious as you are," he muttered, slamming her door shut.

She had only herself to blame for his annoyance. She knew that she couldn't run hot, then cold, when they were together and expect him to understand. Not when she didn't understand her behavior herself. But she could think of no way to smooth Dominic's ruffled feathers without leading him on even more than she already had. So instead, as she drove the short distance to Fabrino's, she talked about his new garage and how best to advertise a grand opening.

"So what do you say? Shall I put together a package for you? I could have something ready to show you in a week or ten days," she offered, glancing at him as she pulled to a stop near his office doorway.

He held her gaze for several seconds, his dark eyes pensive. Then, turning away, he opened the car door. "I told you I'd think about it."

"And?" She smiled what she hoped was an encouraging smile.

"And I haven't made up my mind yet." He got out of the car, then bent down to look her in the eye again. Not a trace of a smile softened his craggy features. "Thanks for lunch." Straightening, he closed the door with a final, quiet click and walked toward his office.

Marti watched him go, wanting nothing more than to call him back to tell him—to tell him what? She'd had so little experience with personal, man-woman relationships that she had no idea at all. All she had was a feeling that no matter what she chose to say, it would only make things worse. At this point it would probably be wisest to just go home. She could always call him about the advertising in a few days. By then neither one of them would be quite so tense.

As she stepped on the accelerator and guided her car off the lot, she risked a glance in the rearview mirror. To her surprise Dominic hadn't gone into his office. Instead he stood outside the unopened door, hands planted on his hips, a frown furrowing his brow as he watched her depart. She almost stopped, almost turned back. But in the end she just continued down the street, goaded by her own uncertainty.

At the house she parked her car in the garage. Then, basket, cooler and quilt in hand, she crossed to the front door. As she turned the key in the lock, she heard a car pull up to the curb and stop. Looking over her shoulder, she saw Dominic's Chevy. Not sure if she was warmed or alarmed by his unexpected arrival, she shoved the door open, set her things in the entryway, then turned back to face him as he started up the walk.

"Is something wrong?" she asked, tucking her hands in her pockets in an effort to still their sudden trembling.

"I need to talk to you, Marti." He climbed the steps, then paused a few feet from where she stood, the uncertainty lurking in the depths of his dark eyes apparent in the pale glow of the porch lights.

Filled with sudden, almost overwhelming remorse, Marti realized that she was responsible for his wariness. And as she met his gaze, she wanted nothing more than to reassure him, as well as herself, that they had nothing to fear from each other. If his kisses and caresses were any indication, Dominic cared for her more than a little. And in the past few weeks he'd come to mean so much to her. But considering how badly she'd behaved again today, how could he know? How could he ever know unless she told him? Maybe now, tonight, the time had come to do just that.

Smiling what she hoped was an encouraging smile, she gestured him into the house and shut the door. When he simply stood in the entryway, silently staring down at her, she groped for something to say.

"You said you wanted to talk to me?" she asked at last, hoping to prod him into going on from there. She didn't want to seem too forward. She didn't want to blurt out anything personal, in case it turned out his reason for being there was strictly business. "About the ads for Fabrino's?"

"No, about us. About this." Reaching out, he gently wrapped his hands around her shoulders and drew her toward him, then bent his head and covered her mouth with his.

As his tongue slid against hers, Marti responded without hesitation. Somehow he'd seen beneath the brittle shell she'd wrapped around herself earlier. And he'd understood . . . again. Sighing with joyous relief, she wrapped her arms around his neck and, threading her fingers through his hair, tasted him with equal ardor. When he moved his hands from her shoulders to her breasts, when he rubbed his thumbs slowly, rhythmically, across her nipples, she arched into him, whimpering softly.

"Ah, Marti, I want you . . . want you . . . so much . . ." He traced the curve of her neck with tiny kisses, his mouth hot and wet, his tongue velvet soft against her skin. Then he tugged at her earlobe with his teeth, making her shiver with desire. "Want you so much." Groaning deep in his throat, he took her mouth again, then caught her hips in his hands, spread his legs and, lifting her slightly, brought her up against him.

The first warning bell went off in her head as she felt the thick, hard length of him between her thighs. Instinctively she clutched at his shoulders, her breath catching in her throat. But before she could drag her mouth from his, before she could ask him to stop, he pressed against her, backing her up, backing her into the wall. His hands rode up her rib cage, up under her sweater to cup her breasts, to knead and squeeze, as his knee thrust between her legs.

A horrible vision of the past flashed back at her, and Marti's thoughts raged. *Oh, no, oh, stop, oh, please, oh,*

*please, oh, please, don't hurt me ... don't hurt me, Brent,
don't hurt me....*

Struggling wildly, she wrenched her mouth free as she
beat against Dominic's chest with her fists. "Let me...go,"
she panted. *"Let me go."*

He moved away from her immediately, raising his hands
in mock surrender as he took a step back, then another and
another. "Hey, Marti, calm down, will you?" As she sagged
against the wall and crossed her arms over her chest, he
stared at her as if she'd dropped down off another planet.
"What the hell's the matter with you? I wanted to make love
with you. And I thought you wanted it, too."

"I... no, I... we can't. I have to work. I told you I have
to work," she finished in a rush, then cringed inwardly as
his eyes narrowed dangerously. How could she have said
that to him? How could she have thrown such a feeble excuse in his face when he'd talked of making love to her?
Only out of desperation, utter desperation—

He gazed at her silently, assessingly, for what seemed like
forever. Anger, hurt and confusion were evident in his dark
eyes. And when he finally spoke, his voice harsh and low,
Marti almost wished he hadn't.

"I don't believe you. There's more to this than your need
to work and you know it. You were scared. I'd like to know
why."

For the space of a heartbeat Marti was tempted to tell
him, to blurt out the ugly truth. But just the thought of
Brent Winston and what he'd done to her made her feel
ashamed all over again, ashamed and dirty. And she simply
wasn't up to confessing to Dominic that she'd not only been
raped, but raped due to her own naiveté. What could he
possibly think of her then? Not much, not much at all.
When all was said and done she'd prefer having him remember her with animosity, rather than pity or aversion.

Drawing on what remained of her hard-earned self-reliance, Marti straightened her spine, tipped up her chin and eyed Dominic unflinchingly. "I told you once that my job is my life. And I don't think I've indicated in any way that that's no longer true. However, if you choose not to believe me there's very little I can do about it, is there?" she said, her voice surprisingly cool and steady despite the dull ache in her heart. She'd never see him again, not after what she'd said, not after what she'd done. But it was better that way. It had to be.

Once again he simply stared at her, and for one long moment Marti considered taking back every word she'd spoken. But then it was too late. And that was just as well.

"Hey, don't sweat it, sweetheart," Dominic replied. "You have to work, go work." He spun on his heel and crossed to the door. As he wrapped his hand around the doorknob he glanced at her over his shoulder. "I won't try and stop you. Not tonight, or any night."

"I think that would be best for both of us," she said, unable to completely will away the slight quiver in her voice.

"You have no idea what would be best for both of us, Ms. Townsend, no idea at all," Dominic shot back. A moment later he walked out the door, pulling it closed firmly behind him.

For several seconds Marti stood alone in the entryway, shivering in the whirl of cold air that Dominic had left in his wake. She wouldn't cry. She *would not* cry. It did no good to cry. She'd found that out seven years ago under not quite similar circumstances. And, as she'd told Dominic, she had work to do, work she couldn't do if her eyes were sore and swollen.

Moving away from the wall, she picked up the quilt and put it on the shelf in the hall closet. Then she retrieved the basket and cooler and carried them into the kitchen. She tossed out the trash and empty cans, wiped out both basket and cooler with a damp cloth and put them in the pantry. Then she crossed to the kitchen table, sat in her chair and reached for a pencil. She tried to focus on the papers in front of her, but couldn't do it. As she blinked her eyes, trying to clear her vision, something hot and wet trickled down her cheek and fell onto the back of her hand.

"Oh, Marti, what have you done?" she whispered, covering her face with her hands as her shoulders began to shake. "What have you done?"

As he roamed from one room of his house to another, Dominic realized that it had been years, three years to be exact, since he'd been this angry at himself as well as someone else. Since he'd found the statement from Diane's gynecologist and learned the depth of her deception, he hadn't been involved with anyone who had mattered enough to make him upset. But Marti had been different. Whether he liked to admit it or not, Marti had been someone special from the first.

"Once a chump, always a chump, right?" he muttered. Bracing his palms on either side of the kitchen sink, he stared at his reflection in the window and tried to see if "stupid" really was written all over his face.

But, no, he wasn't being fair to himself. He hadn't gone after Marti Townsend with his eyes closed. He'd known all along that her job was important to her, and he hadn't begrudged her the status and success she'd achieved. He'd not only admired her for it, but given the chance, he'd have supported her all the way to the top. He'd also believed that she wanted, needed, more to her life than Carter and Caisson had to offer. Despite what had happened tonight, somewhere in the back of his mind he knew that he hadn't been wrong about her, not in the same way he'd been wrong about Diane.

Returning to the living room, he knelt in front of the fireplace, lit a match and touched it to the kindling tucked under the logs stacked on the grate. As the dry wood began to burn, he replaced the fan-shaped screen. Then he eased back into the old, overstuffed chair that had always been his favorite and propped his feet on the hearth.

As he watched the flickering flames, the warmth of the fire washed over him, and as if with a will of its own, the last of his anger abated. He wanted to stay mad at Marti. Really, he did. But suddenly he found that impossible to do. And as he began to think straight, he finally began to realize that no matter what she'd said, she'd driven him away only because she'd been afraid.

And if he had any sense at all he'd stay away, too. But he already knew he had no intention of doing that. Instead, he was going to do his damnedest to find out why she'd been afraid, then do whatever was necessary to prove that she had no need to fear him. He wasn't a callous brute, and he wasn't about to allow her to think of him as one.

She certainly hadn't had such a poor opinion of him earlier, had she? *She* had come looking for *him* that afternoon, not vice versa. And tonight she'd invited him into her home without hesitation. And both times she'd more than welcomed his kisses and caresses. Hadn't she?

He wasn't a rounder by any stretch of the imagination, but he'd been with enough women to know that Marti hadn't been faking her passionate response to his loving. Nor had she been faking the sudden panic that had gripped her when he'd backed her against the wall.

Granted, he'd been hungry for her—he hadn't been with a woman in a long time—but he hadn't been rough or sadistic. He knew how to control himself and he had. He knew how to be gentle and he'd tried. But she'd seemed so hungry, too.

He'd thought she'd been as ready as he had. He'd thought that she'd wanted him, that she'd needed as much as he to take the edge off. But he'd thought wrong. He'd definitely thought wrong. And as a result he'd scared her half to death. Then, allowing his masculine pride to override his common sense, he'd left her that way. Left her thinking he was some sort of insensitive clod. Like whoever it was that had hurt—

As he stared at the leaping, dancing flames Dominic went very still. Why hadn't he realized it sooner? He should have. He *could* have if he'd just given it some thought. She'd been so damned skittish around him at first. And more than once he'd seen a hint of fear in her eyes. How could he have forgotten that? And how could he have allowed himself to get so carried away?

It was simple, it was because *she* had gotten carried away, too. For a while, in his arms, she hadn't been afraid. For a while, at least, she'd trusted him enough to revel in his kisses and caresses.

Yet she hadn't trusted him enough to admit to him her sudden fear. When he'd confronted her about it, she'd refused to answer. She'd crawled behind her cool and distant facade, then made her pretty little speech about work. And he'd done exactly what she'd probably expected him to do. He'd stormed out of her house and out of her life. And she'd agreed it was for the best.

Now, as he looked back, much calmer and more dispassionate, he realized that she hadn't really said it as if she meant it. He'd heard the quaver in her soft voice and seen the glitter of tears in her eyes. But he'd walked out anyway. Hurt and angry, he'd let her chase him away.

But where was it written that he had to stay away? Just because he'd made the threat didn't mean he had to follow through on it. In fact, that was the last thing he intended to do now. He wasn't about to let her equate him with the jerk who'd hurt her. He was going to show her that he could be trusted. He was going to prove to her that he cared for her enough to truly *care for* her in every way. And if it was the last thing he did, he was going to make sure that she realized just how gentle loving could be. He was going to show her how much more there was to life than a job. And he was going to let her know that she could have it all with him, if she wanted.

All he had to do was find a way to slip back into her life, a way that gave her no alternative but to allow him in again—and not just once. Once wouldn't be enough. If he had any hope of restoring her faith in him, he'd have to see her a number of times over a period of several weeks. And he'd need a good reason to do so. He couldn't just show up on her front doorstep. But he could...show up at her office.

She'd all but insisted on helping him with an advertising campaign for the new garage, hadn't she? So if he took her up on the offer, how could she refuse? She was so honorable, she'd probably just grit her teeth and get on with it. And he would have just the opening he needed.

"Good morning. Ms. Townsend's office."

"Ms. Barnes?" Leaning across his desk, Dominic closed the door between his office and the work bays, then sat back in his chair.

"Yes."

"This is Dominic Fabrino. I'd like to make an appointment with Ms. Townsend about an ad campaign for my garage." He paused, all but holding his breath as he waited for Marti's secretary to respond.

"You're calling to make an appointment with her. Jeez, no wonder she looks like something the cat dragged in."

"I beg your pardon?"

"Did you two have a fight or something?"

He hesitated for several seconds, somewhat taken aback by the woman's candid questions. But obviously she was concerned about Marti. And she knew her boss well enough to know about him. But *what* about him? Since she hadn't hung up on him yet, he assumed Marti must have left a few significant gaps.

"Or something," he answered at last. "How is she?"

"Not too good. Either she's got a terminal case of the flu or she's been up half the night crying."

"Ah, hell."

"My sentiments exactly. So how soon can you be here?"

"I think I'd better wait a few days. How about Wednesday afternoon, late afternoon? Make it her last appointment of the day if you can."

"I can. Four-thirty sound okay?"

"Sounds perfect. And, Ms. Barnes—"

"Don't worry. She won't know you're scheduled until you walk through her office door. But you better make it good, Fabrino. And you better not hurt her again. Because I know where you work."

As the receiver clicked in his ear Dominic wasn't sure whether to laugh or bang his head against the desk. He didn't get a chance to do either. The office door opened and Mooch stepped across the threshold.

"Hey, boss, you want to wipe that grin off your face and come out here a minute?"

"Now what?"

"You know that problem Father Duncan's been having with his minivan?"

"Yeah."

"Well, I think we're going to have to pull the engine out after all."

"What do you mean *we?*"

Chapter Seven

Marti had gone through some bad times in her life, but the three days since she'd sent Dominic away definitely ranked among the worst. Once she'd started crying Sunday night, she hadn't been able to stop completely for hours. And she'd been all but useless at the office not only Monday, but Tuesday and today, as well. Though she'd tried to deal with her misery as she had in the past, this time throwing herself into her work simply wasn't . . . *working*.

Luckily, only Heather seemed to realize that the indomitable Ms. Townsend had been faltering lately. And, bless her heart, she'd done her best to cover for her. But Marti knew she couldn't expect her secretary to take up the slack much longer. She had to get a grip, and she had to do it soon. She had to put Dominic Fabrino out of her mind and out of her heart. That was the best thing to do, the only thing to do.

She'd proven once and for all that she was incapable of the kind of relationship he wanted, or *had* wanted until the moment she'd gone slightly berserk in his arms. By now he was probably thanking his lucky stars that he'd found out when he did just how neurotic she could be. At least she hadn't wasted too much of his time, she thought bitterly, turning her desk chair to face the window.

Outside dark clouds scudded across the sky, threatening rain—cold, maybe even freezing rain just in time for the worst of rush-hour traffic. Frowning, she glanced at her watch. It was almost four-thirty, and as far as she was concerned she was finished for the day. Considering her current frame of mind, she wasn't likely to accomplish much in the next hour. And as far as she knew there weren't any appointments pending.

Maybe if she went home, ate a decent meal and made an early night of it, she'd come out of her blue funk by morning. Then again, maybe she'd do what she'd done the past couple of nights. Maybe she'd skip dinner and stare at the walls and have another good cry, all guaranteed to make tomorrow even worse than today.

In any case, she'd sat in her office, staring at the piles of unfinished paperwork mounting on her desk long enough. Hanging around another thirty minutes to an hour wouldn't be productive. But if she left now, at least she'd miss the worst of the rain as well as the traffic snarl that surely would ensue.

Pulling her briefcase off the credenza, she swiveled around to face her desk again. She ought to take something home to work on, just in case her powers of concentration made a miracle comeback. Maybe the proposal for Marco Savings and Loan and the sketches for—

The buzzer for her internal telephone line went off so unexpectedly, and she'd been so wrapped up in her thoughts, that Marti practically jumped out of her chair. Pressing one hand to her pounding heart, she picked up the receiver.

"Yes, Heather?"

"Ms. Townsend, Mr. Fabrino is here to see you," her secretary replied, her tone so calm, so professional that Marti thought she'd misunderstood her.

"Mr. Fabrino?"

"Yes." Heather paused expectantly, then continued when Marti failed to respond. "He'd like to discuss the advertising for his new garage with you."

"But you didn't tell me—" Marti began, anger and confusion warring inside her.

"Gosh, I'm sorry, Marti," the other woman interrupted. "He called early Monday morning to make an appointment. I thought I told you, but it must have slipped my mind. Of course, I've been so busy the past few days since you haven't been feeling very well..."

Though Marti heard the hint of reproach in her secretary's voice, she felt more suspicious than guilty. Heather never forgot appointments, not even when the entire office was in the midst of chaos. And it hadn't been *that* bad the past few days.

"You're meddling again, Heather."

"One day you'll thank me for it," she replied quite confidently.

"One day I'll fire you for it," Marti warned with equal certainty.

"So shall I escort him into your office?"

She didn't want to see him. *She didn't.* She'd only get her hopes up again. She'd only be tempted to dream impossible dreams. And that would be futile since he definitely wasn't there for personal reasons. He was there to hold her to her offer to help with his advertising campaign, an offer she'd made when the future had seemed bright rather than bleak.

Though she hadn't forgotten about it, she'd no longer expected him to take her up on it. Not after Sunday night.

But he had, and for more reasons than one she couldn't be so churlish as to refuse. As she'd pointed out to him, he'd worked on her old car for more than a year at much less than the going rate. That alone gave him the right to a similar consideration in return.

In fact, working with him might actually come to serve as a form of final closure. Once and for all her debt to him would be well and truly paid. And if she dealt with him in a businesslike manner again, perhaps she'd be able to distance herself from him emotionally. Then, when she'd completed whatever work he requested, maybe they could part without any hurt or hostility lingering between them.

Of course, they could never be just friends. She could finally admit that to herself. But they didn't have to be enemies, either.

"Yes, Heather, you can escort him into my office."

She had just time enough after hanging up the receiver to stand, straighten her navy blue skirt and button her matching suit jacket before Heather opened her office door. Unfortunately she'd chewed off her lipstick hours ago and hadn't bothered to replace it. And no amount of makeup would have hidden the dark circles she imagined still lurked under her eyes. But her hair should be fine, she thought, smoothing a hand over it. *All neat and pretty....*

As Heather winked broadly, then stepped back to allow Dominic to enter, Marti gave herself a firm mental shake. She could wallow in maudlin memories all she wanted when she was home alone. But here and now she'd be wise to keep her mind on business or risk making a fool of herself all over again.

He walked into her office as cool, calm and collected as she wished she could be. Wearing a well-tailored dark gray suit, a pale pink shirt and a stylish gray-and-pink patterned silk tie, he looked nothing like the man she'd come to know.

He looked every inch the corporate executive he'd been only a few years ago. And he appeared completely comfortable with the impressive, yet somewhat intimidating, image he projected.

"Hello, Marti. It's good of you to see me," he said, smiling cordially as he paused in front of her desk. "I know you're busy, so I promise not to take too much of your time."

Well, she'd wanted businesslike, and obviously that's what she was going to get. For a moment she wasn't sure exactly how to react. Then she decided it would be best to give as good as she got. Drawing on her years of experience working with impossible clients in improbable situations, she extended her hand in the traditional gesture of greeting and returned his smile.

"Dominic, welcome to Carter and Caisson." His quick, firm handshake only served to underscore his uncompromising demeanor. Sighing inwardly, Marti motioned to the chair angled in front of her desk. She had no reason to be hurt. Yet somehow, despite all her mental gyrations, she'd hoped... "Please, sit down. Would you like something to drink? Coffee or tea, or perhaps a soft drink?"

"No, thank you." He sat back in his chair, cocking an ankle over a knee, and met her gaze, his dark eyes assessing.

"Well, then..." Ducking her head, she sat down and reached for a pad of paper and a pen. "What can I do for you?" she asked as she glanced at him again. For just an instant she thought she saw a flicker of something warm, something wanting, in his eyes, and her heart beat a little faster.

"I'd like to retain Carter and Caisson to work on the advertising for the new garage. You really impressed me with your ideas the other day. However, if you'd rather not work on the ads yourself, I'd be happy to work with anyone else on your staff instead."

"Oh, no, that won't be necessary," she said quickly. "I'd like to do the work myself. As I said, it will keep costs down to a—"

"If you do the work, I expect you to bill me for your time just as you would any other client."

"But you said—"

"I don't want any favors from you. If I couldn't afford to pay for your services, I wouldn't be here."

Talk about being put in your place, she thought, lowering her gaze to the odd scribbles she'd etched onto her pad. But if that was the way he wanted it, that was the way he'd get it.

"In that case, you'll be billed a flat-rate consultation fee for today." Tipping her chin up, she met his gaze again. "After that you'll be billed by the hour for the time I spend putting together a portfolio. We have a fairly simple contract for small companies advertising on a limited basis." She leaned across her desk and handed him one. "As you can see, the fees are on there. If you'd like to take a few minutes to read it, I can—"

"It looks fine to me." Though he'd hardly glanced at the single sheet of paper, he pulled a pen from his shirt pocket and signed on the dotted line.

"All right, then." She took the contract from him and tucked it into a file drawer. "Where would you like to begin?"

"Wherever you would, Marti," he said softly, almost suggestively.

She glanced at him sharply, but his expression was as close to bland as it would probably ever be. He'd meant nothing more than what he'd said, and she'd do well to remember it.

"In that case, why don't we start with print ads and go from there?" she suggested as she ripped off her scribble sheet and picked up her pen again.

"Sounds good to me. What have you got in mind?"

"I thought we could combine an ad with a coupon for some sort of grand-opening special and run it in the *Post,* the *Riverfront Times* and the various neighborhood papers. We could also use the same basic ad, class it up a bit and run it in *St. Louis Magazine.*"

Once she got started, Marti was in her element. She relaxed appreciably and the ideas began to flow, no small thanks to Dominic's honest interest and enthusiasm. He didn't automatically agree with every suggestion she made, but for the most part he allowed her to give her creativity free reign. Within an hour she had outlined several satisfactory strategies for print, radio and cable TV advertising.

"Well, I think that should do it for today. I'll have to get back to you tomorrow or Friday with specific costs for the radio and television spots. Then you can make a final decision on them. And I should have mock-ups of the print ads ready in about a week. Why don't we set up an appointment for next Thursday? Would you prefer morning or afternoon?"

"Afternoon."

"How about four-thirty again? That way you'll be my last appointment of the day. If we run into any glitches, we can work them out right away and save you another trip downtown."

"Sounds good to me." He stood, but didn't immediately turn to leave.

Marti had a feeling there was something else he wanted to say, something she wasn't sure she wanted to hear. Rising quickly, she once again extended her hand. "Good night, Dominic."

"Good night, Marti. Drive safe." Taking her hand in his, he nodded toward the window. "It's getting nasty out there."

Drawing free of his lingering hold, she glanced over her shoulder and saw that her weather forecast had been right on target. Rain beat against the glass in a steady torrent. Traffic would definitely be a mess. If they left now, they'd both be caught in the middle of it. But if she asked him to stay and have a drink at the little pub in the basement of the building...

He'd probably refuse; he had every right to. He'd meant their meeting to be strictly business. Although she often had drinks or dinner with a client, with Dominic it would be different. And he knew that as well as she did.

"Right. You, too," she said at last, turning to face him again.

He hesitated once more, his eyes holding hers, the rain hitting against the window the only sound in the room. For just an instant she was tempted to come out from behind her desk, to walk him to the elevator, or at least to the door. What could it hurt? But common sense won out. Maintaining a certain amount of distance was imperative at this stage. If she didn't, she might end up throwing herself into his arms. And then he really would have reason to pity her.

"I'll call you as soon as I have those costs nailed down," she offered with what she hoped was an air of finality.

"I'll be waiting to hear from you." He smiled almost sadly, as if she'd disappointed him. Then he turned and walked out of her office. He said something to Heather, something that made her laugh. And then the outer door whooshed open and closed, and he was gone.

Still standing, Marti began to sort through the papers on her desk, tucking some into her briefcase, tossing others into various trays on her credenza. As she did so, she realized that for the first time since Sunday night she felt good. Not great, but *good*. And she didn't even try to deny that her lift in spirits was due entirely to Dominic's unexpected appearance.

In fact, it didn't matter why he'd come to see her. All that mattered was that he had, and that this time he hadn't left in anger. Within the next couple of days she'd have a reason to call him, and next week she would see him again. Come to think of it, she'd probably have to see him a number of times over the next few—

"Oh, good, you're smiling. Does that mean you aren't mad anymore?" Heather asked in a teasing tone of voice.

"Not necessarily." Marti snapped the locks on her briefcase, then crossed to the coat tree in the corner. Shrugging into her black wool coat, she eyed her secretary sternly. "You know, Heather—"

"I know, I should have told you he was coming. But he asked me not to say anything ahead of time if I could help it. And you're always stressing how important it is to keep our clients happy."

As Heather flashed an irreverent grin, Marti picked up her briefcase and started toward her. "You're impossible, you know?"

"I know. So are you two meeting for drinks downstairs, then going on to dinner? Gosh, I could have made reservations at—"

"No."

"But you always have drinks and dinner with Neal—"

"Heather?"

"Yes?"

"You're pushing it."

"I know. I'm sorry." She didn't sound nearly as contrite as Marti thought she should. "Are you going to make me walk to the parking garage by myself?"

"Then I'd have to walk to the garage by *myself*," Marti admitted, smiling wryly as she and Heather headed toward the elevators.

"Oh, yeah, right." As the elevator doors opened and they stepped in, she grinned at Marti again. "You know, you never did tell me what happened this weekend. Friday you were happy as a lark, but Monday you looked like..."

As the elevator doors closed, Marti sagged against the back wall, sighed and shook her head in complete and utter despair.

Ten days later, on a deceptively bright and sunny Saturday afternoon, Marti was once again trying to work. Unfortunately she was having just about as much success at getting anything done as she'd had any weekend since she'd agreed to shop for a new car with Dominic. Which meant little or no success at all.

She'd thought about going to the office where the work-oriented atmosphere might have helped to focus her attention. However, that would have meant changing into her Ms. Townsend persona. Faded jeans and a baggy sweater were all right around the neighborhood, but even on a Saturday she deemed that kind of dress unsuitable for Carter and Caisson, especially since she'd probably run into several members of her staff there. And since she'd more than likely end up daydreaming about Dominic anyway, she might as well continue to do it in the comfort and privacy of her own home.

Setting aside the report she'd been attempting to read for at least thirty minutes, she propped her feet on the coffee table and tipped her head against the back of the sofa. Since her first meeting with Dominic she'd talked to him twice on the telephone. Their conversations had been relatively short and to the point. But then she'd been calling about business during business hours and, of course, he'd been...busy.

They'd also gotten together as planned on Thursday afternoon, and their second meeting had gone even more smoothly than the first. She hadn't been nearly as nervous as she'd anticipated. Dominic had shown both interest and enthusiasm for the ideas she'd put together, suggesting only a few changes with which she'd readily agreed.

They'd finished earlier than she'd expected, but once again he'd seemed in no hurry to leave. Once again he'd seemed to be waiting, as if the next move was hers. And she'd almost made it. After a week of careful consideration she'd decided a drink at the pub would be in order, and she'd been on the verge of issuing an invitation when Heather had buzzed her on the intercom. It had been one of the executives in Chicago with a problem only she could handle.

She'd told Heather to put him on hold while she walked Dominic to the outer doors. He'd seemed oddly resigned as he'd taken his leave—resigned to the fact that her job obviously *was* her life. She'd wanted to deny it. She really had. But instead she'd nearly twisted an ankle as she'd raced back to her office to take the call.

Now, sitting alone on a Saturday afternoon, she wondered if it had been worth it. She wanted to believe that she'd made the right choice. But for the first time in almost seven years, she couldn't automatically accept that she had. How different would today be if she hadn't taken the call, if she'd asked Dominic to have a drink with her instead?

With a muttered curse, Marti dragged herself off the sofa and padded toward the stairs. If she didn't get out of the house for a while, she'd end up with the screaming meemies. Though the sun was shining, the air was frosty cold, so riding with the top down was out of the question. But then she was too antsy to drive anyway. A brisk walk would do her more good in the long run.

As she pulled on wool socks and sneakers, then found mittens and a scarf, she considered taking her camera. But she wasn't in the mood to take pictures of other people having fun. This time she wanted to have fun herself. And she knew just where she could do it.

The Catholic church a few blocks away was having a fall festival today. She'd seen the advertisement in the neighborhood newspaper earlier in the week—booths featuring arts and crafts and games of chance, a variety of music and entertainment, a spaghetti supper. Come one, come all . . .

She didn't bother with makeup—it was a Saturday. But she did run a brush through her hair, taking out the worst of the tangles. Then she slipped on her coat, slung her scarf around her neck, pulled on her mittens and grabbed her purse.

"I'm on my way," she murmured, taking a deep breath of the crisp, clean air as she started down the sidewalk.

The game booths had been set up on the church lot, and despite the cold weather quite a few people milled from one to another, trying their best to toss hoops over soda bottles or knock down milk cans with softballs. Marti wandered among them on her way to the hall, pausing now and then to watch the hopeful players test their skills.

At the dunking booth, where mounds of straw had been substituted for the usual tub of water, she thought she saw Dominic's niece and nephew among the children waiting their turn to knock the parish priest off his perch. What if Dominic had come, too? Her heart beat a little faster as she scanned the crowd, but she didn't see him anywhere. Of course, that didn't mean he wasn't there. He could be in the hall.

Trying not to get her hopes up, she headed toward the wide, double doors that opened into the church hall. She hadn't come looking for Dominic. Really, she hadn't. But if she happened to run into him, then . . .

Then, what?

As she walked through the doorway and blended into the noisy yet good-natured throng of people moving slowly from one booth to another, she realized that there was little she could do beyond saying hello. Since their relationship had become strictly business, she couldn't expect him to invite her to join him. Come to think of it, she couldn't even expect him to be there alone. What if he was there with someone else, someone other than his family? If she ran into him, and he was with another woman, what would she—?

"Oh, no. . ."

Standing as if rooted to the spot, Marti stared at the handsome couple ambling through the crowd several yards ahead of her. Though they were moving away from her at an angle, she recognized Dominic immediately. Dominic, with his arm around a gorgeous brunette, talking and laughing, then stopping, turning and...*oh, please, no*...glancing *her* way.

Her heart pounding, her face flushed, Marti whirled around and started toward the door. She could only hope that he hadn't seen her, or that if he had, he'd be kind enough to let her go. She wasn't up to a round of casual greetings and polite introductions. She didn't want to know—

"Marti, wait." An odd hint of urgency in his deep voice, Dominic caught her arm, gently yet firmly halting her hasty retreat.

For just an instant she was tempted to pull away from him and continue out the door as if he hadn't spoken. But that kind of boorish behavior would be unforgivable. He'd done nothing to warrant that kind of response from her. In fact, he had every right to spend his time with whomever he wanted. And she had no cause to be anything but gracious about it.

Forcing herself to smile, she turned to face him. "Hello, Dominic. It's so nice to see you," she murmured inanely, not quite meeting his gaze.

"Oh, really? Then why did you make a run for it the moment you did?" he asked softly, still holding on to her arm.

Her head snapped up and her eyes met his. "I didn't—"

He gazed down at her, his knowing smile admonishment enough. She'd been caught in the act, and denial would only make bad matters worse.

"I didn't want to intrude," she amended, glancing rather surreptitiously at the pretty woman standing beside him. She seemed more amused than upset by their exchange, which only added to Marti's overall embarrassment.

"Hey, don't worry about it. Carmen's not the jealous type. Are you, Sis?" He paused for a moment, a teasing glint in his eyes. Then, as if satisfied by her obvious surprise, he continued. "Marti, meet my sister, Carmen Rozelli. Carmen, meet Marti Townsend."

"Your...sister?" Marti glanced at the woman again and saw the resemblance between her and Dominic at once. If she hadn't been so intent on running away, she probably would have noticed it sooner—just as she might have also noticed that Carmen was pregnant.

"I've been looking forward to meeting you. I've heard so much about you." Carmen's dark eyes glittered with mischief just as her brother's did, but her smile was also equally warm and friendly.

"You have?" Marti smiled tentatively as they shook hands.

"Oh, yes. Not only is my baby brother crazy about you, but you were definitely a big hit with Rose and Drew and the kids. Speaking of which—"

"Oh, *Marti!*"

As Amy suddenly appeared to throw her arms around Marti's waist, Marti gazed at Dominic, her heart fluttering in her chest. He was crazy about her? Maybe two weeks ago, but surely not any longer.

"You're here, you're here," Amy crowed, smiling beatifically as she claimed Marti's attention at last. Then she turned and scowled at her uncle. "Why didn't you tell me she was going to be here, Uncle Dominic?"

"Because she didn't tell *me.*"

"But I really didn't plan—"

"You should have told him. Otherwise we might have *never* found you." Frowning thoughtfully, Amy glanced at Marti again. "Did you just get here?"

"Well, yes..."

"Oh, goodie." Amy's frown disappeared as she smiled and clapped her hands. "We can go to all the booths together. Then we can go outside and play all the games. Okay?"

"I'd really like that, but..." She shrugged, not knowing what to say to the little girl, then glanced at Dominic uncertainly. Though she didn't want to hurt Amy's feelings, at the same time she didn't want to foist herself off on Dominic. Since he obviously hadn't planned to spend the afternoon with her, he shouldn't be forced to—

"I wanted to ask you to come with us, but I wasn't sure how you'd feel about socializing with a...client." He smiled wryly as he smoothed a wisp of her hair away from her face.

"I've been known to do so on occasion," she admitted, returning his smile gratefully. He'd let her know that she was welcome. Yet he'd also given her an out if she wanted it.

"And would this be one of those occasions?"

"Yes, it would." She held his gaze a moment longer, then turned to Amy and extended her hand. "So where shall we start, Miss Gardner?"

Amy giggled as she slipped her small hand into Marti's. "How about over here? They're selling brownies, and Uncle Dominic *loves* brownies, don't you?"

"Among other things," he drawled, looping an arm around Carmen's shoulders as they followed behind.

"You two have a fight or something?" Carmen murmured, nudging him in the ribs.

"Or something," he admitted.

"Going to do anything about it?"

"What do you think?" He raised an eyebrow questioningly as he met his sister's gaze.

"I think maybe it's time I found Tony, and left you to it. I'd offer to take Amy but those two look like they're attached at the hip." Carmen nodded toward Marti and their niece, busily buying an enormous bag of brownies.

"That's okay. They really like each other, and it's kind of fun watching them together."

"Well, then, maybe later you could bring Marti over to the house for dinner. Nothing fancy, but I've got candles and a decent bottle of wine somewhere. Say five-thirty or six?"

"Sounds good to me, but I can't make any promises."

"Aw, come on, Dominic. Losing your touch?"

"Carmen?"

"Yeah?"

"Your husband's looking for you."

"See you later." Grinning up at him, Carmen nudged him again. Then, with a quick wave, she disappeared into the growing crowd milling around the hall.

"Where'd Aunt Carmen go?" Amy asked as Dominic joined her and Marti at a booth selling cookie-dough Christmas ornaments.

"To find Uncle Tony. Did you want to go with her?"

"No, I want to stay with Marti." She exchanged smiles with her idol, then turned her attention back to him. "You're going to stay with Marti, too, aren't you, Uncle Dominic?"

"If it's all right with her," he said softly, his eyes holding hers above the little girl's head.

"Is it all right, Marti?" Amy asked.

"Perfectly all right," Marti agreed as she lowered her gaze.

"I knew it would be." Amy offered them a self-important smile. "Because she likes you, Uncle Dominic. She likes you a whole lot. Don't you, Marti?"

"Well, I . . ." Her face flushing a bright red, she stared at him helplessly, then shrugged. "Yes, I do," she admitted. Then, not giving him a chance to respond, she grabbed Amy's hand and pulled her toward a booth displaying silk-flower arrangements. "Look, Amy, aren't these pretty?"

Trying not to smile quite as smugly as his niece had, Dominic trailed after them. He'd hoped that Marti had wanted to be with him as well as Amy. He couldn't help but be pleased by her affirmation. Yet he knew better than to take anything more than that for granted, at least for the time being.

But he'd seen how she'd reacted when she'd caught a glimpse of him with "another woman." He'd seen the hurt in her eyes before she'd turned away, and it had been all the goading he'd needed to follow her through the crowd. It had almost been enough to make him believe that she cared for him after all.

And now, as they wandered together from booth to booth, he realized that she did care. She'd managed to hide her feelings so well when they'd met at her office that he'd been ready to give up on her. He could only thank his lucky stars that she hadn't found it quite as easy to play it cool here.

Now all he had to do was take it slow, to refrain from rushing her physically or emotionally. No matter how frustrating he might find it, he had to be content with simply being with her until she trusted him again. He'd already frightened her once, albeit unknowingly. But he'd have no excuse if he frightened her again. Second chances were hard enough to come by; he'd have no right to expect a third.

They spent more than an hour in the church hall, stopping at one booth after another, allowing Amy to set the pace. And slowly but surely, the tension between them seemed to diminish. By the time Amy was ready to go outside, they'd even begun to talk to each other and not just to her. And once she insisted they try some of the games, too, they ended up spending the rest of the afternoon trying to see who could win the most stuffed animals for one very canny little lady.

"Something tells me we've been had," Marti grumbled as she tossed her empty wallet into her purse. "I don't know about you, Fabrino, but I'm broke."

"Well, I guess that means I'm the grand-champion stuffed-animal winner of the day." He grinned at her triumphantly.

"Now wait a minute. I won the chipmunk, the frog, the—"

"Uh-uh. *I* won the frog—"

"Oh, no, you didn't."

"I think Marti's right, Uncle Dominic," Amy said, smiling sweetly as she juggled the armload of toys they'd won for her.

"Hey, squirt, where'd you get all the goodies?" Andy demanded, skidding to a halt beside them.

"Marti and Uncle Dominic won them for me. They had a . . . a competition. Right?"

"And I can just imagine whose idea it was." Grinning, Angela tugged on a lock of her sister's hair as she joined them, too. "Come on, kiddo. It's time to go. Dad's waiting for us in the car."

"But I thought Uncle Dominic was gonna—"

"Uncle Dominic's taking Marti to Aunt Carmen's for dinner," Angela stated in her older-and-wiser-sister tone of voice.

Barely restraining the urge to throttle his number-one niece, Dominic glanced at Marti out of the corner of his eye. He'd been working up to dinner at Carmen's, but he hadn't actually invited her yet. He'd been waiting for just the right moment. Unfortunately, thanks to Angela's rather bald statement, that moment had apparently come and gone. But at least Marti didn't seem upset. In fact, she simply stood there, staring at him curiously, the hint of a smile playing at the corners of her mouth.

"I wanna go, too," Amy whined, her lower lip pouting out. "Can I, *please,* Uncle Dominic? Can I, can I?"

"Not tonight, squirt. It's just grown-ups. So give us a big hug. Then you'd better get going 'cause your daddy's waiting. Okay?"

"Okay," she agreed at last. "But Marti first."

As Dominic stood aside, Marti hugged the little girl, whispering something into her ear that made her giggle. Then he moved forward, hugged her, too, and sent her on her way.

"Somebody's going to sleep well tonight," Marti murmured as they watched the children cross the parking lot and climb into Drew's car.

"You, or Amy?" Dominic asked, turning to face her.

"Both of us," she admitted.

"Tired, are we?"

"A little."

As she gazed up at him in the deepening dusk, he wanted nothing more than to put his arms around her and draw her close. But he wasn't sure how she'd respond, and he didn't want to do anything to ruin what had been a wonderful day.

"Listen, about going to Carmen's..." He paused for a moment, choosing his words carefully so as not to put her in an awkward position. "I would have mentioned it earlier, but I wasn't sure how you'd feel after spending all afternoon with Amy. It's not something we have to do. I'll understand if you have other plans, if you have to get back to work or... anything."

To his surprise, Marti didn't even hesitate. "I don't have any plans at all. And I can always work tomorrow, or the next day, or the next," she admitted with a wry smile. "But I really ought to change first." She waved a hand at her faded jeans and grubby sneakers.

"You look fine the way you are," he tried to assure her. When she just stared back at him skeptically, he gave in to the urge to smooth a hand over her hair. "Really, Marti, you do. You look... beautiful."

"Oh, Dominic..." she protested softly, lowering her gaze.

Even in the growing twilight, he saw her blush. But she didn't seem to take offense. And she didn't turn away from him. All good signs, as far as he was concerned. Yet he knew that he had to keep it casual, to keep it friendly, or he'd run the risk of scaring her away again.

"Where's your car?" he asked at last, his tone light. As if by mutual agreement, they headed across the lot away from the church hall.

"I walked from the house." Falling into step beside him, her shoulder brushed against his, but he resisted the urge to put his arm around her.

"Me, too." Though it was in the opposite direction from Marti, Dominic also lived only a few blocks away from the church, as did his sister. "Mind if we walk to Carmen's? Her house is only a couple of blocks from mine. Then later, when we're ready to leave, I'll get my car and drive you home."

"All right," she agreed readily.

They walked the rest of the way in companionable silence, the glow of streetlights and porch lamps guiding their way down the quiet city sidewalks.

Both Carmen and Tony greeted them at the door. Laughing and talking, they took their coats, then ushered them into the living room.

"Dominic wasn't sure if you'd be able to come," Carmen said as she and Marti sat on the sofa. "But I'm really glad you did."

"I'm glad I did, too." Glancing at Dominic, she offered him a whimsical smile, then turned back to his sister. "You have a lovely home."

"Let me check on dinner, then I'll show you the rest of the place." As she and Marti stood, Carmen turned to the men. "You guys want a drink or anything?"

"I'll have a beer," Dominic answered, trailing after Carmen and Marti. "Want me to bring you one, too, Tony?"

"Yeah, sure. I'm going to put a couple of logs on the fire and see if I can get it going again."

As the three of them walked into the kitchen, a flurry of furry bodies came scurrying across the tile floor. Yipping excitedly, four little long-haired dachshunds crowded around their legs, tails wagging a mile a minute.

"Oh, Dominic, they look just like Butch," Marti exclaimed, bending down to stroke first one silky head, then another and another.

"They should," Carmen said as she handed Dominic a couple of beers, then set one on the counter for Marti. "He's their daddy."

"Where's Mama Heidi?" Dominic asked, watching as Marti sat on the floor and allowed the pups to crawl into her lap.

"Out in the yard taking a break." Grinning, Carmen turned her attention back to Marti. "You like dogs, huh?"

"I've never had one of my own. And I probably wouldn't know what to do with one if I did. But I've always liked them," she admitted, cuddling one of the puppies in her arms.

"Dogs are like people. All they really need is love. And I think you've got more than enough to give," Dominic said.

"You do?" She raised her head and met his gaze, her eyes suddenly full of doubt.

"Yes, I do," he reassured her, aware of just how concerned she was. At that moment, he wished he could lay his hands on whoever had made her feel so damned unworthy. But that wouldn't do either of them any good, not in the long run. And that's what really counted. "So when do we eat?" he asked, turning to Carmen, determined once again to lighten the mood, at least for the time being.

"About twenty minutes."

"Well, then, I guess I'll check and see how Tony's doing with the fire." A beer in each hand, he strolled out of the kitchen.

"So, Marti, want to see the rest of the house?"

"Um, sure," Marti replied, her eyes on the doorway through which Dominic had disappeared. He'd given her a compliment, the kind of compliment she'd rarely gotten in her life. And she wanted nothing more than to go off alone somewhere and hold it close to her heart. But right now, sitting in Carmen's kitchen, she knew that was impossible. "What about the little beasts?" she asked, not quite certain how to get them out of her lap without causing an uproar.

"Let's lock them in the laundry room until after dinner. Here, I'll take two if you take two," Carmen offered, scooping a couple of pups into her arms.

"Sounds good to me," Marti agreed, quickly following suit.

After a tour of the house, they had dinner in the dining room. As they ate baked chicken and fettuccine and drank wine by candlelight, Carmen told Marti about the ups and downs of teaching second grade, then quizzed her in turn about the advertising business. Dominic and Tony added an occasional comment, but for the most part seemed content to talk about the football games scheduled for the following day.

By the time they'd finished, and she and Carmen were clearing the table together, Marti felt as if she'd known Dominic's sister all her life. She was so bright and funny, so warm and giving, that Marti wished they could be friends forever. But her relationship with Dominic was tentative at best. And she knew that once it ended, keeping in touch with his sister would put everyone in an awkward position.

"Want to play with the puppies again while I clean up the kitchen?" Carmen asked as they set the last of the dishes on the counter.

"I really ought to help you—"

"Oh, go on, you're dying to get your hands on them again, aren't you?"

"Well...yes." Marti laughed as she headed toward the laundry room.

"Would you like to take one home with you? They're weaned and paper trained. I'd planned to advertise them in the paper next week anyway. Although I'm going to miss them, I'd really like to sell them before Christmas."

As she sat on the floor and allowed the puppies to crawl into her lap again, Marti was almost tempted to say yes. A dog would keep her company and help to ease her loneliness. But she spent most of her time at the office, and when she was at home she worked there, too. She wouldn't be much of a companion. And once she moved to Chicago... What would she do with a dog then? Here she had a yard, but there she'd have to live in an apartment, at least for a while.

"I don't think so, Carmen. But thanks anyway."

"Think about it for a week or so. If you change your mind, give me a call. Okay?"

"Okay."

They had coffee and dessert—the most wonderful Italian cream cake Marti had ever tasted—in the living room. And then, though it was still relatively early, Dominic asked if she was ready to go. She wasn't, really, but it had been a long day, and she'd seen Carmen yawning, so she said that she was. When he offered to get his car, however, she suggested that they walk instead, and he readily agreed.

They said their good-nights, then, bundled up against the cold, they headed toward her house, walking quickly to keep warm.

"Maybe we should have driven," Marti said after they'd gone a couple of blocks.

"Are you cold?" He moved a little closer to her and put an arm around her shoulders.

"Not really. But I didn't think... you'll have to walk back." She wanted to spend as much time with him as possible, but she hadn't considered how she might have inconvenienced him. "I could drive you home," she suggested, smiling up at him.

"Uh-uh. I want you in your house, safe and sound, not driving home from my place all alone."

"But I should—"

"No arguments," he interrupted as they started up the walkway toward her front porch. "Got your key handy?"

"Right here." She handed it to him, then stood aside while he unlocked her front door.

"There you go." He returned her key as he swung the door open for her. "Good night, Marti." He stuffed his hands in his jacket pockets and took a couple of steps back.

She hesitated, wanting to say so much more than good-night, wanting to *do* so much more than watch him walk away... again. "I had a really nice time today. Thanks for including me."

"My pleasure."

"I really liked Carmen and Tony."

"And the puppies?" he teased softly.

"Them, too," she admitted with a smile.

"They liked you, too."

She couldn't put it off any longer. She had to let him go. Especially since he didn't seem inclined to stay. "Well, good night."

"Good night," he said again, then turned and walked down the steps.

"Dominic, wait." Before she could stop herself, she followed him down the steps.

Once again he turned to face her, meeting her gaze. "What is it, Marti?"

"I . . ." She shook her head, not sure what to say, then settled for the simple truth. "I've missed you."

"I've missed you, too." Smiling, he tucked a wisp of hair behind her ear, then drew his hand away again. "Now go inside, will you? Please?"

Nodding once, she spun around and ran up the steps. Not daring a backward glance, she walked through the doorway, then quietly shut the door and leaned against it. He hadn't held her or kissed her. But he'd said that he'd missed her; he'd said that he'd missed her, too.

Chapter Eight

The layouts for the print ads for the new Fabrino's garage were ready the following Friday afternoon. As Marti went over them one last time, checking for errors, she had to admit that they were quite good. While she'd written the copy herself, and set up the basic layouts, the art department had added just the right finishing touches. Now it would be up to Dominic to choose the ads he liked best, then make a final decision as to where and when to begin running them.

Glancing at her watch, Marti saw that it was already after three o'clock. She had a meeting at four, but that probably wouldn't last more than thirty or forty-five minutes max. Still, she couldn't count on being able to meet with Dominic before five o'clock. And she didn't feel right about asking him to come downtown so late on a Friday afternoon. Better to have Heather call him and set up an appointment for Monday or Tuesday of next week.

But Marti didn't want to wait until next week to see Dominic. She wanted to see him today. Almost a week had passed since they'd been together, and in that time she hadn't heard a word from him. Not that she'd had any reason to think that she would. They'd had a nice time on Saturday, but he hadn't said that he'd call. He'd simply said that he'd missed her. And the more she'd thought about it, the more she'd come to think that he'd only said so to be gracious. Considering she'd all but thrown herself into his arms, what choice had he had?

Still, somewhere deep in her heart, she wanted to believe that he'd enjoyed being with her as much as she'd enjoyed being with him, and that he'd meant what he'd said on Saturday night. Perhaps he'd just been busy, as busy as she had been the past few days. With Thanksgiving next week, he and his crew had more than likely been working overtime, trying to get as many of his customers' cars as possible ready for holiday travel. And if that was the case, he certainly wouldn't want to take time off to come downtown next Monday or Tuesday.

So why not stop by Fabrino's with the layouts on her way home from work tonight? The garage was normally open until six or six-thirty, and if he was dealing with a preholiday rush, Dominic would probably be there even later than that this evening. It shouldn't take him long to look at the ads and make a few decisions. And not only would she save him a trip downtown, she'd have a chance to see him again, at least for a little while, under circumstances that shouldn't cause either of them any discomfort.

Having made her decision, Marti closed the portfolio and set it beside her briefcase. She'd attend her meeting as planned. Then, as soon as it was over, she'd go to Fabrino's. But she wouldn't get her hopes up, not at all. She was going there on business, *strictly business,* something she'd have to try to remember whether she actually believed it or not.

"Hey, Dom, doesn't Ms. Townsend drive a little red Mustang convertible?" Eddie asked as he propped a hip against the car that Dominic had been working on most of the afternoon.

"Yeah. Why?" he asked, not bothering to come out from under the hood. No telling what Eddie had in mind. Probably more nonsense about how he ought to conduct his—

"She just pulled onto the lot. She's getting out of her car. She's heading—"

Dominic straightened so fast he hit his head on the hood. "Here, Eddie. Since you've got time to stand around giving play-by-plays, why don't you finish replacing the spark plugs?" He tossed the plug he'd just pulled out to Eddie. Then, grabbing a rag to wipe his hands, he turned and headed toward his office.

He couldn't imagine why Marti had come to the garage. But whatever her reason, he was glad that she had. He'd wanted to call her all week. Yet each time he'd started to dial her number, he'd talked himself out of it halfway through.

He'd vowed not to rush her. And after Saturday night, when he'd used up a year's worth of willpower walking away, he didn't trust himself to be satisfied with a telephone call. One thing would have led to another, and he'd have found an excuse to go back to her house, to take her in his arms and...to scare the living daylights out of her. Again.

So he'd forced himself to wait awhile, to give her time, and to give himself time, as well. But now she'd come to him. And no matter why she had, he intended to make the most of it.

He stood in his office doorway, watching as she crossed the lot, her briefcase in one hand. Ah, of course, the ads for the new garage, he thought. But if she only wanted to talk business, surely she'd have set up an appointment at her office rather than go out of her way to come and see him on a Friday night. It wasn't as if he'd been in any hurry for the work to be done. In fact, as far as he was concerned, the longer it took, the better, since it gave him a plausible reason to keep in touch with her.

"Hey, Marti, what brings you here? Not having problems with your car, are you?" Smiling, he gestured her into his office, then shut the door to keep out the cold.

"Oh, no, the car's running fine." She smiled tentatively as she met his gaze. "I just stopped by to show you the layouts for your print ads. The art department finished them this afternoon, and I thought you might like to see them. What with the holiday next week, I figured you'd be pretty busy. I wasn't sure if you'd have time to come downtown. And since you're on my way home anyway..." She shrugged, her words trailing away.

"You're right," he agreed, shifting some of the mess on his desk off to one side. "We've been pulling overtime all week, and next Monday, Tuesday and Wednesday won't be any better."

"Oh, well, if you're really busy now, we can just wait until after—"

"We're just about finished for today," he assured her, barely resisting the urge to reach out and grab her as she edged toward the door. "And I've really been looking forward to seeing the layouts."

"In that case..." Smiling once more, she joined him behind his desk, opened her briefcase and took out the portfolio. She arranged the layouts on his desk in no particular order, then adjusted the lamp to show them to their best advantage. "Here they are."

He'd expected them to be good and, indeed, they were. In fact, choosing one over the others was virtually impossible, he liked them all so much. But after some deliberation, he finally decided on which ads to run where, as well as when and for how long.

"So what do you think?" he asked as she marked the appropriate layouts, then jotted down a few notes in her memo book.

"I agree with your choices, but if you have second thoughts, just let me know. Since we won't be running any of the newspaper ads for several weeks, we can still make changes. However, the magazine ad has to be submitted no later than Wednesday afternoon. So if you have any doubts about it, be sure and call me as soon as possible."

"The magazine ad's the one I like the best," he admitted.

"Me, too," she agreed, tucking the portfolio back into her briefcase. "Thanks for taking the time to go over these with me. I hope I didn't keep you from anything." She lifted her briefcase off the desk, smiling as she glanced up at him.

"Just replacing a set of spark plugs, but I can do that anytime." Shoving his hands in the pockets of his jeans, he returned her smile. "Actually, I should be thanking you for saving me a trip downtown. I'm sure you have better things to do on a Friday night."

"Not really." Her smile faded a bit as she turned toward the door.

"Going home?"

"Yes."

"Had dinner yet?" He'd take her to a restaurant, they'd eat, they'd talk, then he'd leave her at her front door again. What could it hurt?

"No."

"Want to have dinner with me? I'll have to stop by the house first and get cleaned up. But then maybe we could try Gian-Tony's. It's not far and I've heard the food's good."

She faced him again, her eyes meeting his. "I'd like that, Dominic. I'd like that a lot."

He hadn't realized he'd been holding his breath until she spoke. But when she did, he sighed with relief. "Want to follow me to my place? Or would you rather go home? It'll take me about thirty minutes to shower and change. Then I could swing by for you."

"Why don't I just follow you to your place? It'll save a little time. And I'd...I'd like to see where you live," she admitted, a hint of pink creeping up her cheeks as she lowered her gaze.

Whatever her reasons, she trusted him enough to go home with him, something he doubted she'd have done a few weeks ago. Somehow he'd managed to redeem himself in her eyes. Barely controlling the urge to grab her and hug her and kiss her, he sauntered over to the closet and retrieved his jacket, then stuck his head out of the doorway leading to the bays.

"Hey, Eddie, I'm going home. You and Mooch can close up about six-thirty, and I'll plan to see you guys again in the morning around eight or eight-thirty, okay?"

"Yeah, right. In the morning, Dom."

Shrugging into his jacket, he crossed to the outer door where Marti stood waiting. "All right, we're out of here," he said, slipping an arm around her shoulders to shield her from the cold. Or so he told himself.

As agreed, she followed him to his house in her car. When they arrived, she didn't hesitate at all about going in with him. She seemed to approve of his simple furnishings as he showed her around. Then, accepting a beer, she offered to wait in the living room while he showered and changed.

He did so as quickly as possible, not wanting to give her too much time to have second thoughts. Yet when he returned to the living room she was no longer there.

"I'm in the kitchen," she called out, just as he started toward the front window to see if her car was still parked in his driveway.

"What are you doing?" he asked, pausing in the doorway. Actually, he could see what she was doing. She was setting the table with plates, silverware, napkins and glasses. He could also see that she'd kicked off her shoes, slipped out of her suit jacket and unbuttoned a couple of buttons on her plain silk shirt.

"I hope you don't mind." She glanced at him for a moment, then turned back to the table. "I called Imo's and ordered a pizza to be delivered. I thought it might be nice to eat here, just the two of us, instead of in a restaurant, surrounded by strangers."

He didn't say anything for several seconds. He simply stared at her, his heart too full for words, as he realized how very easy it would be to fall in love with her.

Fall in love with her?

"I ordered half pepperoni and half Italian sausage. Is that all right?" She had turned to face him again, and as he met her gaze, he saw the uncertainty in her eyes.

"That's fine, just fine," he assured her, moving into the kitchen. "Would you like some wine to go with it? I just happen to have several bottles of a very nice red that someone sent me several weeks ago." He offered her a teasing grin as he opened the pantry and waved a hand at the bottles filling one of the shelves.

"Wine *would* be nice," she agreed, smiling, too.

The pizza arrived a few minutes later, and although Marti tried to insist on paying for it, since she'd ordered it, Dominic managed to beat her to it.

They ate in companionable silence for a while, both hungrier than they'd thought. But as the pizza disappeared, piece by delicious piece, and they each had a second glass of wine, they began to talk a bit about how they'd spent the week they'd been apart.

"I thought you might be busier than usual with the holiday coming," Marti said as she helped him clear the table. "But I had no idea you were working twelve-hour days. And I heard you say that you're working tomorrow, too."

"And Sunday," he admitted. "A lot of people are going to be on the road, and they all want to be sure their cars are all right before they head out. Unfortunately they all wait until the last minute to have them checked over. But I'm not complaining. It'll slow down again after the first of the year."

"I wish I could say the same thing. Although I guess I shouldn't complain, either. I imagine I'd be bored if I weren't so busy." She leaned against the counter, watching as he stacked their dishes in the dishwasher.

"Not necessarily. You could always spend more time on your photography," he suggested.

"I could, couldn't I?" she said in a wistful tone of voice as she gazed off in the distance thoughtfully.

"You're very good at it. Have you ever considered it as an alternate profession?"

"Not really. Although I have sold a few photographs to local newspapers and magazines." She shrugged noncommittally, then waved a hand at the coffeemaker. "Coffee's ready."

"Why don't we have it in the living room?" As he opened a cabinet and reached for a couple of mugs, Dominic realized that Marti didn't seem very enthusiastic about the track their conversation was taking. She didn't seem to want to talk about her job or anything related to it. And, frankly, neither did he. There were more important things they needed to discuss, and the sooner the better.

"That would be nice," she readily agreed, accepting a mug of the steaming brew.

He poured a mug for himself, then they walked to the living room together. Not wanting to crowd her, Dominic held back a bit at the doorway, allowing her to choose where she wanted to sit. Without hesitation, she headed for the sofa, curling comfortably into a corner of it. As he moved to join her, she glanced at him, her shy yet inviting smile making his heart beat a little faster. Then she lowered her gaze and took a sip of her coffee.

Trying not to read too much into the longing he'd seen in her eyes, he sat down beside her, leaving a bit of space between them as he did. They needed to talk more than anything else, *before* anything else. And he could only hope that she knew it as well as he. Unless they talked, he wouldn't know how or why he'd frightened her. And without that knowledge, he couldn't risk touching her, *wouldn't* risk touching her, for fear that he'd do it again.

"I'm glad you stopped by the garage tonight," he said at last, breaking the silence stretching between them. "And not just because you saved me a trip downtown." If he let her know how he felt, maybe she'd trust him enough to do the same.

"I'm glad I did, too." She took another sip of coffee, then set her mug on the table. "I wanted to show you the layouts." She folded her hands in her lap and shifted slightly so that she faced him. "But I also wanted to talk to you." Her eyes met his for a moment, then she ducked her head. "I . . . I owe you an apology."

"For what?" he asked, gently tracing the line of her jaw with his fingertip.

"For the way I behaved a couple of weeks ago when you…when we were…when we started to…" She glanced at him again as her cheeks turned crimson.

"Get intimate?" He set his mug on the table, too, then slipped his arm around her and drew her close.

"Yes," she murmured. Leaning against him, she rested her head on his shoulder.

"I frightened you, didn't I?" he asked softly.

"Yes."

"In what way?"

Twisting her hands together in her lap, she shrugged and shook her head wordlessly.

"Were you afraid that I would hurt you?" he prodded as gently as he could. "Were you afraid I'd force you—"

"Not you…never *you*," she cried, tipping her face up and meeting his gaze.

"But you *were* afraid, Marti. You were with *me*, and you were *afraid*."

"Believe me, Dominic, I know you'd never hurt me. I've known it from the first. But when you…when you…backed me against the wall, in my head you were…you were—"

"I was someone else, wasn't I?" Tightening his hold on her, he rubbed his cheek against her hair, soothing her. "Someone who hurt you," he added, his voice rough with anger. If he could only get his hands on the bastard who'd hurt her so badly. He'd like to shove *him* up against a wall and beat the living daylights out of him.

"It happened a long time ago. I thought I'd gotten past it." She sighed and shook her head again. "But I guess I haven't. I guess maybe I never will," she admitted in an anguished tone of voice.

"Want to tell me about it? Sometimes talking helps," he urged. Knowing how reserved she was, he wondered if she'd ever told anyone about it. Sharing her pain wouldn't be easy for her. But if she trusted him, really trusted him as much as she seemed to, maybe she wouldn't shut him out.

"I'm not sure I can," she whispered, staring straight ahead of her.

"Did you know him?"

"His parents and my parents have been the best of friends for as long as I can remember. My father plays golf with his father as least once a week. My mother and his mother were sorority sisters. Brent Winston and I practically grew up together. I thought he was my friend. I thought I could trust him."

"Did you date?"

"Not until after I graduated from college. By the time we reached our teens we only saw each other occasionally. Neither of us really enjoyed going out with our parents, and once we were old enough to stay home alone that's what we usually did. And since we didn't go to the same schools, we never socialized with the same crowd.

"I hadn't seen him in almost two years when he called one night. I'd moved into my own apartment and been working at the bank about six months. He'd been working in Dallas, but had recently moved back to Kansas City to start a new job. Apparently he'd seen my parents, and they'd suggested we get together. I wasn't dating anyone at the time, so I agreed to have dinner with him, mostly out of curiosity."

As she paused for a moment and drew in a deep breath, Dominic brushed his lips against her hair. He had a good idea of what was coming, and his heart ached for her. But he knew that if she didn't tell him what Brent had done, she'd never be able to let it go. And until she did, how could she start to heal?

"What happened?" he asked quietly.

"Nothing, really. We had dinner and went to a movie, then he dropped me off at my front door. He asked me out a couple more times, and I went. But after our third date he suddenly seemed to expect more than a good-night kiss, a lot more. And I realized that although I liked him, I didn't want to sleep with him. Somehow I managed to put him off. And when he asked me out again, I told him I was busy. He accepted my excuses at first, but then he finally confronted me. So I told him I'd rather not see him again at all.

"When I didn't hear from him for almost a month, I assumed he'd found someone else. But then one night he showed up at my apartment uninvited. He said that he just wanted to talk, that he needed my advice about something. I . . . I didn't even think twice. I just let him in.

"I didn't realize he'd been drinking until he grabbed me in the entryway and started backing me against the wall. I asked him to let me go, and he—he just laughed in my face. He said I was a cold bitch and he knew how to . . . how to warm me up. I tried to get away from him. But I couldn't. . . ." Sobbing now, she pressed her face against his chest.

"Marti, honey, don't—"

"He raped me, Dominic. I'd never been with anyone, and he . . . he raped me."

Raging silently, Dominic held her in his arms, letting her cry. She'd been young and innocent, and she'd been brutally violated by someone she'd trusted. No wonder she'd been so hesitant the first few times they'd been together. Just getting into a car with him must have taken a monumental act of faith on her part. That she'd allowed him into her home, that she'd welcomed his kisses and caresses, suddenly seemed like nothing short of a miracle.

Yet she had. And although he'd frightened her, however inadvertently, she was here with him now, sharing the darkness that had haunted her soul in a way she'd probably never done before. Surely that had to count for something. Surely there really was hope for them yet. He'd thought he'd been wishing for the moon, but maybe he hadn't been after all.

As her tears finally began to subside, he dug out his handkerchief. Then, pressing it into her hands, he spoke to her gently. "You've never told anyone, have you? Not the police, not even your parents."

"At first, I couldn't. I felt so... ashamed. Because I *had* let him into my apartment," Marti said, blotting her face with the handkerchief he'd given her.

She wasn't sure why she'd told Dominic about Brent. It hadn't been something she'd really *wanted* to do. But now that she had, she felt as if a weight had been lifted from her shoulders. And she realized that she wasn't nearly as mortified by her revelations as she'd imagined she'd be.

"After a while, I tried to say something to my mother," she admitted at last. "She said that it was obvious that my sexual initiation hadn't lived up to my romantic fantasies, and as a result, I was probably just overreacting. She reminded me that I'd always been too sensitive. She also reminded me that Brent and I *had* been dating. Because of that, I don't think she could believe that he actually forced me.

"When I realized it was futile to try to convince her otherwise, I just let it go. I applied for the job at Carter and Caisson, and I moved to St. Louis. And I just...tried...to forget."

"But you couldn't, could you?" he asked, gently stroking her arm.

"I kept it all bottled up inside me. Until now." Aware that she'd probably laid more on him than he'd ever bargained for, she tipped her head back and met his gaze. "I'm sorry. I never should have—"

"Don't apologize, Marti. Not to me." Bending his head slowly, he kissed her cheek. "You've kept your hurt to yourself too long. Maybe now that you've talked about it, you can let it go. Maybe you can finally start to heal."

"I hope so," she whispered fervently, resting her head on his shoulder again. "But I'm still afraid that I'll always be...*afraid.*" Dominic had been more patient and understanding than she'd believed any man could be. But she couldn't expect him to put up with her fearfulness for an indefinite amount of time. Yet neither could she guarantee that she wouldn't panic in his arms again.

"You probably always will be," he agreed quietly. "But a little fear isn't all bad, not at the right time, in the right place. And I think maybe you're over the worst of the fear— the fact that you could talk about it, share it...with me..."

"But when you—" she started to protest, not wanting to deceive him in any way.

"Before I backed you against the wall, were you afraid of me? Were you afraid when I kissed you and caressed you?"

"No..."

"What about now? We're here alone in my house, sitting together on the sofa. Are you afraid?"

"No..." He was trying to restore her faith in herself. Yet she couldn't dismiss all her uncertainties, not when they might cause both of them grief in the long run. "But what if I can't...can't...?" Closing her eyes, she shook her head helplessly, unable to put her thoughts into words.

"Make love?" He did it for her, his voice infinitely soft and gentle.

She nodded wordlessly, curling close to the warmth and reassurance he offered her.

"Why don't we cross that bridge when we come to it?"

"But if I can't—"

"If you can't, we won't. We won't do anything you don't want to do. Not ever," he vowed. "Believe it or not, I'm happy just being with you, Marti. As long as you're happy being with me...."

"Happier than I've ever been," she admitted, smiling shyly as she lifted her face to meet his gaze.

"Then why don't we just take it from there? One day at a time...." He traced the curve of her cheek with his fingertips, then bent his head and took her mouth slowly, completely, as she willingly parted her lips for him.

When he finally eased away from her, Marti wanted to protest. But she'd been so unsure of herself and her feelings for so long that her intrinsic reserve won out. Resting her head on his shoulder once again, she sighed deeply. Then, lulled by the slow, steady beat of his heart, and the feather-light stroke of his hand on her arm, she closed her eyes.

They sat together, just so, for what seemed like a wonderfully long time, lost in their own thoughts. Finally, realizing that it was getting late, and recalling that Dominic had to work the following day, Marti straightened and reluctantly swung her legs to the floor.

"I'd better go." She wiped the last trace of tears from her cheeks with his handkerchief, then frowned thoughtfully. "Where are my shoes?"

"In the kitchen along with your suit jacket. I'll get them for you."

Grateful to have a few moments alone, she tried to pull herself together, physically as well as emotionally. Standing, she smoothed a hand over her wrinkled skirt, rebuttoned the top buttons of her blouse, then tucked a few wayward wisps of hair back into place. Now if only she could collect her thoughts with equal ease. But that would be impossible until she was alone.

"Sure you're ready to go?" Dominic asked. He set her shoes on the floor, then slipped his arm around her waist so she could step into them without losing her balance.

"We both have to work. And if I don't go now…" If she didn't go now, she'd be tempted to ask him to let her stay the night. And she didn't want to do that until she knew she was ready for all that would entail.

"I know what you mean." He smiled wryly as he held out her suit jacket. "Slip this on while I get our coats."

"*Our* coats?" She followed him into the entryway.

"You're not driving home alone." He held her black wool coat for her, then shrugged into his leather bomber jacket.

"But I do it all the time," she protested, collecting her briefcase from the table where she'd left it.

"Well, that doesn't mean you're doing it tonight." He caught her arm, turned her around and planted a kiss on her lips. "Now are you going to give me the keys, or will I be forced to frisk you for them?" he growled, his eyes glittering with mischief.

"They're in my briefcase," she retorted tartly, opening it to retrieve them.

"Ah, just my luck." He took them from her with a rueful shake of his head, then escorted her out the front door.

"Oh, please. You're just looking for an excuse to drive my car, and you know it."

"Actually, I'm just looking for an excuse to be with you a little longer," he muttered, nuzzling her ear as he opened the car door for her.

She slipped into the passenger seat without a word, the sudden warmth of his breath against her sensitive skin making her shiver all over. When she risked a glance at him, he grinned and waggled his eyebrows, then closed the door. And to her surprise, she laughed out loud.

"What's so funny?"

"What do you think?"

"Tonight I think I'm better off not knowing." Reaching over, he covered her hand with his for a moment and squeezed it reassuringly. Then he started the engine and pulled away from the curb. They rode in silence for several seconds before he spoke again. "I guess you're going to Kansas City to spend Thanksgiving with your family."

"Not this year. My parents are going on a cruise with the Winstons. Since I don't really have any other family or close friends there anymore, I thought I might as well just stay here."

"Are you doing anything special here?" He glanced at her thoughtfully as he pulled into her driveway and punched the garage-door opener.

"I'm not doing anything at all." To be honest she'd tried not to think about the holiday weekend too much. Even though she'd be seeing them at Christmas, she'd been hurt that her parents had made other plans for Thanksgiving. Thursday was also her thirtieth birthday, and she hadn't really wanted to reach that particular landmark all alone.

"Well, you are now." He drove her car into the garage, then got out and opened her door.

"So what am I doing?" She eyed him suspiciously as they walked to her front porch.

"You're having dinner with me and my family."

"Oh, Dominic, I appreciate the invitation. But I don't want to intrude."

"Don't be silly," he admonished, wrapping an arm around her shoulders and giving her a quick hug. "My parents have been wanting to meet you. And Carmen and Tony and Rose and Drew and the kids will all be there. Just think how happy Amy will be to see you." As they reached her front door, he paused, turning her to face him. "Say yes, Marti. And I promise you a day to remember."

"You're sure no one will mind?" she hedged.

"Positive."

"All right, then. Yes."

He hugged her again, then drawing back a bit, kissed her softly on the mouth. "Amy will be thrilled . . . among others. . . ."

"I hope so."

"I know so." He kissed her once more, then opened her front door. "I'll call you, okay?"

"Okay."

He touched her face with his fingertips, hesitating a moment longer, his dark eyes full of longing. Then, taking a deep breath, he shoved his hands in his jacket pockets and turned away. "Good night, Marti."

"'Night, Dominic."

She almost asked him to stay. But in her heart she knew that it wouldn't be wise. Though she wanted him to hold her, to kiss her and caress her, she wasn't ready for the rest of it. Not yet. But she would be soon, she thought, very soon.

Telling Dominic about the pain and humiliation she'd suffered at Brent Winston's hands had soothed the wounds she'd lived with for so long. And, as Dominic had predicted, she'd already begun to heal. Finally she could believe that anything was possible. With love. . . .

Love?

"Oh, Marti..." She stood in the entryway, still clutching her briefcase, as the truth dawned on her at last. She'd fallen in love with Dominic Fabrino. In spite of herself and her rigid goals, she'd fallen in love. And she had no idea what to do about it.

She'd worked so hard to achieve success. But suddenly it seemed like nothing compared to what she might have with Dominic. If he loved her, too....

With a weary shake of her head, she set her briefcase on the hall table and unbuttoned her coat. She wouldn't think about it any more tonight, she *couldn't*. She'd dealt with enough problems already. And, as a result, her emotions were altogether too close to the surface. Weighing her options for the future now simply wouldn't be smart. Better to wait until she was cool, calm and collected again. Then common sense would have at least half a chance.

As she headed for the staircase, she knew she was only postponing the inevitable. But at the moment, all she wanted was to go to bed, to sleep...to dream....

He called Saturday night, but it was late, and they only talked for a few minutes. From the sound of his voice and some of the things that he said, Marti knew that he'd had a hard day. So, although their conversation was the high point of her own day, she didn't keep him long.

He called again late Sunday afternoon to ask if she had plans for dinner. When she said that she didn't, he offered to stop by her house around six-thirty or seven with burgers and fries. She readily agreed.

He arrived just after seven, carrying a sack of goodies from the steak house in one hand and a bottle of fine red wine in the other. He looked almost as weary as he'd sounded on the telephone, yet he was as full of nonsense as ever. As they ate by candlelight in the dining room, using her best china and crystal, he told her about his day, making her laugh as he related some of Mooch and Eddie's more entertaining antics.

When they finished, he helped her clear the table. Then, since he seemed almost ready to drop, she sent him into the living room to relax while she put on a pot of coffee. He didn't have far to drive home, and he'd only drunk one glass of wine, but she didn't want him on the road without at least a little caffeine to keep him going.

However, by the time she walked into the living room, carrying a steaming mug in each hand, Dominic had already fallen asleep. Stretched out on her sofa, snoring softly, he suddenly appeared more vulnerable than Marti had ever imagined he could. In the past he'd always seemed invincible. But in reality he wasn't. He had feelings, too. And he, too, had been hurt, just as he could be again. Until now she'd been too self-involved to realize it. But in the weeks ahead, she knew that she couldn't allow herself to forget it.

As quietly as possible, she returned to the kitchen and set their mugs aside. Then she went upstairs, fetched a blanket and pillow and walked back to the living room. There she slipped off his sneakers, slid the pillow under his head and tucked the blanket around him, all without waking him. She knelt on the floor for a minute or two, just watching him sleep. Finally she leaned forward and kissed his cheek. Then, reluctantly, she returned to the kitchen and the paperwork she'd left on the table.

At ten-thirty she decided to call it a night. On her way upstairs, she checked on Dominic, but he was still sleeping soundly. The thought of waking him hardly occurred to her, at least not to send him home. She had no qualms at all about his spending the night on her sofa. Although he'd probably be more comfortable in her . . . in a bed.

"Go to your room, Marti," she muttered softly as she headed for the stairs. "Go directly to your room. Do not pass Go. Do not collect two hundred dollars. And do not, under any circumstances, return to the living room before daybreak."

If he awoke during the night and wanted to leave, he could always let himself out. If he was still there in the morning... Well, at least it would be morning. And since they both had to work, they wouldn't have time for... for anything. Anything at all. Or so she told herself as she showered, then slipped into a long, flannel nightgown and crawled into bed.

She thought she might have trouble sleeping, but she didn't. In fact, she drifted off without any tossing or turning at all and slept deeply until just before dawn.

She came awake slowly, and in the pale gray light, saw him sitting on the edge of her bed. For just an instant, fear flashed through her. But then she realized that it was Dominic. And she knew that he would never hurt her.

"I didn't want to wake you," he murmured, rubbing her cheek with the back of his hand. "But I couldn't go without seeing you, without saying thank-you for letting me stay."

She reached up and covered his hand with hers. Then, turning her face, she pressed her lips against his palm. "You're welcome... anytime."

"I didn't mean to be such lousy company."

"Actually, you weren't company at all," she teased softly. "If it hadn't been for your snoring, I wouldn't have even known you were here."

"I don't snore," he protested. "Do I?"

"Next time I'll get it on my tape recorder."

"Next time I won't be sleeping on the sofa. In fact, I won't be sleeping at all, and neither will you," he vowed, his voice dark with promise as he threaded his fingers through her hair and bent to kiss her.

She opened her mouth for him, her tongue gliding over his, then arched instinctively as his hand skimmed over her breast. He drew back a little, kissing her cheek and the curve of her neck, his whiskers rough against her skin. Then, sliding his thumb over her nipple, he took her mouth again.

Moaning softly, Marti twisted under him, the sensation of his hand on her heightened almost unbearably through the fabric of her gown. "Please, Dominic..." she whispered urgently, not sure what she wanted, only knowing she wanted more.

"Ah, Marti, sweetheart." Drawing her into his arms, he held her close for one long moment, brushing his lips against her hair. Then, settling her back against her pillows, he slowly eased away from her. "I'm sorry. I shouldn't have done that. You're still half-asleep. I...I think I'd better go."

"But, Dominic—" She didn't want to him to go. She wanted him to take her in his arms again. She wanted him to finish what he'd started. She wasn't afraid...she *wasn't*.

"When we make love I want you with me all the way, beginning to end. I don't want to feel that I'm taking advantage of you, or that I've caught you unawares. And I don't want you to end up feeling that way, either." With obvious reluctance he moved away from her bed. "I want us to be together more than anything, Marti, but only if you're sure you want it, too."

She *was* sure that she wanted to be with him. Yet she said nothing for several seconds. Because somehow she knew that he wasn't talking about their being together for just a day or a week or a month. And where Dominic was concerned, she hadn't allowed herself to think much beyond that. Now she realized that the time had come when she must. Otherwise *she* could end up hurting *him*.

"What time is it?" she asked at last.

"Just past six."

"I... I have to get ready for work," she murmured. Although it was the last thing she wanted to do, Marti knew that at the moment it was the best thing she could do... for both of them. Her work had always been her refuge, and that's what she needed, at least until she got a few things sorted out in her head.

"I know. Me, too." Dominic backed slowly toward the door. "Mind if I call you tonight?"

"Not at all." She propped herself up on her elbows, forcing herself to smile.

"Then I'll talk to you later."

"Yes, later..." she murmured, wanting him to stay, yet letting him go. For his good as well as her own.

Chapter Nine

Although they talked on the telephone for several minutes each evening, Marti didn't see Dominic again until Thursday. With the preholiday rush at Fabrino's and her own need to get through some of the work she'd let slide lately, they were both putting in twelve-hour days. By evening they were too tired to do more than exchange a few words about their days. And that was just as well. Or so Marti tried to tell herself.

After their encounter early Monday morning, she'd thought it wise to put a little distance between them, physically as well as emotionally. She needed time to weigh her options, to consider what she wanted as opposed to what she could have now or in the future. And she had to face up to the possible consequences of whatever choices she made before her relationship with Dominic deepened.

Unfortunately, knowing what she had to do and doing it were altogether different. For once in her life she didn't want to think. With all her heart and soul, she simply wanted to *feel*. It took every ounce of willpower she possessed to stay away from Fabrino's. But she knew if she went there, she'd find a way to lure Dominic back to her house, up the stairs and into her bed. And then she'd be tempted to allow herself to believe in happily ever after, even when common sense warned that odds were against it.

"And you've never been much of a gambler, have you? At least, not where love's concerned," she mused early Thursday afternoon as she checked on the spinach-and-artichoke casserole she'd popped in the oven twenty minutes earlier. Satisfied that it would be ready by the time Dominic arrived, she closed the oven door. But perhaps she was being rather hard on herself, she reflected as she headed back to her bedroom to finish dressing.

It wasn't as if Dominic had ever said anything about always or forever, she thought, slipping into her long-sleeved, royal blue sweater dress, then adding the gold chain and button earrings she'd chosen to wear with it. Looking back, she had to admit that all he'd really said was that he wanted to make love with her. And despite her lack of experience, she knew that men and women made love all the time with no promise of anything resembling permanence between them.

More than likely her mental gyrations would end up being all for naught. Though she'd never said anything specific about Chicago, she had made it clear from the first that her job was her life. Considering what had happened with his ex-wife, Dominic had probably assumed their relationship would be temporary all along. And an affair might be all he really wanted. Surely she could understand that, as well as accept it. He couldn't know how much she'd once wanted a husband and family, simply because she'd never told him.

But you could tell him now....

She gazed at herself in the mirror for several seconds, then slowly turned away. Mentioning marriage and children at this stage would be the same as asking for a commitment, the kind of commitment he might not be willing to make to someone like her. And that she could never do. Not as long as there was a possibility that he didn't really care for her as much as she had begun to care for him.

Better to enjoy whatever time she had with him in whatever way seemed right. Better to take it day by day, and not think too far ahead. He wanted to make love with her, and she with him, and for the time being she wouldn't allow anything else to matter.

Determined to obey her personal dictates, Marti ran a brush through her hair, then started down the stairs to check on her casserole again. As she reached the hallway, the doorbell rang, and for the first time in what seemed like forever, she smiled. *Dominic.* A little early as usual, but she was more than ready.

Opening the front door, she offered him a cheerful greeting, then stepped back to allow him to enter. When he stood where he was, eyeing her solemnly, her smile started to fade. Nervously she twisted her fingers around the simple gold chain she wore, wondering what was wrong.

"Never again," he muttered after several seconds.

"What—"

He didn't give her time to finish. He strode into the entryway, grasped her shoulders gently, pulled her toward him and took her mouth in a long, slow, deep kiss. Finally, raising his head, he met her gaze, his dark eyes full of the devil.

"Never again am I going for three days without you," he vowed. Bending his head, he gave her another quick kiss. Then, with obvious reluctance, he released her. "You look gorgeous. And something smells good. Carmen said you were bringing a vegetable dish.''

"Spinach-and-artichoke casserole." Flustered by his kisses and compliments, Marti waved a hand toward the kitchen. "I'd better get it out of the oven before it burns."

Not bothering to take off his jacket, Dominic followed her down the hallway and into the kitchen. As she found a pair of pot holders and opened the oven door, he crossed to the table. "Mmm, I knew it. You baked brownies, too," he said, snitching one out of the tin she'd left there.

"I thought the kids would like them ... among others." Grinning, she glanced at him over her shoulder. "Don't eat too many or you'll spoil your dinner." She carried the covered dish to the counter, set it in a basket and tucked a towel around it to keep it warm.

"Not possible." He palmed another of the chocolate goodies, then replaced the lid on the tin. "Unless I eat them all," he added, a mischievous twinkle in his eyes.

"Don't even think about it." She took custody of the cookie tin, setting it on the counter beside the basket.

"Okay, I won't. I'll think about you instead." He came up behind her and put his arms around her. Drawing her back against him, he nuzzled her neck. "Just like I've been doing." He turned her to face him and brushed his lips against hers. "Ah, Marti, I've missed you."

"I've missed you, too," she admitted, sighing deeply as she rested her head on his shoulder. She'd been so sad, so lonely without him. But it didn't matter anymore because he was here with her now, holding her close, warming the hollow places deep in her heart.

"Guess we'd better go," Dominic muttered, his cheek pressed against her hair. "Although I must say I'm tempted—"

"Your family will never forgive us if we're late," Marti cut in as she eased away from him. Much as she would have loved having him all to herself for the rest of the day, not to mention the night, they simply could not miss his family's Thanksgiving dinner. "Why don't you grab the basket and tin while I get my coat?"

"You're bringing your camera, too, aren't you?"

"You don't think they'd mind if I took some pictures?" More than anything she'd wanted to capture his family on film, but she hadn't been sure how they'd feel about it.

"I think they'd be thrilled to have a few good photographs of the family. Half the time when we get together no one remembers to bring a camera. And when someone does, the results are usually pretty poor."

"Maybe I could do a few portrait shots," she suggested, slipping into her coat, then reaching for the camera case on the closet shelf.

"Do you have a tripod?"

"Sure."

"Bring it. Then you can be in some of them, too."

"But—"

"Bring it. Please . . ."

"All right."

Although they were actually a little early, Dominic and Marti were the last to arrive at his parents' house, but no one seemed to mind. Amid a chorus of cheerful greetings and a flurry of hugs and kisses, they were relieved of Marti's basket, cookie tin and camera case, as well as the wine and the rather mysterious white bakery box that were Dominic's contributions to the family feast.

Taking a moment to offer her a reassuring smile, Dominic helped her out of her coat. After hanging it in the hall closet along with his own, he slipped an arm around her waist and drew her close. Then he moved toward the elderly couple standing off to one side and, his voice full of warmth and affection, introduced Marti to his parents.

Both Mary and Sal welcomed her into their home so graciously that Marti's lingering doubts about intruding vanished immediately. In fact, their kind words and shy smiles put her so at ease that she gladly accepted Mary's invitation to join her and Rose and Carmen in the kitchen to help with the final preparations for the big meal.

Dominic's mother and sisters made her feel right at home. Before she knew it, she was laughing and talking with them as if she'd known them all her life. Much to Marti's amusement, Dominic checked on her a couple of times, only to be chased out of the kitchen by Rose and Carmen. On his third foray he finally suggested that she photograph the family before dinner rather than after.

"It's the only way they'll let me spend some time with you," he grumbled darkly, ignoring his sisters' teasing comments as he all but dragged her into the living room.

Hilarity and hoopla followed as Dominic arranged everyone in a variety of poses, first in the living room, then around the huge dining-room table. In between formal shots, Marti took candid pictures, catching Carmen and Tony in a clench, Andy and Angela making faces at each other, Sal and Mary quietly holding hands, Rose playfully ruffling Drew's hair, and Amy whispering in Dominic's ear.

As the shutter clicked again and again, she realized just how comforting it would be to have a truly warm and loving family like the Fabrinos. Granted, they probably had their fair share of problems. But when all was said and done, she knew they'd always be there for one another, as well as anyone else who became a part of their extended circle.

Pausing for a moment to put a fresh roll of film in her camera, Marti tried to will away the longing that welled up deep inside her. She should know better than to want what she couldn't have. And she couldn't be a Fabrino. Not unless she married—

"Hey, Marti, here's your tripod." Interrupting her reverie, Dominic came up beside her, opened the three-legged camera support and adjusted the height for her. "Set the timer on your camera so you can be in some of the pictures, too."

"Oh, but I don't think—"

"Good idea," Rose agreed, not giving Marti a chance to protest. With a grin, she slid out of her chair and onto her husband's lap, then patted the empty seat beside her. "You can sit right here in the middle."

"Oh, yes," Amy piped up, clapping her hands gleefully. "Right here in the middle between me and Uncle Dominic."

Trying valiantly to blink back the tears that suddenly filled her eyes, Marti bent over the tripod and fiddled with her camera. They wanted her to be in their family photographs—not just Dominic and Amy, but all of them. She'd seen it in their faces and heard it in their voices as they'd eagerly made a place for her in their midst. And no matter what happened tomorrow or the next day or the next, she'd never forget how wonderful they'd made her feel here and now.

"You okay?" Dominic asked softly, touching her shoulder.

"Yes." Positioning the camera atop the tripod, she gazed through the lens and adjusted the focus. Then, taking a deep breath, she glanced up at Dominic and smiled. "Go sit down so I can set the timer, all right?"

He hesitated a moment, eyeing her curiously. Then, obviously satisfied that she really was okay, he returned her smile. "All right," he agreed as he moved away from her and joined the others.

Marti took half a dozen photos in the next fifteen minutes. By the fourth or fifth shot everyone was getting kind of silly. Even she couldn't help but laugh as she set the camera on automatic, then made one mad dash after another around the dining-room table. A couple of times Dominic grabbed her and pulled her onto his lap. And just as the shutter clicked on her final shot, he bent his head and kissed her smack on the mouth, causing a fresh round of laughter and a smattering of applause from the others. Though she blushed a bit, much to her surprise Marti wasn't embarrassed at all. She'd been with the Fabrinos long enough to know that public displays of affection were not only accepted, but encouraged.

Shaking her head in mock despair at her son's antics, Mary advised Sal that it was definitely time to carve the turkey. Everyone heartily agreed, and within a relatively short time they were seated around the now-laden table once again, hands joined as they bowed their heads and gave thanks for one another and all that they had. Seated between Dominic and Amy, her hands gently clasped in theirs, Marti closed her eyes and clung to the moment, wanting nothing more than to seal it deep in her soul.

Thanksgiving dinner with the Fabrinos was a unique experience for Marti. Even when her grandmother had been alive, her family's holiday meals had been small, quiet, rather formal affairs. And, more often than not, they'd been held at an elegant restaurant to save her mother any undesired muss and fuss.

But Dominic's family, sprawled around his mother's huge dining-room table, laughed and chattered all at once as they passed platters and bowls from one to another. No one seemed to mind when Andy tossed a roll to Angela, sitting across the table from him, or when Amy landed half a spoonful of spinach casserole on her grandmother's linen tablecloth rather than her plate.

They finally quieted a bit as they settled down to feast on turkey and all the trimmings. But by the time everyone, including Marti, had eaten seconds of everything, they were once again talking and teasing one another, their warmth and good humor tangible evidence of the love and trust they shared.

Since everyone claimed to be as stuffed as the turkey had been, they decided to postpone dessert for a while. The men retired to the living room, as was their tradition, while the women cleared the table. They were storing leftovers and scrubbing pots when Amy, Angela and Andy wandered into the kitchen, each one carrying a favorite board game.

All three clustered around Marti as she scooped sweet potatoes into a plastic container, and they begged her to play with them. When she demurred about leaving the others with all the work, Mary, Rose and Carmen insisted she go with the children, exchanging knowing smiles as they did so.

Following Amy into the dining room, Marti wondered what they were up to. Then, with a quick shake of her head, she dismissed her suspicions as silly. What *could* they be up to? They'd probably played board games with the children so often they were glad to have someone else do it for a change. And Marti truly enjoyed spending time with Dominic's nieces and nephew. Angela and Andy's constant quibbling made her laugh, while Amy's sweet smiles and quick hugs warmed her heart.

Gradually, as the first game ended and they started a second, the adults began to filter back into the dining room, drawing up chairs around the table. As they did so, the children began to exchange what Marti was sure were furtive glances. When they started to nudge one another and giggle, Marti sat back in her chair and eyed Amy with a quizzical smile.

"What's going on?" she asked, more certain than she had been earlier that a conspiracy was afoot.

"It's time." Amy smiled whimsically as Angela and Andy gathered up the game pieces and stashed them, along with the board, back in the box.

"Time for what?" Marti turned to look at Dominic. He stood near the doorway leading into the kitchen, meeting her gaze, his dark eyes full of mischief. Oh, yes, he was definitely up to something, but she had no idea what—

"Time for your birthday party," Amy crowed.

"My birthday...?" Startled, she glanced at the little girl, then turned back to Dominic.

"Happy birthday, Marti," he murmured. As he moved away from the doorway, Rose entered, carrying a decorated cake complete with lit candles, and everyone began to sing "Happy Birthday."

"Oh, my..." Pressing her fingers to her lips, Marti gazed at their smiling faces, not quite sure if she was going to laugh or cry. She hadn't had a birthday party since she'd turned sixteen, and the last thing she'd expected was to have one today.

As they finished the final chorus and Rose set the cake in front of her, Marti eyed Dominic once again. "How did you know?" she asked softly, her voice wavering slightly.

"The same way I knew where you lived—your driver's license. I even know how old you are, but I promise not to tell." He offered her a teasing grin, then gestured toward the cake. "Better make a wish and blow out the candles."

"Be sure and take a *big* breath because there are *thirty* of them," Amy advised. "I counted them for Uncle Dominic."

"Gee, thanks, Amy." Marti shook her head ruefully as everyone laughed. Then, closing her eyes for a moment, she made a wish, not for herself but for those around her, for their good health and happiness. With one deep breath she blew out all the candles.

"Oh, Marti, you did it," Amy cried, clapping her hands with delight. "Now you'll get your wish."

"I hope so," she replied, hugging the little girl hard as tears misted her eyes. "I really, truly hope so." Then, sitting back in her chair, she smiled at the others again. "You have no idea how much this means to me. Thank you, all of you." She lowered her eyes for a moment as she plucked a few of the candles from the cake. "Well... I guess I should cut this masterpiece, shouldn't I?"

"Not until you open your presents," Angela advised. "We always open presents *before* we have cake and ice cream."

"Presents?" She glanced Dominic's way again, but he was no longer standing in the kitchen doorway. Somehow he'd managed to slip away without her noticing. "But you've done so much already," she protested quietly.

"Hey, what's a birthday without presents?" Sal called out, grinning in a way that reminded her of his son.

"Oh, yes, you have to have presents," Amy agreed, then raised her voice several decibels. "Hurry up, Uncle Dominic, Marti's waiting."

"Okay, okay, I'm coming," Dominic replied, striding through the doorway, holding a covered wicker basket in his arms. As Marti eyed him suspiciously, he moved around the table and paused beside her chair. "For you, from me," he said, setting the basket in her lap. Then he bent and kissed her cheek and whispered in her ear. "With love."

"Dominic, you shouldn't have..." Her words trailed away as the basket jiggled a bit beneath her hands. "What in the world...?" She glanced at him, somewhat disconcerted, but he only smiled and shook his head, refusing to spoil the surprise.

"Open it, Marti, open it," Amy urged, dancing from one foot to the other, her eyes bright with anticipation.

Marti hesitated a moment longer, staring at the basket, her heart pounding as she thought of what Dominic had said. *For you, from me. With love.*

Then, as everyone quietly crowded closer, she released the latch and slowly lifted the lid. Inside, nestled on a folded blanket, was a little long-haired dachshund puppy. He stared at her for several seconds as if taking her measure. Then, yipping joyously, he scrambled out of the basket and into her arms, and licked her chin with his velvety tongue.

"Oh...oh, no..." she murmured. As one tear, then another, trickled down her cheek, she ducked her head, burying her face in the little dog's silky fur. A puppy...her very own puppy. She'd never realized just how much she'd wanted one. Until now....

"I hope you like him because I think he really likes you," Dominic teased. Hunkering down beside her, he dabbed at her tears with his handkerchief.

"Of course I like him," she chided, offering him a watery smile. "I like him a lot." Making a valiant effort to get her emotions under control, she took several deep breaths. Then she shifted the basket onto the floor and settled the puppy in her lap. With a sigh of contentment he curled up in a furry ball, yipped one more time and closed his eyes.

Everyone, including Marti, laughed. Then, as if by magic, several gaily wrapped packages in various sizes and shapes appeared on the table before her.

"More presents," Amy said. "Open mine first, okay?" She offered Marti a small oblong box with at least half a roll of tape securing the wrapping paper and three homemade bows decorating the top.

Touched once again by the kindness and generosity of Dominic and his family, Marti nodded wordlessly as she took the package from the little girl and gently worked to remove the wrappings. Inside she found a blue leather collar for her puppy.

"Oh, Amy, it's just perfect," she murmured. Drawing the child close, she hugged her. "Thank you so much."

"Now mine," Angela insisted.

"And then *mine*," Andy added eagerly.

By the time Marti finished opening the remaining gifts she had everything she needed for her new pet. Angela had given her a leather leash to match the collar she'd gotten from Amy. Andy had given her a bag of rawhide chew bones. And Dominic's parents and sisters had given her a little wicker dog bed, food and water bowls and ten pounds of puppy food.

Eyeing her loot as she gently stroked the little dog's silky ears, Marti shook her head wryly. "You shouldn't have," she said. Then, sure that he'd instigated the entire affair, she met Dominic's gaze. "But I'm so glad you did. Thank you." Reaching out, she took his hand in hers and squeezed it gently. "Thank you, all of you," she added, smiling shyly as she turned her attention to the others gathered around the table.

"Now all he needs is a name," Angela said. "Got any ideas?"

"Gosh, I haven't had time to think about it," Marti admitted.

"How about Max?" Amy suggested. "He looks like a Max to me."

"Yeah, Max is good," Andy agreed.

"What do you think, Angela?" Marti asked the older girl.

"I like it, too."

"Then Max, it is," she decreed, much to Amy's delight. "Now how about some cake?"

"And ice cream, too. Grandma has chocolate and vanilla *and* spumoni," Andy advised as he helped Dominic move her gifts from the dining-room table. "I'm having a scoop of each and a giant piece of cake and one of Marti's brownies."

"Oh, no, you're not," Rose admonished.

"But, Mom, it's Thanksgiving."

As the kids followed Rose into the kitchen, Dominic slid into the chair next to Marti. "Having a good time, Birthday Girl?" he asked, scratching Max's ears.

"A very good time." She took his hand in hers and lifted it to her lips. "Thanks to you."

"My pleasure, sweetheart." Threading his fingers through her hair, he tipped her face up and kissed her. Then, as the others filed back into the dining room, carrying dessert dishes and cartons of ice cream, he eased away from her. "So you want cake and how many scoops of ice cream?"

What she wanted, what she *really* wanted, would have to wait until later. But for now... "One scoop of chocolate—for starters."

They finished dessert, then Marti let the kids take Max out in the backyard to play, while she returned to the kitchen with Dominic's mother and sisters to help with the final cleanup. After the last pot had been dried and put away, they joined the men in the living room. Along with the children, they watched a holiday special on television. And then it was time to go.

Following a round of hugs and kisses and fond farewells, Marti and Dominic headed back to her house. She sat in the passenger seat of his Corvette with Max cuddled contentedly in her lap. The trunk of the car was loaded with the rest of her gifts as well as a grocery bag full of leftovers for them to share. Or so Carmen had said, offering a knowing smile as she'd walked them to the car.

"You're coming in, aren't you?" Marti asked, feeling suddenly shy as Dominic pulled into her driveway.

"If you want me to."

"I thought you could help me get Max settled for the night. Then maybe we could have a cup of coffee or a brandy or... or something." She glanced at him out of the corner of her eye, glad that it was too dark for him to see the blush burning her cheeks.

Or something.... She couldn't have sounded more ingenuous if she'd tried. Only that wasn't the way she wanted Dominic to think of her tonight. She wanted him to realize, once and for all, that she'd put the past behind her, that she was capable of trusting him, as well as loving him in every way a woman could love a man.

"Coffee sounds good. For that matter so does a brandy. Or something...." he teased softly, reaching out to brush a wisp of hair away from her face. "Why don't you go unlock the door while I get Max's gear and our leftovers out of the back?"

"All right," she agreed, more than happy to have a few moments alone to collect herself. She might be unschooled in the art of seduction, but she wasn't completely inept. If worse came to worst, she could simply *tell* him how much she wanted to make love with him. Couldn't she?

"Oh, sure, nothing to it," she muttered, clutching Max in one arm as she unlocked the front door and stepped into the house.

At Dominic's suggestion, they spread newspaper on the laundry-room floor just to be safe, added Max's bed and a bowl of water, then set up the baby gate Rose had lent them. Afterward Marti started a pot of coffee while Dominic took the little dog out for a last romp around the yard. When they didn't return immediately, Marti put on her coat again and joined them. Together she and Dominic did their best to wear out the frisky puppy, laughing as he ran and rolled and tumbled between the two of them.

By the time Max finally began to flag they were more than ready for the coffee she'd brewed. Leaving him curled up in his bed, they carried their steaming mugs into the living room and collapsed side by side onto the sofa.

"He's a real sweetie, isn't he?" Marti mused, kicking off her pumps and tucking her legs under her so that she shifted a little closer to Dominic. As she gazed at him out of the corner of her eye, he sipped his coffee, then set his mug on the table and folded his hands in his lap.

"You're going to spoil him rotten, aren't you?" he asked.

"Probably," she admitted softly, tightening her grip on the mug she held as a wave of disappointment washed over her. Though he sat beside her he hadn't put his arm around her, much less kissed her or... or anything. Apparently he wasn't planning to stay, and unfortunately she wasn't experienced enough to—

"Before you know it, he'll be sleeping in the bed with us, won't he?"

"In bed with... us?" Slowly she raised her eyes and met his dark, tender gaze, her heartbeat quickening as she realized exactly what he was saying.

"Mmm, yes." He took her mug from her and set it next to his, a hint of a smile tugging at the corners of his mouth. "But not tonight. Tonight I'd like it to be just you and me." Wrapping his arms around her, he held her close as he smoothed a hand over her hair. "I want to make love with you, Marti. Slow, sweet, gentle love...."

There were so many things she could say, so many things she *should* say. But as she rested her hands against his chest and pressed her lips against the bare skin at the base of his throat, she settled for the same simple statement he had. "I want to make love with you, too." She brushed her lips against his neck and along the curve of his jaw. Then she tilted her face up and smiled invitingly. "More than anything, Dominic, anything at all."

Drawing back a bit, he rested his hands on her shoulders and solemnly met her gaze. "I won't hurt you, Marti. I swear I won't. If you want me to stop, now or later, just say so, and I will." He ducked his head and kissed her slowly, gently, as if sealing his vow of tenderness.

Beneath her fingertips Marti could feel the tension thrumming through his body. Though she knew that he was holding back for her sake, she also realized how little it would take to ignite his mounting passion. To her surprise she felt no fear at all. He'd said that he wouldn't hurt her and she believed him with all her heart. He would love her as deeply and completely as she wanted. And, oh, how she wanted ...

"I know, Dominic, I know," she murmured as she reached up and cradled his cheek in her palm. Leaning toward him, she brushed her mouth against his, then traced his lips with the tip of her tongue, tempting him.

With a low sound he gathered her into his arms again, opening his mouth over hers, sliding his tongue between her teeth possessively. As she curled her fingers into his hair

Marti tilted her head to give him easier access. Pressing close to him she welcomed the deep, velvety thrust and parry of his tongue with her own as pleasure coursed through her.

Too soon for her liking, Dominic once again eased away from her, ignoring her murmured protest. "Marti, sweetheart..." Smiling roughly, he kissed the tip of her nose. "When you kiss me like that..." He hesitated, resting his cheek against her hair. "Let's go upstairs...okay?"

"Okay," she agreed, giving him a quick hug before she moved away from him.

He took her hands in his and helped her up. Then he slipped an arm around her waist and together they walked up the stairs without a word. At her bedroom door, however, Dominic hesitated. When Marti glanced up at him questioningly, he smiled and tenderly brushed a hand across her cheek.

"Before we go any further, I just want you to know, you don't have to worry about protection. I have something with me."

Despite the sudden heat warming her cheeks, Marti tilted her head to one side and met his gaze with an impish grin. "So do I," she admitted. "Being a mature, responsible adult, I bought something on my lunch hour Tuesday, and let me tell you, deciding on color, size and texture was no easy—"

"You're something else, you know?" Dominic said, shaking his head in admiration as he slipped an arm under her knees and lifted her into his arms. "Something...no, *someone* special," he corrected as he carried her to the bed and settled her against the pillows.

"You, too." Wrapping her arms around his neck, she pulled him down beside her, then turned toward him as he bent his head to claim her mouth.

He kissed her slowly, sensuously, as his hands skimmed down her back and along her sides, then over her breasts and belly, tantalizing her in an almost unbearable way. As she arched against him she mentally cursed the layers of clothing that came between them. She wanted, *needed*, more, so much more. To touch him, really touch him, and to be touched by him in turn. Moving restlessly, she plucked at the buttons of his shirt, opening one after the other, then fumbled with his belt buckle.

"Take your clothes off, Dominic. *Now*," she whispered.

"I will if you will." As he unzipped the back of her dress, she saw him smile in the pale moonlight glimmering through the bedroom windows.

"Oh, I will, *I will*."

With sighs and murmurs, kisses and caresses and a hint of soft, sweet laughter, they undressed each other, then slid beneath the blankets.

"All right?" Dominic asked, cradling her in his arms as he stroked her breast with his fingertips.

"Mmm, yes." Moving against him invitingly, she threaded her fingers through his hair and drew his head down so she could kiss him once again.

With infinite care he deepened his caresses, using his hands and his mouth to pleasure her. And Marti followed suit, her desire to give as well as receive overcoming her natural reserve in a way that surprised them both.

Thanks to her loving ministrations, his restraint finally began to wane. Breathing hard, he eased away from her and smoothed her damp hair away from her face. "I want to be inside you, Marti." He slid his hand over her breast and across her belly, then between her legs, stroking her. "Do you want it, too?"

Marti twisted sinuously, reveling in the heat of his touch. Yet it wasn't enough, not nearly enough. "I want...you, Dominic. I want you."

Turning away from her, he took a foil packet from the nightstand and opened it. When he turned to her again, she opened her arms to him, drawing him close as she eased onto her back. He settled himself between her legs, yet still he seemed to hold back as he gazed down at her for several seconds. "All right?" he asked at last.

Without a word, she arched into him as she ran her hands down his back to his buttocks, her eyes holding his. And then, as he entered her slowly, gently, completely, filling her aching emptiness, she closed her eyes and sighed with soul-deep satisfaction.

"Still all right, sweetheart?"

"Oh...yes..." she murmured, wrapping her legs around him as she nuzzled his neck. Then, stirring restlessly beneath him, she rolled her hips provocatively as a new kind of urgency pulsed through her. "Dominic?"

"I'm here, Marti, right here," he muttered.

As she clung to him, he began to move, slowly at first, then faster and faster. She moved with him, trusting him, loving him enough to follow wherever he led until suddenly, unexpectedly, ecstasy overwhelmed her. With a soft cry of surprise and delight, Marti gave herself up to it as Dominic called her name and thrust into her one final time.

They lay together for a long while afterward without speaking, neither seeming to want to break the new yet fragile bond between them. Finally, however, despite Marti's murmured protest, Dominic eased away from her and sat up.

"I didn't hurt you, did I?" he asked, pulling the blankets up around her.

"No." She took his hand in hers and pressed her lips against his palm. "Not at all. Although I am a bit sore," she admitted, wincing slightly as she shifted a bit.

"I think I know what might help." He bent over and dropped a quick kiss on her forehead, then disappeared into the bathroom. He returned a few minutes later with a washcloth he'd soaked in warm water. Sliding under the blankets with her, he gently tucked it where she was most tender. "How's that?"

"Mmm, much better, thank you." She curled close to him, resting her head on his chest as he slipped an arm around her. Then, much to her chagrin, she yawned. "Oh, my, I'm sorry. It's definitely not the company."

"Maybe I ought to go so you can get some sleep."

"But I thought..."

Marti hesitated, unsure of what could be construed as proper etiquette under the circumstances. Somehow she'd simply assumed he'd spend the night, but perhaps that was acceptable only when you shared a more permanent relationship. And surely, she reminded herself firmly, one night together didn't constitute any sort of permanency. Although now that they'd been together in such an intimate way, Marti couldn't imagine them ever being truly apart again.

"Thought what?" Dominic prodded, his voice low.

"That you'd spend the night," she admitted. "But if you'd rather—"

"There's nothing I'd rather do than stay here with you, Marti. Nothing at all. As long as you want it, too."

"I do," she murmured, sighing wistfully as she nuzzled against his neck. *Tonight and every night from now until forever.*

Astonished by the thought she'd had, Marti stared into the moonlit darkness as understanding suddenly dawned on her. No matter how she'd tried to warn herself against it, she'd fallen in love with Dominic Fabrino. Not tonight, but days ago, *weeks ago*. And she'd done it so deeply and completely that the mere thought of going on with her well-orchestrated life without him tore at her heart.

For seven long, lonely years she'd been sure that she would never trust any man enough to allow him to make love to her, and she'd adjusted her goals and expectations accordingly. She'd set aside her dream of having a husband and family of her own, striving instead for success in her chosen profession. She hadn't counted on a man like Dominic Fabrino coming into her life. But he had, and in so doing, he'd turned her well-ordered world upside down.

For one long moment she thought of Benson's job. She thought of moving to Chicago alone. And she wondered how she would ever be able to do it when the time came.

"Something wrong, Marti?" Stroking her arm gently, Dominic brushed his lips against her hair. "You seem kind of tense all of a sudden."

"No, nothing's wrong," she replied, willing herself to relax as she forcefully put all thoughts of Chicago out of her mind. For tonight she and Dominic were together and, as she'd vowed earlier, that was all that mattered. She'd worry about tomorrow . . . tomorrow.

"Sure?"

"Absolutely." She snuggled closer to him as his hand drifted from her arm to her breast, then tipped her face up. "Of course, a kiss *would* be nice."

"Ah, Marti, if I kiss you..." He did, then shook his head. "Sweetheart, you're too sore."

"You'll be gentle. Trust me."

He did. And he was.

* * *

All things considered, Dominic should have slept until noon. Instead, he awoke just after five o'clock Friday morning, alone in Marti's bed.

Alone?

Turning onto his side, he smoothed a hand over the place where she'd lain beside him until . . . when? The sheets were cool, indicating that she'd been gone for a while. But where? And more important, why? After they'd made love a second time, she'd fallen asleep in his arms. And eventually, aware of how very much he loved her, he'd slept, too.

As he sat up and reached for his pants, he wanted to believe that the feeling was mutual. Despite the cruelty she'd suffered at another man's hands, she'd trusted him enough to make love with him. And she'd done so with a passion that had taken his breath away. Yet sometime during the night she'd left him, and though he couldn't say why, her going worried him more than he liked to admit. He'd begun to believe that she wanted them to be together as much as he, both now and in the future. But as he left her bedroom and walked slowly down the stairs, he couldn't help but wonder if he'd been wrong.

He found her in the living room, sitting on the sofa in the semidarkness. She'd put on a long-sleeved robe and a pair of fluffy slippers, and she was cuddling a sleeping Max in her lap. As he moved toward her she turned her head, and he sensed more than saw her smiling up at him.

"I'm sorry. I didn't mean to wake you," she said, her voice just above a whisper. "I heard Max crying and came down to check on him."

"That's okay. I woke up on my own." He sat down beside her, close enough to touch without touching, giving her the space he thought she needed. "How's he doing?"

"Fine now." Laughing softly, she shook her head with obvious dismay. "I took him outside for a few minutes.

Then he wanted to play for a while. I was wondering if he'd ever wear himself out again when he finally fell asleep.''

"How about you? How are you doing?''

"I'm...fine, too.'' Without hesitation, she scooted closer to him, then turned and pressed her lips against his bare skin. "More than fine. You, too?''

"Me, too.'' As she rubbed her cheek against his chest, he put his arm around her at last.

Surely, after tonight, when they opened themselves to each other in such an intimate way, she'd be honest with him. Surely now, more than ever, she trusted him enough to tell him if she had a problem or, more important, *they* had a problem. Just because he was so damned afraid of losing her didn't mean he would.

And he *was* afraid, more afraid than he'd ever been about anything. Splitting with Diane had been painful. But looking back he realized that the love they'd shared had been too young and frivolous to stand up to the test of time. What he felt for Marti was something else altogether, something deep and rich and overwhelmingly *right*. Four years ago he hadn't been willing to give up anything for his ex-wife. But for Marti...

If necessary, he knew that he'd give up everything he had for her. She meant that much to him. And in the days ahead, in his own quiet way, he intended to make sure that she knew it. Because losing her would not only break his heart, ultimately it would shatter his soul.

"Are you sure?'' she asked, her voice suddenly full of uncertainty as she gazed up at him.

"Yes, I am.'' As she uttered a soft sigh, he gave her a reassuring hug. "Still tired?''

"Mmm, a little.''

"Come back to bed, then.''

"What about Max?''

"Might as well bring him, too." Standing, he took her hand and drew her to her feet. "The more the merrier."

"Actually, I'd rather he slept in his own bed," she suggested shyly. "We could put it on the floor by the foot of our bed."

"That we could," he agreed, trailing his fingers along the line of her jaw. "Go on up and warm a place for me while I get Max's bed."

"My pleasure." She leaned forward and kissed his chin.

Before she could move away, he caught her shoulders in his hands and took her mouth possessively. "I hope so, sweetheart, I hope so...." Then, reluctantly, he let her go.

Chapter Ten

A little more than three weeks later, on the Saturday night before Christmas, Dominic pulled up to the curb outside Marti's house. As was the case whenever he met her, he was early, but tonight even more so than usual. But he had his reasons. Unlike the past few weekends, he hadn't seen her at all that day, so waiting until the prescribed time of seven o'clock had been more difficult than he'd anticipated.

He'd left Mooch and Eddie at the garage at five-thirty and by six-fifteen he'd already showered and dressed in his black tuxedo. Finally, unable to cool his heels at home any longer, he'd climbed into his Corvette and, taking the scenic route, which added at least three minutes to his drive time, headed toward her house.

Of course, he didn't have to sit in the car for the next fifteen minutes. She'd given him a key to her house a couple of weeks ago so he could look after Max on evenings when she was late getting away from the office. Those nights he usually started dinner, too, among other things. . . .

But tonight they were going to Carter and Caisson's gala Christmas party and, knowing how important the evening was to Marti, Dominic had every intention of doing it right. Key or no key, he'd wait until seven sharp, then call on her as a proper gentleman should. Until then, he didn't mind sitting in the Corvette alone. With another holiday upon them, he'd been so busy lately that he relished having a little quiet time to think about Marti and all they'd shared since Thanksgiving.

They'd spent the remainder of the long weekend together. Friday and Saturday he'd gone home only to change clothes. And aside from an all-day shopping trip to the mall with his nieces and nephew on Saturday, an outing he'd promised them weeks earlier, he and Marti hadn't really gone out at all. They'd sat in front of a fire, sharing bits and pieces of their pasts. They'd played with Max. They'd nibbled on leftovers and pigged out on pizza. And they'd made love on the sofa and in the shower and once, at Marti's insistence, against the wall in the entryway.

He hadn't wanted to leave her Sunday night, hadn't wanted to interrupt his quiet campaign to convince her that they belonged together. But he'd silently sworn that he wouldn't rush her into anything, and the only way he could be sure of that was by giving her the time and space he felt she needed. To his knowledge, she'd never been involved in a relationship as intimate as theirs had become. Loving a man physically, as well as emotionally, was completely new to her. And though she seemed to delight in it on every level, he knew it was too soon for her to be sure enough of herself and her feelings for him to commit to any kind of permanency.

On a more practical level, they'd also had to go to work on Monday morning, something neither of them would have been capable of doing without getting a little rest. He'd also known that Marti had wanted some time to prepare for what she'd admitted would be a busy day. And so, albeit reluctantly, he'd gone home early Sunday evening.

In the three weeks that followed, they'd managed to see quite a bit of each other despite their busy schedules. During the week, at her invitation, he had stopped by her house each evening on his way home from work. Depending on who arrived first, one or the other of them would start dinner, they'd eat, take Max for a walk, then sit and talk for a while. Occasionally he'd spent the night, again at her invitation. Most evenings, however, aware that she had work to do, he'd leave her sometime around eight-thirty or nine with a good-night kiss or two. Though he'd found that more and more difficult to do lately, he'd simply remind himself of how much her job meant to her. He wanted her to be happy, and if Carter and Caisson made her happy, he could and *would* live with it.

Each weekend they'd been together constantly from Friday night until sometime Sunday, and Marti had seemed as determined as he to pack as much into those days and nights as possible. With Amy's help they'd bought two Christmas trees, one for Marti's house and one for his, then spent an entire afternoon decorating them. She'd introduced him to her darkroom and taught him the basics of film developing. They'd also gone bowling with Rose and Drew and the kids, to the symphony with Carmen and Tony, and a holiday open house at Heather's. They'd had Sunday dinner twice at his mother's, once just the two of them and once with the rest of the family. And they'd made love with an intensity that had only added to his determination to have her for his own.

Yet, despite the undeniable joy they took in each other, despite their steady progression from friends to lovers, as well as their growing intimacy, somewhere at the back of his mind Dominic knew that all was not as well as it should be between them. More and more often lately Marti had seemed preoccupied. Granted, she'd had a lot on her mind, including the company Christmas party, which she'd organized, and her upcoming trip to Kansas City to see her parents. But Dominic had begun to sense that something else was bothering her, something that concerned him.

He'd tried to question her about it a couple of times. But on both occasions, before he'd been able to probe too deeply, she'd managed to allay his uncertainties just enough to make him wonder if his imagination had gone into overdrive. Now, sitting alone in the dark outside her house, recalling all that had occurred over the past few weeks, Dominic realized he wasn't imagining things.

Too often lately he'd caught her staring into space, her eyes shadowed with sadness. At times, when they'd made love, she'd clung to him with an urgency that had bordered on desperation. And occasionally when he'd spent the night, he'd awakened alone in her bed. More often than not he'd find her sitting on the sofa with Max, just as he had that first night. But once she'd been standing by the window, gazing into the darkness, her face wet with tears. She'd claimed that they were tears of happiness, and he'd wanted to believe her so much that he had. But suddenly he wasn't quite so sure.

No matter how he'd like to convince himself otherwise, Marti was worried about something, and he had to find out what it was. Only then could he help her to deal with it. Whether it was something simple like her trip to Kansas City, or something more involved, he wanted to know. For his peace of mind, as well as hers, he *had* to know.

Of course, he'd wait until after the party tonight, until they could be alone together for a while. But he wouldn't allow her to put him off again. Whatever her problem, to-night they'd solve it once and for all. Or else he'd know the reason why they couldn't.

Shifting restlessly on the leather seat, Dominic glanced at his watch. Relieved to see that it was almost seven, he took a moment to check his appearance in the rearview mirror, then left the car and headed up the walkway.

Drawing in a deep breath of the cold night air, he eyed the brightly colored lights twinkling around the windows and peeping out of the shrubbery on either side of her front porch. Suddenly his mood lightened considerably.

For as long as he could remember, Christmas had been his favorite time of year. He'd always enjoyed the good food and good fun of the holiday season. But his enjoyment had increased a hundredfold the last few weeks as he'd shared it all with Marti. She'd added her own special touch of magic to everything they'd done together. Yet he had a feeling that she didn't even know it. Maybe the time had come to tell her. Maybe later, when they were alone, he would.

He rang the doorbell, expecting to have to wait a minute or two for Marti to answer. But a few seconds later the front door swung open and she stood before him, her blue eyes bright with excitement as she smiled up at him.

"Hi," she murmured, stepping aside so he could join her in the entryway.

"Hi, yourself." He gazed at her for one long, admiring moment, then continued softly. "You look . . . wonderful, just wonderful, Marti."

She wore a simple yet elegant, close-fitting, emerald green velvet sheath with narrow rhinestone straps that bared her shoulders. The only jewelry she'd added was a pair of long, dangly gold-and-rhinestone earrings that shimmered when she moved. And, as she'd been doing more and more often, whether at home or at work, she'd left her hair loose. In the gentle glow of the hall light it gleamed like gold silk as it curled softly around her shoulders.

"You're not too shabby, either, Mr. Fabrino," she teased. "That tux looks like it was made for you." Blushing prettily, she fussed with his lapels a bit. Then, pretending to straighten his black bow tie, she stood on tiptoe and kissed him on the chin.

"It was, several years ago." He wrapped his hands around her shoulders, bent his head and took her mouth slowly, deeply. "Luckily I can still get into it," he muttered, suddenly wanting more than anything to get out if it and into—

Giving himself a firm mental shake, he eased away from her. They'd have all the time they needed to make love later. But for now they had a very special party to attend, one that meant a lot to Marti in many ways. Tonight was her night to shine, and he'd be damned if he'd do anything to ruin it, including making her late.

"Ready to go?" he asked, gesturing toward the door.

She sighed almost wistfully, then smiled again. "I guess we'd better. I promised Heather I'd be there by seven-thirty to make sure everything was in order. Just let me say goodbye to Max."

"What? He's not going with us?" Dominic asked with mock surprise as he followed her into the kitchen.

"He absolutely, positively refused to wear the little suit I bought him. Didn't you, sweetie?" Bending over the baby gate that kept the little dog confined to the laundry room whenever she was gone, Marti cooed to him as she scratched his shaggy ears. Wriggling with delight, Max flopped onto his back and wagged his tail.

"We're both alike," Dominic muttered darkly. "Putty in your pretty hands."

Straightening, Marti shook her head and smiled wryly. "You are not."

"Am, too." Slipping his arm around her, he led her back to the entryway. "You're wearing a coat or a jacket, aren't you?" Secretly he hoped she had a jacket to match her dress, one she'd wear all evening. She looked too sexy in that skimpy little number by itself for her own good.

"A black velvet cape." She took it out of the closet and handed it to him.

As he swirled it around her shoulders, he bent and kissed her neck. "Lovely," he murmured, savoring her delicate shiver. "Why don't you leave it on when we get there?"

"Then I wouldn't be able to show off my new dress."

"My idea exactly." With a teasing grin, he tucked her hand in the crook of his elbow.

"You don't like it?" she asked coyly.

"I love it," he vowed as he escorted her down the walkway. "But so will every other guy at the Ritz Carlton tonight."

"Don't worry. You're the only one who matters." For an instant she rested her head on his shoulder, as if to reassure him, then slid into the car.

"You, too, Marti," he admitted as he gazed at her solemnly for several seconds. Then, smiling once again, he closed her car door. Less than a minute later, he slipped into the driver's seat and they were finally on their way.

They arrived at the Ritz Carlton Hotel just before seven-thirty. With a good-natured warning to watch it, Dominic handed over the Corvette's keys to the parking valet. Then, taking Marti's hand in his, he led her into the elegantly appointed hotel lobby and on to the ballroom where the party was to be held. While he checked her cape at the nearby cloakroom, she went ahead to make sure that everything was in order for the more than two hundred guests they were expecting.

As he wandered around the ballroom, waiting for Marti to finish with Heather, Dominic realized it had been quite a while since he'd attended such a posh affair. Not only had all of the Carter and Caisson employees been invited, but also all of the clients with whom the company dealt on a regular basis. According to Marti several of the executives from C and C's corporate headquarters in Chicago were also scheduled to attend. And from what he could see, Marti had done her utmost to ensure that the party would be perfect.

A huge Christmas tree decorated with red bows and tiny white lights filled one corner of the room. Arrangements of red and white carnations tucked among branches of dark green holly graced each of several dozen linen-covered tables set for eight that had been spaced around the room. Two open bars, as well as two cocktail buffet tables full of steaming hors d'oeuvres, had been set up on either end of the room. And a four-piece string quartet warmed up on a small dais centered near a bank of sumptuously draperied windows.

As the first early arrivals began to filter through the wide double doorway, Marti came up beside him and slipped her arm through his. "What do you think?" she asked, slanting a smile his way.

"I think I'm glad I wore my tux." He squeezed her hand as he offered her a teasing grin. Then he continued on a more serious note. "You did a great job putting it all together. You should be proud of yourself."

"I wish I could take more credit for it, but Heather did most of the work. I don't know what I'd do without her." She paused for a moment, gazing around the room, obviously pleased with what she saw. Then she turned to him again. "Want to help me meet and greet?"

"I'd be honored," he admitted, touched that she'd offered to include him in the business side of her life in such an overt way.

They stood together near the ballroom entrance for more than an hour, smiling and shaking hands as well as exchanging a few words with the guests as they arrived. And though Marti introduced him as her friend, she did so with such possessive pride that no one could have doubted the true nature of their relationship. Touched once again by her obvious regard, he felt his heart swell with love. And he wondered if maybe he'd read her wrong after all. Maybe she'd simply been worried about the party and hadn't wanted to bother him with it.

Once Marti was sure that most of the guests were there, they moved into the crowd and began to mingle. Since she was the hostess, he stood back and let her take the lead, admiring her grace and charm as she moved among her peers with such aplomb. Occasionally, when one client or another seemed to want her undivided attention for more than a few moments, he'd wander off to refill her drink or replenish her plate. He knew that she was having a wonderful time. And so was he. At least, he was until he had the misfortune to overhear a conversation concerning Marti.

He hadn't intended to eavesdrop on the two men standing ahead of him at the bar. But he knew that they worked in the art department at Carter and Caisson, and when they mentioned Marti's name he couldn't help himself. Her employees liked and admired her, and it pleased him to hear them say so. But this time, although the men were more than complimentary, Dominic was literally left dumbfounded by what they said.

"She looks great tonight, doesn't she?"

"Yeah, who'd have thought it?"

"She's been offered Benson's job, you know."

"So she'll be moving to Chicago, huh?"

"Sometime after the first of the year."

"Any idea who'll take her place?"

"As far as I know she hasn't said anything about it yet. And she probably won't until after the holidays. But she met with the guys from the corporate office all day yesterday. Rumor has it everyone was smiling afterward."

"Well, she certainly deserves it."

"Yeah, but I hate to see her go. It won't be the same around here without her."

They collected their drinks and drifted away without even glancing at him. He watched them go, barely restraining the urge to follow them and demand some sort of explanation. When the man standing behind him cleared his throat, he turned back to the bartender and ordered a club soda for Marti. He considered ordering a Scotch on the rocks for himself. Something to soothe the sudden aching emptiness that had settled deep in his soul. But the alcohol would only end up loosening his tongue, and he couldn't risk saying anything to Marti without thinking it through first. And even while sober, thinking had suddenly become something extremely difficult to do.

Benson's job...Chicago...smiling...not the same without her... Without her...

The other men's words tumbled through his head as he moved through the crowd. If they were right, if she'd not only been offered a job in Chicago, but agreed to take it, why hadn't she told him? Had she been afraid that he'd be upset about it? Granted, moving to Chicago with her wouldn't be the easiest thing he'd ever done. He'd have to sell his business and he'd miss his family. But surely she'd realized by now just how much he cared for her. Surely she knew that he'd go with her anywhere, if only she asked.

Yet she hadn't asked. And that's what really hurt. Because it meant that she had probably already decided to go without him. So when was she planning to say something about it? After the holidays when she announced it to her staff? Maybe that was why she'd been so adamant about going to Kansas City alone. Perhaps she wanted to tell her parents first, and if he were there she wouldn't be able to do so without telling him, too. Better to let him cool his heels in St. Louis.

His heart twisting bitterly, Dominic paused a few feet away from her. As she had been most of the evening, she was surrounded by several clients. Her head tipped to one side, she smiled as she listened to something one of the women had to say. Even at a distance he could see that she was genuinely interested in whatever it was.

Genuine. Sincere. Honest. Looking back over the past several weeks, recalling all that they'd shared, Dominic realized that was how Marti had been with him all along. So why was he suddenly so willing to believe that she'd begun to deceive him?

Maybe she hadn't made a decision about the job in Chicago yet. Maybe that was the problem she'd been wrestling with in the dark hours before dawn. And maybe she was going to Kansas City alone to think it through on her own, away from whatever unintentional influence he might have over her.

She'd trusted him with her gravest fears. Perhaps it was time for him to trust her, too. To believe that she loved him enough to tell him all that he needed to know just as soon as she could. And in the meantime... In the meantime, he'd remind her as often as he could of how much *he* loved *her.* He'd not only show her but tell her again and again. He'd start to say the words, tonight, and he wouldn't stop until she made him.

As he started toward her again, she glanced over her shoulder, frowning slightly, then smiled when she met his gaze. Despite all the people clustered around her, she'd been looking for him. Reassured, he stopped beside her and slipped an arm around her shoulders. Taking the club soda from him, she put her arm around his waist and moved a little closer.

"I guess there isn't any chance of leaving early, is there?" he asked, his voice cued for her ears only.

"What time is it?"

"Ten-thirty."

"I'll have us out of here in an hour," she promised, her eyes glimmering with warmth as she gave him a quick hug. Then, easing away from him, she took his hand in hers. "I have to talk to a couple more clients. Come with me?"

Squeezing her hand gently, he held her still for a moment. "Wherever you want, Marti. Whenever you want." He met her gaze for a heartbeat or two, then smiling once again, he gestured toward the milling crowd. "Just lead the way."

They got back to Marti's house just after midnight. He parked in her driveway, grabbed the overnight bag he'd packed, then walked with her to the front door. Together they checked on Max and found him sleeping soundly in his little bed. Not wanting to wake him, they moved out of the kitchen as quietly as possible. Marti turned to go upstairs, but before she'd gone more than a couple of steps, Dominic caught her hand in his and pulled her toward the living room.

"I want to kiss you under the mistletoe," he murmured, stopping beneath the little bunch of greenery they'd hung in the archway. The lights on the Christmas tree in the corner twinkled merrily, and the spicy scent of pine wafted around them.

"Why?" She gazed up at him quizzically as she slid her arms around his shoulders.

"Because it's almost Christmas." He nibbled at her earlobe. "And there's something I want to tell you." He brushed his lips over hers lightly. "I love you, Marti. I love you." Not giving her a chance to reply, he gathered her close and took her mouth with an intensity that stunned them both.

Raising his head at last, he scooped her into his arms and headed for the staircase. In her room he set her on the bed and slowly, deliberately, undressed her. And then, despite the urgency welling up inside him, he made love to her with a measured tenderness, taking her gently to the edge and over, drinking in her sweet cries of ecstasy as he filled her with his love.

"So much for spending Christmas with my family," Marti muttered as she wandered from one elegantly appointed room to another in her parents' house just after one o'clock Christmas Day.

She'd been there almost two days, and she doubted if she'd actually seen her mother and father more than ten hours total. Her father had rounds at the hospital and her mother was preparing for a showing at a New York gallery in February. And, of course, they'd just gotten back from their cruise.

So sorry we missed your birthday, darling. But we know you understand. We did think about you, though, and we bought you some gorgeous emerald earrings in St. Thomas.

After thirty years she should have known better than to expect things to be different. But obviously she hadn't learned. She'd honestly thought that today, of all days, they'd be together. And they had been for as long as it took them to have brunch at a downtown hotel. Then her mother had gone up to her studio and her father had gone back to the hospital.

You know how it is when you're a professional, Martha. Your work has to come first.

Oh, she knew, all right. But she also knew that it didn't have to be that way. Men and women everywhere managed to combine meaningful work with a full and happy home life. And Dominic had given her reason to believe that she could, too. In his own quiet, gentle way he'd taught her to love. And he'd let her know that she *could* have it all, if she wanted.

I love you, Marti. I love you....

Pausing by one of the living-room windows, she tilted the shutter to let in a bit of sunshine. For several moments she gazed at the huge Victorian Christmas tree centered against the far wall. Then, turning away, she rested her head against the window frame and stared at the wide expanse of manicured lawn that sloped down to the street.

Her mother had insisted that the elegantly appointed pink and cream and gold creation was all the rage. It really was gorgeous. But Marti much preferred her shaggy, needle-dropping, kind-of-crooked pine filled with cookie-dough ornaments, strings of popcorn, dozens of twinkle lights, and what Dominic referred to as Amy's mess of tinsel.

Dominic ...

She'd known that he had wanted to come with her, yet she'd resisted the urge to let him do so. She'd had to talk to her parents about the future and she hadn't thought it would be wise to have him there when she did. Not because she didn't want to share her plans with him. She intended to do just that when she got back to St. Louis.

She hadn't asked him to come with her because she'd had a feeling that her parents would be upset with the decisions she'd made. And she hadn't wanted them to vent their frustrations on him. Though he'd had a hand in her change of heart, she'd made her choices without his knowledge. And she was going to stick to those choices regardless of what happened between them in the future.

As she'd told her parents at dinner last night, much to their chagrin, she wasn't taking Benson's job. In fact, she was leaving Carter and Caisson altogether within the next six months to concentrate on her photography. And, as she *hadn't* mentioned to her parents, if Dominic Fabrino asked her to marry him—

The ringing of the telephone interrupted her reverie, and she hurried across the room to answer it. He'd called late Thursday afternoon, ostensibly to report on Max's well-being, and had promised to call again today. Hoping it was him, she caught the receiver on the third ring and offered a breathless hello.

"Merry Christmas, sweetheart."

"Merry Christmas." For just a moment she closed her eyes and wished with all her heart that they could be together. She'd been lonely before, but it had been nothing compared to how she felt right now with several hundred miles separating them. "I miss you."

"Miss you, too, and so does Max. We both slept in your bed last night." To cause the little dog the least amount of upset they'd agreed that Dominic would stay at her place while she was gone.

"Where is he now?"

"Here with me and the rest of the family at my parents' house. He's eating up all the attention."

"I thought I heard barking in the background." She heard quite a bit of laughing and talking, too. She could just imagine everyone gathered around the dining-room table or huddled in front of the TV.

"Yeah, the kids are chasing him around the kitchen." He paused for a moment, as if unsure what to say next.

"How is everyone?"

"Fine. They miss you, too. Especially Amy. She wants to say hello."

Marti talked to the little girl for a few minutes, assuring her that she'd definitely be home on Sunday and they'd exchange gifts upon her arrival. Then, much to her surprise, one after another, Dominic's relatives came on the line to say a few words until she'd talked to all of them.

By the time Dominic spoke to her again, she was almost in tears. Why she'd insisted on coming to Kansas City when she could have been with them, she had no idea. For all the warmth and concern, not to mention understanding and acceptance, her parents had shown her, she might as well have talked to *them* on the telephone.

"Are you okay? You sound kind of weepy," Dominic asked softly.

"I'm fine, really," she murmured. "Just remembering Thanksgiving, and thinking how lucky you are to have such a wonderful family."

"Are your folks around?"

"My mother's in her studio working. My father's at the hospital."

"You're not doing anything special?"

"We had brunch earlier at a hotel downtown, and we've been invited to dinner at some friends' house."

"Not—"

"No, not them."

"Want to see if you can get a flight out tomorrow instead of Sunday? Max and I can be at the airport waiting for you anytime you say."

She was tempted, sorely tempted. But one more day with her parents wouldn't hurt, not really. It was Christmas, and for now they were all the family she had. And maybe in that time she'd be able to convince them that she was finally doing what was right for her. Maybe she could tell them about Dominic and the true extent of her hopes and dreams for the future.

"I wish I could," she admitted, unable to prevent a hint of wistfulness from creeping into her voice. "But I think I'd better stay until Sunday as planned. I'll...I'll see you then."

"If you're sure that's what you want..."

Dominic didn't sound sure at all. He sounded as if he was getting ready to argue, and that she couldn't handle right now.

"That's what I want," she replied firmly.

"Then I'll see you Sunday."

"She didn't sound too happy, did she, Uncle Dominic?" Amy asked, plopping down next to him on the back porch steps.

Though it was a bright, sunny day, the air was crisp and cold, too cold to be sitting on concrete steps. But after talking to Marti the general chaos that marked every Fabrino family holiday had begun to get to him. He'd had to get away for a while to collect his thoughts, and taking Max out to play had been as good an excuse as any.

Of course, he should have known that Amy would catch up with him eventually. She'd been worried about Marti since last night. And obviously she still was. But she did have a point. Marti hadn't sounded too happy at all. Whatever was going on in Kansas City, he had an idea it wasn't what she wanted or needed. Yet she'd been so insistent about staying.

"Uncle Dominic?" Amy tugged on his jacket sleeve, demanding his attention. "I said—"

"I know what you said." Reaching out, he scooped his niece onto his lap. "She didn't sound too happy."

"You don't sound too happy, either."

He shrugged wordlessly. He *wasn't* happy, and trying to fool Amy would be futile. When she knew she was right she could be like a dog with a bone.

"But you're always happy when you're together, you *and* Marti. Aren't you?"

"Yes."

"Well, then, I think you ought to go and get her."

"Oh, really?"

"Momma said it's not *real* far to Kansas City. She said you could drive there in your 'Vette. I bet if you hurry you could be back tonight. Then tomorrow we could give her our presents."

"I don't know, Amy...."

"Please, Uncle Dominic, *please?*" She tipped her head back and gazed at him, her dark eyes full of pleading.

He shook his head in bewilderment. Out of the mouths of babes... But, hell, at this point, what could it hurt? Neither he nor Marti were having much of a Christmas as it was. At the very least he'd get to meet her parents, maybe spend some time with them. And if Marti really was as unhappy as she'd sounded, he'd convince her to drive back with him. Either way they'd be together again and, though he couldn't speak for Marti, that alone would lift *his* spirits plenty.

"All right, squirt, I'll go and get her."

"Yippee!" Amy jumped off his lap and began to dance around the yard.

"But I can't guarantee we'll be back tonight or even tomorrow. She told her parents she'd stay until Sunday."

"Oh." Amy frowned for a moment, then brightened again. "Well, just call me when you get here, okay?"

"Okay." He stood and stretched, then called to Max. "Come on, dog. Looks like we're going for a ride."

Twenty minutes later, with Max settled on a blanket on the passenger seat and his entire family waving from the front porch, Dominic pulled out of his parents' driveway and headed for Kansas City. He made the drive in just under four hours, a more than reasonable amount of time considering the circumstances. He hadn't wanted to end up with a speeding ticket. But then, he hadn't wanted to arrive at Marti's parents' house after they'd left for their dinner party, either.

As it was he got into the Kansas City area around five-thirty. Luckily Marti had given him her parents' telephone number and their address. He simply stopped at a gas station, bought a city map and ended up having no trouble at all finding their place.

They lived in an exclusive suburban area south of the central business distract. The streets were more like country lanes, and the homes, as imposing as they were impressive, sat on long, wide landscaped lawns. Pulling into the driveway of the Georgian-looking minimanse that bore the address for which he'd been searching, Dominic couldn't help but wonder how Marti had been satisfied with her little house on the Hill after growing up in such elegant surroundings. Or maybe that was exactly why she had been satisfied.

As he thought of her rattling around the huge house alone all afternoon, any doubts he'd had about arriving unannounced vanished into thin air. Suddenly he was very, very glad he'd come. Slipping into his black leather jacket, he grabbed Max in mid-stretch, tucked the little dog under his arm and climbed out of the car. He strode up the winding

path that served as a walkway, hesitated only a moment
when he reached the tall, carved wood double doors, then
rang the bell.

Before he'd counted to ten a light went on in the foyer and
he sensed rather than saw someone eyeing him through the
peephole. An instant later the door swung open and, with a
soft cry of delight, Marti flew into his arms.

"Dominic, oh, Dominic. And Max, little Max, too. I
can't believe you're here. But I'm so glad...so...glad," she
murmured, burying her face in his neck as he hugged her
close. "But why...?" A puzzled expression on her pretty
face, she eased away from him, cradling Max in her arms.

"It was Amy's idea. She said we both sounded sad, and
she thought it was because we weren't together. I, for one,
had to agree." He smoothed a wisp of honey blond hair
away from her face in his by-now-familiar manner, and offered her a wry smile.

"Me, too." Returning his smile, she leaned toward him
and brushed a gentle kiss over his lips.

Accepting her sweet invitation, Dominic drew her into his
arms again and covered her mouth with his, kissing her in a
way that could leave no doubt of just how happy he was to
be with her once more.

"Martha, is someone here? I thought I heard—"

Muttering a curse, Dominic moved away from Marti. He
hadn't intended to be in the midst of a passionate embrace
with her the first time he met her mother. And the elegantly
attired, aging yet attractive blond woman eyeing him dis-
tastefully from across the foyer couldn't be anyone else.

"Mrs. Townsend? I'm Dominic Fabrino, a friend of
Marti's."

As if prompted by his words, Marti closed the distance
he'd put between them. Slipping an arm around his waist,
she faced her mother proudly. "Let me introduce you

properly. Mother, I'd like you to meet someone very special, Dominic Fabrino. Dominic, my mother, Eleanor Townsend."

"Mr. Fabrino." Mrs. Townsend acknowledged him with a regal nod, but refrained from offering him her hand. Then, turning to Marti, she frowned reprovingly. "Where on earth did you get that animal? Do you realize you have dog hair all over your dress? And you don't have time to change. We're supposed to be at the hospital to pick up your father—"

"Max was my birthday gift from Dominic. Dog hair has never bothered me nearly as much as it has you. And I'm not going to the Osbornes' unless Dominic goes, too." Tipping her chin up, Marti eyed her mother defiantly.

"But that's out of the question. I insist—"

"Fine. We'll stay here. Give my love to every—"

"He's not staying in this house, Martha." Though she spoke to her daughter, Eleanor Townsend glared at Dominic, making no attempt to hide her growing hostility.

"Marti, maybe I'd better go—"

"If you go, Dominic, I'm going with you." She gazed up at him, her eyes holding his steadily for several seconds, assuring him that she meant every word she'd said.

"He's the reason you're doing it, isn't he? He's the reason you're throwing away—"

"I'm not throwing away anything," Marti retorted quickly, not giving her mother a chance to finish her vindictive diatribe. Then, turning to Dominic, she thrust Max into his arms as she continued. "Give me a couple of minutes to get my things and we can leave."

"Martha, don't do this," Eleanor warned, trailing after her daughter as she walked out of the foyer. "Your father will be furious...."

Wondering if he'd made a monumental mistake, Dominic stood where he was. He hadn't meant to stir up trouble. But then, never in a million years would he have anticipated the kind of "welcome" he'd received from Marti's mother. The woman was cold as stone and just as hard. He should have known from the little Marti had said about her, but seeing truly was believing.

For the first time since he'd met her, Dominic finally had a good idea of just what kind of upbringing she'd had. He had a feeling that love and laughter had been sadly lacking even when her grandmother had been alive. And then she'd been raped by a man she'd known for years. No wonder she'd thrown herself into her job. For her, Carter and Caisson had been more than a place to work. It had been a safe haven from emotions she'd never been truly allowed to express.

But since they'd been together that was no longer the case. So maybe Carter and Caisson was no longer as important to her as it had been. Given what he knew about her now and the depth of his feelings for her, he could understand if it was and accept it. Yet if it wasn't—

"I'm ready." She stood before him, wearing her coat, clutching her purse and an overnight bag, smiling valiantly.

"Maybe you ought to try—"

"I've tried, Dominic. For thirty years I've tried. As far as I'm concerned, it's just not worth the effort anymore. I'm used to being hurt, but I refuse to stand by and allow you to be hurt, as well. Let's go home and share what's left of Christmas, just the three of us," she said, setting her bag down so she could hold Max again.

"Have I told you lately how much I love you?" he asked, overwhelmed by an emotion deeper and sweeter than any he'd ever experienced.

"Tell me again, anyway."

"I love you, Marti, more than words can say."

"And I love you, Dominic, with all my heart."

As if by mutual agreement they made the drive back to St. Louis in virtual silence, each wrapped up in their own thoughts. For his part Dominic was more determined than ever to talk with her about the future. He'd been patient as long as he could. Now he wanted his relationship with Marti solidified in some way. He wanted to look ahead instead of back, and he wanted to do it with her. But how could he expect her to know how he felt unless he had the courage to tell her?

They got to her house just before ten o'clock. As always, they saw to Max's needs first. Then, when the little dog was finally settled in his bed, they wandered into the living room. While Marti curled up on the sofa, Dominic plugged in the lights on her Christmas tree. He stood before it for a minute or two, watching them wink on and off. Finally, knowing the time had come to talk to Marti, he turned and sat down beside her.

"I'm sorry about your mother. I had hoped that we'd get along."

"Why?" She gazed at him curiously.

"Because I want to marry you." He hadn't intended to say it so baldly, but the words slipped out before he could stop them. Not giving her time to protest, he met her incredulous gaze and continued quickly. "You know I love you, and more than anything I want to be with you, even if it means moving to Chicago. I'll sell Fabrino's—"

"Oh, Dominic..." Her eyes misting with tears, Marti laid a hand along his cheek. In all her life no one had ever made her feel quite so cherished as she felt at that moment. Nor had anyone ever given her quite so wonderful a gift.

She had no idea how Dominic knew about Chicago, but somehow he did. And he was offering to give up everything he had to go there with her. For her, he'd sell his business and move away from his beloved family. For her . . . just for her.

"You don't have to say anything one way or another yet. Just promise me you'll think about it." He took her hand in his and kissed her fingers.

"I'm not going to Chicago, Dominic."

"What?" He eyed her quizzically, as if unsure that he'd heard her right.

"I'm not going to Chicago. I turned down the job last week. In fact, I told my boss that I'd be leaving sometime within the next six months, so they could start searching for my replacement. I want to work on my photography, really work on it, and see what happens." She smiled confidently as she met his gaze. "I also want to marry you. And have babies. . . ."

"You . . . do?"

"Mmm, yes, lots of babies." She leaned forward and kissed him on the cheek. "Because we've got lots of love to go around."

"We do, don't we?" he agreed. Still holding her hand, he stood and drew her to her feet, then led her across the living room. Pausing in the archway under the mistletoe, he turned to face her. "Merry Christmas, Marti." He put his arms around her and kissed her ever so gently.

"Merry Christmas, Dominic," she whispered joyfully, and not quite so gently kissed him back.

Epilogue

"I didn't think we'd ever get those two to bed," Marti muttered as she and Dominic wandered into the living room arm in arm, Max tagging along after them.

They'd been married almost two years and once again it was Christmas, a very special Christmas for both of them because this year they'd made two new additions to their growing happiness. The twins, Jonathan and Jamie, hadn't quite understood why they were doing it, but brother and sister had had a wonderful time trying to take down the tree—tearing up ribbons and wrapping paper, crawling into boxes and adding to the holiday chaos in general, both at home and at their grandparents' house.

Proud parents that they were, Marti and Dominic had delighted in their antics. And though they were both worn-out, neither could recall ever having had a better Christmas. Except perhaps the first one they'd shared when they'd promised to love each other always. Now, as then, they sat together on the sofa, arms around each other, basking in the warmth of their love as they watched the tiny lights twinkle on the tree.

"Now that we're finally alone, I have a little something special for you," Dominic said.

"But you've already given me so much," Marti protested. "A new coat, a sexy nightgown, a gold bracelet, *twins . . .* " As he switched on a lamp, she offered him a teasing smile.

He'd also given her the opportunity to make a success of her photography. She was selling photographs nationally now, and her first show at a local gallery was scheduled for the spring. But she never could have done it if Dominic hadn't turned Fabrino's into such a success story. A third garage to be located in the west county area was now on the drawing board.

"This is something I've wanted you to have ever since the first time you invited me to dinner." He handed her a flat, medium-size square box wrapped in gold foil and tied with a bright green ribbon.

She frowned thoughtfully as she took the gift from him. "What is it?"

"Open it and see."

Her fingers trembling slightly, she untied the ribbon, then carefully peeled off the paper and lifted the lid. Inside, cushioned by several layers of tissue, was a sterling silver frame, and in the frame was a photograph. It wasn't a studio portrait, nor was it one of hers.

As she trailed her fingertips over the smooth, cool glass, tears filled her eyes. "Oh, Dominic . . . it's beautiful." She gazed at him, then at the photograph. It was of her and the twins and Max, curled up together against a pile of bed pillows. "Thank you. For the photograph, and for making my life complete."

"It was the least I could do, considering how much I love you. Speaking of which, now that we're finally alone..."

"Oh, yes," she agreed, setting aside the photograph she knew she'd treasure always. She stood, took her husband by the hand, and pulled him to his feet. "Now that we're finally alone..." Threading her way through the empty boxes, ribbon, and mounds of wrapping still littering the floor, she led him toward the hallway. In the archway, under the mistletoe, she turned to face him. Putting her arms around him, she drew him close and kissed him. "Let's have our own special celebration...."

* * * * *

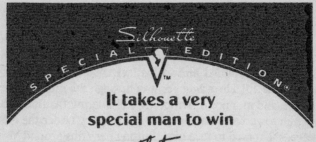

Silhouette

SPECIAL EDITION

It takes a very special man to win

That SPECIAL Woman!

She's friend, wife, mother—she's you! And beside each Special Woman stands a wonderfully *special* man. It's a celebration of our heroines—and the men who become part of their lives.

Look for these exciting titles from Silhouette Special Edition:

January   BUILDING DREAMS by Ginna Gray
Heroine: Tess Benson—a woman faced with single motherhood who meets her better half.

February   HASTY WEDDING by Debbie Macomber
Heroine: Clare Gilroy—a woman whose one spontaneous act gives her more than she'd ever bargained for.

March   THE AWAKENING by Patricia Coughlin
Heroine: Sara McAllister—a woman of reserved nature who winds up in adventure with the man of her dreams.

April   FALLING FOR RACHEL by Nora Roberts
Heroine: Rachel Stanislaski—a woman dedicated to her career who finds that romance adds spice to life.

Don't miss THAT SPECIAL WOMAN! each month—from some of your special authors! Only from Silhouette Special Edition!

TSW

VOWS
A series celebrating marriage
by Sherryl Woods

To Love, Honor and Cherish—these were the words that three generations of Halloran men promised their women they'd live by. But these vows made in love are each challenged by the tests of time....

In October—Jason Halloran meets his match in *Love #769*;
In November—Kevin Halloran rediscovers love—with his wife—in *Honor #775*;
In December—Brandon Halloran rekindles an old flame in *Cherish #781*.

These three stirring tales are coming down the aisle toward you—only from Silhouette Special Edition!

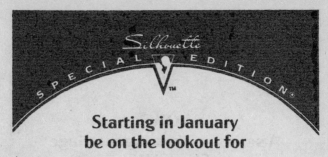

Silhouette

SPECIAL EDITION ™

Starting in January
be on the lookout for

MAVERICKS

LISA JACKSON'S
MAVERICK MEN

They're wild...they're woolly...and
they're as rugged as the great outdoors.
They've never needed a woman before,
but they're about to meet their matches....

HE'S A BAD BOY (#787)—January
HE'S JUST A COWBOY (#799)—March
HE'S THE RICH BOY (#811)—May

All men who just won't be tamed!
From Silhouette Special Edition.

SEMAV-1

Fmc 8/8/94